W9-AAU-562

SEVEN BLACK STONES

MYSTERY NOVELS BY JEAN HAGER

Featuring Molly Bearpaw

SEVEN BLACK STONES
THE REDBIRD'S CRY
RAVENMOCKER

Featuring Chief Mitchell Bushyhead

GHOSTLAND
NIGHT WALKER
THE GRANDFATHER MEDICINE

SEVEN BLACK STONES

JEAN HAGER

THE MYSTERIOUS PRESS

Published by Warner Books

A Time Warner Company

Copyright © 1995 by Jean Hager
All rights reserved.

 Mysterious Press books are published by Warner Books, Inc.,
1271 Avenue of the Americas, New York, NY 10020.

A Time Warner Company

The Mysterious Press name and logo are registered trademarks of Warner Books, Inc.

Printed in the United States of America

First U.S. Printing: April 1995

10 9 8 7 6 5 4 3 2 1

Library of Congress Cataloging-in-Publication Data
Hager, Jean.
    Seven black stones / Jean Hager.
        p.   cm.
    ISBN 0-89296-565-7
    1. Cherokee Indians—Fiction.   I. Title.
PS3558.A3232S48   1995
813'.54—dc20

94-26821
CIP

In loving memory of my sister.
Jo, this is for you.

SEVEN BLACK STONES

1

Sunday

Two miles south of old Highway 51, midway between Stilwell and Tahlequah, a row of rusted bedsprings, upended and wired together, formed a listing barrier between the construction site for the Cherokee Nation's new bingo hall and Zebediah Smoke's property. It was the ultimate study in contrasts, spiritual as well as material.

The exterior walls of Zeb's one-room shack were scrap lumber covered with tar paper and old automobile hubcaps. A tail of smoke drifted from the stovepipe. The roof, a slanting rectangle of corrugated tin, reflected blinding shafts of afternoon sunlight through the windshields of cars traveling the country road a hundred yards in front of the shack.

During the past month, the frequent passing of construction vehicles five days a week had sprayed most of the gravel into the bar ditches and cut deep, washboard ruts in the road. Cars bumped and bounced over it, as though crossing a series of cattle guards, shaking and rattling everything that would shake or rattle.

Eyeing the piles of junk near the shack, Will Fishinghawk steered his new Ford Taurus carefully onto the rounded shoulder. "Blasted road would tear up a car in a week," he grumbled to his companion, Professor Emeritus Conrad Swope. Will did not want to be there. He was missing his Sunday nap, for one thing.

"Never mind the car," Conrad said as he winced and shifted uncomfortably in the passenger seat. "It's my kidneys I'm worried about."

Will grunted and coasted another little distance, staring at the shack with disgust. Finally, he braked but made no move to get out of the car.

No human being should have to live in such conditions, Will thought, but then Zeb really didn't have to. Zeb had built the shack himself twelve years ago, after the four-room house on the property had been destroyed by a tornado. He'd lived in a tent while he built it, even though his welfare check would cover a rental in town—a modestly priced efficiency apartment, but it would at least have modern plumbing. The shack had electricity, but water came from a pump outside and the bathroom was an outhouse.

Will had listed for Zeb the advantages of a move to town countless times.

"I ain't moving in somebody else's house," Zeb had insisted. "This here is *mine*, and if you don't leave me be, I'll make a will and give it away to my brother's grandson instead of you. Even if I ain't laid eyes on him for twenty years."

"I wish you would," Will had bridled. He didn't want anything to do with Zeb's property. The market price for the few acres of rocky land—provided he found somebody stupid enough to buy it—wouldn't be worth the trouble. But Zeb continued to think—or so he alleged every time

Will brought up moving—that Will secretly coveted this piece of worthless real estate.

Sometimes he thought Zeb stayed here to spite him. Most of Will's friends and colleagues knew he was Zeb's only kinsman in the area, and Zeb's living conditions embarrassed him.

He felt responsible for the old man, which was totally illogical. Zeb was older than dirt, but he wasn't about to let anybody else make decisions for him.

Still, the situation was a constant irritation rubbing off the scab of Will's guilt.

Conrad, who had been studying Will's abstracted face, broke the silence. "Are you planning to sit here all day, or are we going in?"

Will could think of no good reason to delay any longer. "Let's walk from here. Don't want to pick up a nail or a piece of wire."

The two men got out and walked down the pebble-strewn dirt lane toward the shack. Conrad wore a gray cardigan sweater over his yellow, button-down oxford-cloth shirt and carried a burgundy briefcase with his name lettered in gold. Will was in shirt-sleeves.

The temperature had been in the sixties the past two days, freakishly warm for the first week of December. It had lured people out of doors to stroll or bike or just sit; the clement weather was a gift that, given the vagaries of Oklahoma climate, could be snatched away at any moment.

"He may not let us in," Will warned, more to voice his own hope than to douse Conrad's. He'd agreed to accompany Conrad because he feared Zeb wouldn't let Conrad in the house unless Will was with him. He might not, anyway.

"He's suspicious of everybody these days." Will tapped his temple with an index finger.

"Hardening of the arteries?"

Will shrugged. "Could be." But truthfully he thought Zeb was just a stubborn old man who took pride in opposing anybody who tried to help him.

The grass on the south side of the shack had been scorched, possibly with intent. More probably the old man had burned a pile of rubble and the fire had gotten loose and spread to within inches of the house before he could put it out. Whichever, it had occurred in the past two weeks, since Will was last there.

Old fool shouldn't be shambling around setting fires, Will thought and felt a stab of anger dig a little deeper into his guilt.

As they reached the concrete-block steps, the door scraped open a crack.

"Huh," Zeb greeted them. His gray hair was cut above his eyebrows in front and hung straight down the sides of his brown face. Wrinkles etched spidery roads through his sunken cheeks, over high cheekbones, and across a prominent brow. A corncob pipe was clenched in the corner of his mouth between short, stained teeth. Three of his front uppers were missing. Several months ago, Will had hauled him to the dentist and paid for a partial plate, which Zeb then refused to wear.

His tough brown flesh had shrunk back against the bone, as if readying itself to start the decomposition process, revealing the shape of the skeleton beneath.

Zeb wasn't sure of the exact year of his birth, but Will estimated he was eighty-seven, give or take a year on either side.

Will produced the six-pack of Budweiser he'd been holding behind him and said with forced heartiness, "It's good to see you, Uncle." Actually, Zeb was his great-uncle, his grandmother's eldest brother.

"Still running with white devils, I see," Zeb grunted as he grabbed the six-pack. He hadn't once looked directly at Conrad, but there was the sense that he would welcome a protest, so that he could engage Conrad in argument.

"Good afternoon, Mr. Smoke," Conrad said, taking no offense.

Zeb ignored him.

"May we come in?" Will inquired, furious at having to ask.

Zeb's eyes snapped shut. After a moment, he opened them and said, "Reckon so, but you have to leave when I say. I got things to do."

Ornery old coot, Will thought. Always had to be the boss. Zeb stepped back and gestured for them to enter.

Inside, three small holes in the back wall had been stuffed with rags. A twin-sized bed covered with a faded patchwork quilt hugged one wall. A cast-iron stove loomed in a corner, filling the room with the pungent scent of wood smoke. It was too warm in the shack. Conrad removed his sweater and unbottoned the top button of his shirt.

Without acknowledging Conrad by so much as a glance, Zeb laid the corncob pipe on a small metal table and popped the tab on a can of beer. He took a long swallow and smacked his lips.

He didn't offer the visitors a beer, which was fine with Will. The Budweiser hadn't been chilled. Since Zeb's old refrigerator had conked out, he'd acquired a taste for warm beer, which he was only able to indulge when Will thought to bring the brew. Lately, Will hadn't thought to very often.

Will didn't begrudge the old man an occasional beer but, unreasonably, it seemed like a bribe to him. In exchange for what? he wondered. Simple civility?

As if he'd read Will's thoughts, Zeb waved the hand that was wrapped around the Budweiser can toward a couch that might have once been brown. The couch, pushed back against the wall facing the bed, was propped up on one end with a block of wood.

"Might as well sit."

By pressing down with his palm, Conrad found a spot where the couch's broken springs wouldn't stab his skinny derriere. He draped his sweater over his knees and set the briefcase at his feet. With his shock of white hair, trim white mustache, freshly starched and ironed shirt, and knife-creased trousers, he looked comically out of place.

Instead of joining Conrad on the couch, Will perched on one of the flat arms, the one with the most padding intact. Even with the padding, the arm was as hard as a board, but there were no broken springs to jab him.

"You remember Professor Swope, Uncle. I brought him out to meet you a couple of weeks ago." He hadn't remembered to bring Budweiser on that occasion, and their reception had been even chillier than today's.

Zeb squinted at Conrad, as though trying to place him. His shrewd black eyes were as shiny as marbles. He shook his head. "Nope."

Will was sure the old man remembered Conrad, but he had decided to be difficult.

What else was new?

"Professor Swope—" Will began.

"Conrad," Conrad corrected, meeting the old man's hostile glare with a friendly smile. But he made no move to open the briefcase and get out his tape recorder. A wise decision. Zeb would be sure to balk if Conrad seemed to take anything for granted. Maybe Conrad could bring out the recorder later, if Zeb warmed up to him a little.

And maybe pigs were about to sprout wings.

Nevertheless, Will went through the motions. "Conrad," he said, "used to teach history at the university in Tahlequah. He was one of my professors. Now he's working on an oral-history project for the Tribal Studies Institute. He'd like to record what you can remember of your younger days and some of the old stories you used to tell me. I explained all of this to you when we were here before." Will heard himself begin to sound exasperated. Next, he would get exasperated because he was exasperated. Zeb always did that to him.

Conrad picked up on Will's vexed tone and raised a hand to silence him. His reproving look said young people were too impatient. Well, he hadn't had to deal with Zeb all his life.

"We can come back another time, Mr. Smoke," Conrad said, "if that suits you better."

Zeb tilted his chair back against the wall, took another swig of beer, and wiped his mouth with the sleeve of his flannel shirt. "Since when does what suits me mean shit to a *hi-yo'-ne'ga*?" He glared a challenge at Conrad. "Don't matter, no way," he muttered forebodingly, "'cause there might not be another time for any of us."

"What do you mean by that?" Will asked, reining in his impatience with difficulty.

"We might be dead is what I mean. I can feel the evil forces getting stronger with every nail they drive."

Will turned to Conrad and mumbled out of one side of his mouth, "The bingo hall."

Many Cherokees, having been raised in conservative Christian denominations, objected to gambling in any form. Of course, Zeb would get fighting mad if Will suggested his aversion to the bingo hall came from teachings instilled in the Southern Baptist Sunday School Zeb had attended as a child.

The majority of tribal members, however, had overcome whatever qualms they'd once had. Indian bingo was big business in Oklahoma. The Cherokee Nation's Roland Bingo Outpost in Sequoyah County was pouring half a million much-needed dollars annually into the Nation's coffers; and the new Catoosa Outpost was predicted to bring in even more.

The fifty-thousand-square-foot bingo hall under construction next door would cost $2.5 million, seat more than fifteen hundred people, employ two hundred, and increase the Cherokee Nation's annual revenue by an estimated million dollars.

To the old man, Will said, "Well, Uncle, I guess you're safe here."

"How do you figure that?" Zeb demanded.

"You told me you made medicine to protect yourself."

Zeb let the front legs of his chair hit the bare pine floor with a crack. "You poking fun at me?"

"You know I'm not," Will said, sighing.

Zeb sucked air through the gap in his front teeth. "Hah. You don't believe my medicine works. You and your white man's schooling."

The old man's mood seemed even more contentious than usual. "That's not the point, Uncle. I thought *you* believed in your medicine, so what's all this stuff about evil forces?"

Zeb shook his head and muttered something unintelligible in Cherokee, probably an oath. Getting up, he shuffled to a shelf nailed to the back wall and rummaged through a few plastic dishes, cooking utensils, cornmeal, flour, sugar, and canned food. Mostly the old man lived on fry bread, canned tuna, corn, soup, and rabbit or squirrel now and then.

On the same wall with the shelf a few articles of clothing hung on nails.

Zeb selected an empty Folgers coffee can and dumped his pipe ashes in it. Pulling a small cloth bag of Bull Durham from his pocket, he refilled the pipe and tamped it down with his finger. From another pocket, he produced a match and struck it against the wall. He lit the pipe, sucking loudly with his eyes closed.

It all had the feel of a ritual performed for the benefit of an audience and seemed to take forever.

When he had the pipe going to his satisfaction, Zeb turned his back on the visitors to gaze out one of the shack's two windows at the construction site. The naked steel framework of the bingo hall reminded Will of the skeleton of some giant prehistoric beast.

"Two nights ago, they set my yard on fire," Zeb said, "Tried to burn my house down with me in it."

"Who?" Will asked.

"Them." Zeb pointed a bony, yellow-nailed finger in the direction of the construction site.

The old man was getting more paranoid every day. "How do you know who it was? Did you see them?" Will asked.

"Don't have to see 'em."

Will didn't believe it, but he let it pass. "Well, they're afraid of you, Uncle. They think those medicine ceremonies you've been doing around the bingo hall are meant to curse them. To tell the truth, I wouldn't be surprised if that's what you're up to myself."

Removing the pipe from his mouth, Zeb turned around. "You don't think I can put a curse on nobody. You think I'm jest a crazy old man."

"Now, Uncle—"

"Mr. Smoke," Conrad interrupted, unknowingly stumbling on fresh ground for contention, "if somebody deliberately set that fire, you should report it to the sheriff."

Zeb snorted and pointed at Conrad with the stem of his pipe. "Don't want no white law nosing around here," he said combatively. He returned to his chair, finished the beer, and popped another tab. "Don't want no *hi-yo'ne'ga* dying on my land."

"Dying?" At this second mention of death, anxiety edged Will's impatience. If Zeb had finally crossed the line between contentious and crazy, no telling what he might do. And Will would have to deal with the consequences.

Zeb nodded and switched to Cherokee. "The Apportioner sees what's going on over there and she don't like it. When she gets mad enough, she'll send a punishment, like she did in the old days. Lot of people are going to die."

Will wondered uncomfortably if Zeb had decided to help the Apportioner along, but he refused to humor him by replying in Cherokee.

"If you keep talking about people dying," Will said in English, "somebody'll report you and next thing you know you'll be forced into a nursing home." Which was probably where he ought to be, Will thought, but seeing the old man's black scowl, he tried to soften the effect of his words by adding, "I tell you this for your own good." Zeb was a contrary old rascal but, confound it, the last thing he wanted was to see him hauled off, kicking and screaming.

Zeb's mouth curled in contempt. "Have you forgot the old words then?" he asked in Cherokee.

"I remember them all," Will replied in Cherokee, then added in English, "I haven't forgotten anything."

Zeb stared back at him with his black-marble eyes. "You talk like a *hi-yo'ne'ga*. Telling me things for my own good." He was speaking English now, for Conrad's benefit. "That's what they always say. We must speak the white man's words for our own good." His voice gained volume as he warmed to his subject. "And give up our land and take up the white man's religion and stop making medicine." He peered darkly at Conrad. "Look it up in your white man's books, Nephew, and you'll see I'm right."

Will didn't have to look it up. Until well into the twentieth century, the government aided by Christian missionaries had tried to wrest the tribes from their cultures in the name of "civilizing" them, but that was ancient history. "You can't turn back the clock."

"We should have fought them to the last man."

Will heaved a weary breath. "The time for fighting is long past and everybody knows it but you. I worry about you, Uncle." When he wasn't mad enough to shake him until the rest of his snaggledy teeth fell out.

Zeb's expression said he was trying to choose from among several replies. "Is that why you come see me so regular?" he asked finally.

Zeb's eyes reproached Will. Hell, his mere existence was

a reproach. Guilt stung Will's conscience, and he dropped his eyes. "I've been busy, with the end of the semester coming up."

Zeb snorted. "Never mind. I ain't going to no old-folks home. They'll not take me alive." With gnarled fingers, he unbuttoned the pocket flap on the bib of his overalls and took out a plastic pill bottle. It was filled with what looked like tobacco "See this? It's *tso:lagay'v:li*. I been saving it a long time."

Will exchanged a glance with Conrad. They both knew that the Ancient One, or Indian tobacco, was extremely scarce because of the difficult conditions governing its growth. When remade with the proper ritual and incantation, it became Grandfather Medicine, the most powerful medicine of all.

"Where did you get that?" Will asked.

Zeb cackled wickedly. "My business. You don't need to know." He tucked the pill bottle back in his overalls pocket and smoothed down the flap, grinning as though he'd put something over on somebody. "It ain't nothin' but tobacco to you."

"Whatever you say." Will stood and jammed his hands in his trouser pockets, jingling coins restlessly. "Uncle, I want you to promise me you'll stay away from the construction site."

Zeb sucked on his pipe, his narrowed gaze sliding to Conrad, who had been following the conversation with rapt interest.

"What do you know about promises, Nephew? You don't keep yours."

Will stifled a groan of frustration. Zeb delighted in reminding him that, at the age of twelve, he had vowed to become a medicine man, like Zeb. But by the time he'd finished high school he was more interested in book knowledge than in Cherokee medicine.

"Uncle, you better think about whatever it is you're doing out here."

Zeb shooed away Will's caution with his pipe. "All I been doing is protecting myself and watching them build that monster." He waved the pipe wildly toward the construction site, and he was speaking in Cherokee again. "Most of 'em over there are Cherokee on the outside, but they're white in their hearts." He squinted up at Will. "This morning it came to me."

"What came to you?"

"What we need."

Will cringed to imagine. "What's that, Uncle?"

"Brave heroes, like in the old days. Like Tsali back in the old Cherokee country. He died so the ones who had the courage to defy the white soldiers could stay in the land where their ancestors were buried. They didn't let the army drive 'em out here like cattle, like most of the people did."

More ancient history. "Uncle—"

Zeb overrode him. "I'm an old man, outlived almost everybody I know, except you." He studied Will intently. "And you done sold out to the enemy, like everybody else. Me, I'm gonna be like Tsali."

Will bristled at the criticism, even though he always promised himself he wouldn't. He sat back down on the couch arm. "Die, you mean?"

Zeb didn't turn a hair. "If it has to be. But before that, the bingo hall will be destroyed, and a lot of other things. I wish people didn't have to be killed too, but I don't see no other way."

Killed? What was he talking about? Will glanced nervously around the shack. Zeb used to have an old twelve-gauge he'd used for hunting small game, but Will didn't see it. "What happened to your shotgun?"

Zeb blinked at him. "Haven't been hunting in a coon's age. I got it hid in a good place. If them workers break in my house, they won't find it."

Will almost laughed at Zeb's paranoia. "If they wanted to steal a gun, they'd find one in better shape. That thing used to jam sometimes. If you aren't careful, you'll blow your own head off."

"I told you, I don't use it no more, but it ain't me you're worried about, is it? You think I'm planning to shoot somebody with that gun."

Will wondered if Zeb would have mentioned it otherwise, and his anxiety increased. "Are you?"

"I don't have to. All I have to do is sit here and wait for the Apportioner's judgment."

Zeb continued to speak in Cherokee, confident that Conrad wouldn't understand. Will wasn't so sure. Conrad knew some Cherokee, but maybe not enough to follow all that Zeb was saying.

"When it comes," Zeb continued, "I'm ready to die, but some will escape and go to the underworld. There is another world under this, and it is like ours in everything—animals, plants, and people—except the seasons are different. The streams are the trails to the underworld, and the springs at their heads are the doorways. But to enter there, you must fast and go to water. And you can never return here to live because when you go down there you take on the nature of the underground people, and you will die in this world in seven days."

Will had heard all this many times before. "Uncle—"

"Listen! When the destruction comes, remember what I tell you, Nephew. I know you don't believe me, but do as I say. Fast and go to water." He shrugged eloquently. "If I'm wrong, you've lost nothing."

Zeb had made crazy predictions before, but never on such a grand scale. Maybe Zeb did have hardening of the arteries, Will thought; he wasn't getting enough oxygen to his brain. Sitting out here alone, eating an improper diet, staring at that bingo hall, and getting madder every day as he watched it take shape wasn't helping him think any straighter, either.

It would have saved Will a lot of worry if they'd built the bingo hall somewhere else. To Zeb, the construction going on next door was a personal insult.

"They're going to blacktop this road from here to Highway 51," Will said. "There'll be a lot of traffic when the bingo hall opens for business."

"If it opens," said Zeb.

Will ignored the implied threat. "Night traffic, Uncle," he continued. "It'll keep you awake."

"I can't sleep but in fits and starts, anyway."

"You can still leave here. You can get an apartment in Tahlequah or Stilwell. I could arrange it for you."

"Let 'em run me off, you mean. I told you, Nephew, we been giving way to them too long. That's why we're in the sad shape we're in now."

If Zeb was in sad shape, it was by his own choice. As for Will, he wouldn't go back to that old primitive way of life for anything. He liked new cars and central heating and air conditioning and being called doctor by his students. But he would never make Zeb understand. He didn't even try anymore. The life Will had chosen had fixed an un-spannable chasm between them. He regretted the chasm, but not the choices that had put it there.

"You're talking about the whites, but most of the people working on the bingo hall have Cherokee blood."

"Cherokee on the outside, like I said," Zeb grunted. "That don't make 'em real Cherokees"—he touched his chest—"in here."

Will dragged a hand through coarse, close-cut hair and gave Conrad a helpless look. "I don't think he'll let you tape him today. He's too worked up over the bingo hall."

"Don't talk about me like I ain't here," Zeb snapped.

"Well, it's true, isn't it? Will you talk for the recorder today?"

"Huh! Why speak of that time, when it's right now we have to worry about?"

"See?" Will said to Conrad.

"Anyway, I'm busy."

Busy smoking that filthy pipe and drinking Budweiser, Will thought, and working up more resentment. But con-tradicting Zeb would be an exercise in futility.

Conrad picked up his briefcase, concealing his disap-pointment well. "Maybe another time."

Zeb stuck the pipe between his teeth and clamped down hard. He stared at Conrad.

"I'm very interested in what you have to say, Mr. Smoke. I'll record anything you want to get off your chest, and fu-ture generations of your people will hear you long after both of us are dead."

"How do I know you speak the truth?" he asked around the pipe.

"I give you my word."

Zeb's stare made it clear how much stock he put in Conrad's word.

"We have to go," Will said, eager to leave now that it was clear there would be no taping. "Good-bye, Uncle."

Zeb followed them to the door with a sullen look, no doubt frustrated because he hadn't goaded Conrad into defending the whites.

2

They walked back down the lane to the road. Will's shoulders slumped as if from a sudden weight. Only Zeb could make him feel this way, as though some essential part of himself had been lost in the past. As if he stood naked in an alien world.

Assimilated Cherokees and the whites in the university circles where he lived his life treated him with respect. Only Zeb could make him feel disloyal—like a traitor to his people—and, at the same time, angry for letting the old man get under his skin. When he was honest with himself, he knew these feelings were the real reason he didn't visit Zeb often.

On the other hand, staying away only increased his sense of guilt because he didn't think Zeb had many visitors these days. He was damned either way. As long as he was being honest, he wished the old man would go ahead and die. Or go down to that underground world he was always talking about.

Anything as long as Will never had to cope with him again.

They drove west on Highway 51 toward Cherokee County and Tahlequah, stretching their necks to keep the sun visors between them and the blinding sun.

The two-lane highway wound lazily between wooded hills. It was pretty country, especially when the leaves were out. Even in December, the huddled hills, like the backs of huge guardian beasts, seemed to offer protection and security. Protection from what, Will couldn't have said, but he couldn't shake an irrational feeling that dark clouds were gathering and these hills would not stop the rain of trouble that was coming.

Vexed, he pulled his thoughts back to the present. Uncle's ranting had affected him more than usual. He glanced at Conrad. "Another wasted trip. Sorry about that, Professor."

"No problem. I enjoyed the drive—and the company." Conrad was a widower who lived alone and rented his garage apartment to Molly Bearpaw, who worked for the Cherokee Nation.

Will managed a smile. He felt his spirits lifting, now that Zeb was several miles behind them. "Uncle's a rude old codger, but he's never boring."

Conrad scratched his chin. "I didn't catch all of what he said when he switched to Cherokee. Something about destruction and the underworld."

Will repeated the gist of Zeb's conversation, then said, "He's always going on about how the Cherokees have lost their way and angered the old gods. But today was the worst I've ever seen him. He gave me a real uneasy feeling."

"Is that why you asked about the shotgun?"

Will nodded.

"I understood him to say he would wait for the Apportioner's judgment," Conrad said.

"Wish I could believe him."

Conrad looked over at him. "Could be he was trying to aggravate you. I couldn't help noticing that you rub him the wrong way."

"Yeah," Will said glumly. "He doesn't think I'm good for much, but he keeps trying to salvage something." After all the years, it still stung that Zeb had no conception and certainly no appreciation for how hard he'd struggled to become a tenured professor.

They fell silent and watched the road, a lazy gray ribbon that curved gently one way, then looped back the other, again and again. Ahead, where the road started another S-curve, a half-grown coyote loped across the blacktop and disappeared into the trees on the other side. The quiet hum of the car's engine had a lulling effect. Will covered a yawn.

Finally Conrad broke the silence. "I have an idea, Will. Would you let me record you telling some of the stories you've heard from Zeb? Like the one about the underworld. We'd note the source for the record."

Will shrugged. "Sure, but it won't seem as authentic, coming from me."

"I know, but the more sources I have the better. And I'm not giving up on Zeb yet. I'll go back. No offense, but next time I think I'll go alone. If you're not around for him to insult, maybe he'll cooperate."

Will tapped a finger on the steering wheel. "He might agree to talk in the end, but he'll take his sweet time about it."

"I expect that. I've heard the Cherokees say they operate on Indian time."

"Which means whenever they get around to it," Will said.

"It's not a bad way to live."

Will did not comment. He himself had lived in the white world so long that he was a confirmed clock-watcher. Sometimes he wished he could go back, just for a while, to his childhood when time had been an endless river, flowing forward so slowly that you didn't notice its progress. "Even if uncle eventually agrees to be recorded, he may not necessarily let you pick the topics."

Conrad nodded. "That's okay. But I don't believe he's as averse to being recorded as he lets on. I thought I saw a flicker of interest when I said his words would be saved for future generations of Cherokees."

Will chuckled humorously. "You white devils are gluttons for punishment."

3

Four miles south of Tahlequah, Molly Bearpaw and her grandmother, Eva Adair, were working in the Park Hill Cemetery, taking advantage of the pleasant weather to clean up around the graves of Molly's mother and grandfather, Eva's daughter and husband. A cemetery fund paid for keeping the grass mowed all spring and summer, but the care of individual graves was left to the families.

The cemetery sat on a little knoll between a shallow wooded valley and an infrequently traveled country road. Beyond the road a few Hereford cows roamed a pasture, nosing the dead grass for scarce green blades. The pale-blue sky was cloudless, though it changed to hazy white near the horizon. The cemetery was a sad, lonely place to Molly. Given a choice, she would never visit a graveyard.

She spent half an hour picking up dead limbs and empty drink cans and adding them to the pile beneath a blackjack oak tree near the cemetery's tall wire fence. Dropping the last armload of limbs, she blotted her sweaty forehead with the tail of her baggy sweater and wished she'd worn a cotton shirt instead. She pushed up the sleeves and watched her grandmother, who was kneeling between the graves of her husband and daughter, pulling up clumps of dead grass and weeds from around the bases of the tombstones. Eva's birdlike body was lost in a pair of olive-drab coveralls that were several sizes too large.

In the last few minutes, Molly had noticed that Eva's dark eyes, behind her wire-rimmed spectacles, looked tired. Returning to the graves, Molly asked, "Are you about finished here, Grandmother?"

Eva sat back on her heels and swiped at her wrinkled brown brow with her sleeve. "Almost. All I have left to do is clean Josie's name plate." She pushed her glasses up her nose with an index finger.

Recessed in the granite marker above Molly's mother's grave was a metal square containing raised letters and numerals. The metal embossing held up over time better than carved stone; some of the oldest stone markers were worn so smooth that you could no longer read the names of those buried beneath them. Even the carving on the stone of Molly's grandfather, which had been in place for only twenty-one years, was beginning to blur. The name looked like "Echo John Ada," instead of "Echols John Adair."

But the problem with metal was that rust built up and it had to be cleaned and treated regularly or the words would be obscured.

"I'll do it," Molly said. She pointed at a crude bench a few feet away. "You sit over there and rest."

To her surprise, Eva did not argue. Molly helped her up, and Eva put her hands at her waist and straightened her back slowly, grunting with the effort. At seventy-five she had no business crawling over graves on her arthritic knees, but Eva was too proud to admit that she was failing physically.

Molly watched her settle on the bench. Except for being worn out, Eva seemed to be all right.

She reached for the can of cleaning fluid and wire brush they'd brought with them and knelt, facing the words on the marker:

> *Josephine Martha Adair Bearpaw*
> *Beloved daughter and mother*
> *Born March 21, 1946*
> *Died September 7, 1971*

Four brief lines to summarize a life that had spanned twenty-five years. The second line only hinted at the bare facts—that Josephine had been raised by loving parents and borne a child whom, by Eva's account, she had wanted and loved. Since she had died after the disappearance of Molly's father—Josephine's high-school sweetheart whom she'd married at eighteen—there was no mention of a husband in the brief tribute.

The facts preserved on the marker gave no hint of the dark shadow that, at some point, had come to sit on Josephine's shoulder. What had gone wrong? When had the darkness become her constant companion?

When she took the first drink? When she'd progressed to regular drinking sprees? When Molly's father walked out? Or was it as Eva had always insisted? Josephine had been drinking and playing around with the gun and it had gone off. It was a tragic accident, not suicide.

Eva's reality, unfortunately, did not jibe with anyone else's, not even Molly's. True, Josephine had been drinking, but Molly believed she'd known exactly what she was doing. She had waited until six-year-old Molly was with her grandparents, got the gun from the closet shelf, loaded it, put it to her head, and pulled the trigger.

Either way, it wouldn't have happened if there had been no gun in the house.

Josephine's suicide was the source of Molly's aversion to guns of any sort and, consequently, her reluctance to carry a gun in the line of duty.

A couple of close calls in the performance of her job as a Native American Advocacy League investigator, and the repeated urging of Sheriff's Deputy D. J. Kennedy, had not yet changed her mind.

Besides, she might not be performing those duties much longer, a fact that was a constant weight on her spirit. Several weeks ago, the principal chief of the Cherokee Nation of Oklahoma had summoned her to tribal headquarters and warned that the federal grant that paid her salary might not be renewed for another year.

Molly hadn't mentioned that meeting to anybody but D.J. Time enough to tell Eva if the grant was canceled. In the interim, Molly had half-heartedly phoned to inquire about a few jobs advertised in the *Tulsa World* and had followed up on the calls by mailing résumés.

So far she had no interviews scheduled, although a couple of people had written to say they weren't interviewing until after the first of the year and she should check back with them then.

One had brightened her day no end by passing along the gratuitous information that they'd already received a hundred and fifty inquiries about the advertised position. But that news wasn't as disappointing as it should have been.

The position in question was for an insurance-adjuster trainee. Before going to work for the Nation, she'd been employed in a Tulsa insurance-claims office and had hated every boring minute of it. As an adjuster trainee she would, at least, be out of the office part of the time, but she couldn't work up much enthusiasm over the prospect. If, by some grand stroke of luck, she was the one picked from among the mob of applicants, she would have to move to Tulsa.

Meanwhile, she managed to shove the prospect of jobless-ness to the back of her mind most of the time, and she did so now as she attacked the metal plate with the wire brush.

Instead of her professional predicament or the painful questions behind the metal words she was cleaning, she fo-cused on the fresh-baked lemon pie waiting for them at Eva's house. She'd have time for a piece and a cup of coffee before going home. Later, D.J. was taking her to dinner. Tomorrow he would leave for Colorado, where his ex-wife, Gloria, and daughter, Courtney, lived. Gloria had remarried and, while she honeymooned, D.J. and Courtney were going skiing.

D.J. had wanted Molly to go with him. Her refusal had hurt him, which she regretted, but she wasn't ready to share a vacation with D.J., particularly not in the company of his daughter, whom she'd never met.

4

Ed Whitekiller parked his pickup truck two blocks from
the motel, on a side street lined with fifties-style wood bun-
galows and giant elms, whose roots were destroying the
sidewalk. He pulled the collar of his windbreaker up
around his ears and kept his head down, for fear of being
recognized. He walked fast over the cracked and crumbling
pavement, hurrying to get inside, out of sight.

Now that he was here, he worried about his recklessness
in suggesting this rendevous. He must be nuts, meeting
Susan in Stilwell, which was even smaller than Tahlequah.
He knew too many people in this town. Did he have a sub-
conscious wish to get caught? Get it out in the open? Call
Dot's bluff?

He shook his head. He'd never gone in for all that psy-
chology mumbo jumbo. The fact was, meeting in Tahlequah, where Susan lived, was an even greater risk and he
hadn't had time to think of a safer alternative. His wife had
waited until they were eating lunch to tell him she and
their daughter were going to Tulsa for Christmas shopping.

Personally, Ed thought that was a pretty stupid idea, seeing as how he was out of a job and Dot's teacher's salary

plus his unemployment compensation barely covered the basic living expenses. But suddenly he had an afternoon free. He wasn't about to argue with her.

Dot had asked if he'd like to come shopping with them. He'd pretended to consider it, then said no, he'd watch a football game on TV, hang around the house as he had all weekend. She'd looked at him sharply and her skin seemed to grow taut across her cheeks.

"Of course," she'd said and pressed her lips together.

Meanwhile, Ed was making calculations. An hour-and-a-half's drive each way to Tulsa, a couple of hours shopping time. Make it five hours they'd be gone. Maybe longer; all the malls had had extended weekend shopping hours since Thanksgiving. There would be plenty of time for a little excursion of his own.

As soon as his wife and daughter drove away, he phoned Susan. "Hi, sweet thing."

"Who *is* this?"

So it was going to be like that, then. She knew very well who it was. "Your favorite Cherokee, darlin'."

"You'll have to be more specific than that."

He really needed this after the weekend he'd had. He described what they'd done the last time they were together. That ought to be specific enough for her.

"Oh. Ed," she said in a bored tone.

"Right, sugar. And guess what. Dot and Maggie went to Tulsa."

"Well, gee whiz, thanks for sharing that, Ed. Wish *I* was on the way to Tulsa. Or somewhere."

"My point is, I have the afternoon free."

"Bully for you."

She was still pissed because he'd stood her up Friday

night. Her husband had left on a business trip Wednesday afternoon and wasn't due back until Monday. She was lonely and had wanted him to meet her in Siloam Springs for dinner. He'd meant to, but when he told Dot he had to go see a man about a job, she'd said, "What kind of job interview is conducted at night?" and called him a liar and some other things and said if he walked out the door he needn't bother coming back.

Dot was into issuing ultimatums these days. The previous week, they'd had words over his coming home late— again.

She'd met him at the door. "Where were you?" Her words had the ring of an accusation.

"I drove to Tahlequah," he'd said with admirable patience. "Played some pool and went for a couple of beers with friends."

She swallowed and her lower lip quivered. "Ed, if I find out you're having another one of your nasty little flings, we're through."

"Maybe I stay out late because I know when I get here you'll start up with me. Did you ever think of that, Dot?"

She'd stared at him. "I mean it, Ed."

He'd brushed past her then and stopped short. Maggie was standing, frozen, in the doorway to the den, having heard every word.

The next few days, the three of them gave each other wide berths. Until he said he had to go out Friday night for a job interview and Dot had blown her top. "What's the employer's name?" she'd sneered. "Susan?"

That shook him. It was the first hint he'd had that she knew who he'd been seeing. "Who's Susan?" he'd asked.

She'd just glared at him. So he'd stayed home Friday

night and Saturday to convince her that he wasn't messing around with another woman. He'd made a show of being hurt by her mistrust and pretended to call the nonexistent employer to cancel the meeting.

"Are you satisfied?" he'd asked when he hung up. "That probably cost me a job."

Dot had snorted and walked away.

A few minutes later, he'd heard Maggie saying to Dot in the kitchen, "Mom, why are you always on Dad's back? He wants to spend time with his friends or go see about a job and you go ballistic." He could always count on Maggie.

He hadn't heard Dot's mumbled reply.

Meanwhile, Susan drove to Siloam Springs and waited an hour in the restaurant. When he finally got out of the house for ten minutes Saturday afternoon and called her, she'd hung up on him.

Now she'd had almost forty-eight hours to cool off, but apparently it hadn't been quite long enough. The fact that she hadn't hung up was encouraging, though.

"I can think of something much more fun than Christmas shopping," he said.

"Oh, yeah?"

"Uh-huh."

"Like what?"

"Meet me in Stilwell and I'll show you."

"Sit and wait an hour for you again, more likely, and then come home by myself. Yippee. That's just how I want to spend my Sunday afternoon."

He was proud of the way he kept his temper. She had to get it out of her system. He'd have to play along. "I explained how that happened and apologized. I don't know what else I can do."

She said nothing.

"Look, sugar, I swear I won't let anything interfere this time. I'm dying to see you."

"You mean you actually worked a few hours for me into your busy schedule? Wow, am I supposed to be flattered by all this attention or what?"

Her voice had that whiny twang that he hated. Nag, nag, nag. You'd think they were married. "I'm the one who should be flattered that you'll even talk to me, darlin'." He sounded very contrite. A horny man is a determined man.

It took Ed about three minutes to sweet-talk Susan into meeting him in Stillwell. Granted, it was too close to home, but they didn't have all day. He'd called ahead to make a reservation and stopped by the office to pay in cash before going to the room.

Susan was already there when he arrived, peeking out around the corner of the motel. Couldn't wait to see him. He didn't see her car. She must have parked in back.

From the look on her face, she was still sulking. Her eyes didn't light up at the sight of him. Her mouth turned down at the corners. And he'd swear she'd gained a few pounds since the last time they were together. The woman did love to eat.

Suddenly he saw what she'd look like in ten years, when she really got that middle-age spread, and for an instant his desire wavered. One thing you could say for Dot, she took care of herself.

"Where's your pickup?" Susan asked.

"Parked around the corner." He unlocked the door, kicked it shut behind them, and kissed her hungrily. That brought the old soldier back to attention.

After a few moments, she pulled away and sat down on

the foot of the bed. Her mouth was puckered up like a big red prune as she looked around with disdain.

"Not exactly five-star accommodations, is it?" Like she lived in the lap of luxury. Like he hadn't seen the four-room kit-built house her husband had provided for her. It was about half the size of a good chicken coop.

Besides, what did she expect in Stilwell, county seat of one of the poorest counties in Oklahoma? The Hilton? "I didn't notice. You're all I can see, sweetheart."

She wrinkled her nose. "It stinks in here."

Okay, so the place smelled like stale cigarettes, but that sort of thing had never bothered Susan before. He really was crazy, trying to keep two women happy. And not doing a terrific job on either front.

"Is that a new dress?"

"Uh-huh."

He could tell she was pleased he'd noticed. "Pretty."

He sat down beside her and nibbled her ear lobe. She'd dabbed perfume behind her ears. It was the same scent she always wore; he'd never had the nerve to tell her he hated the stuff. "Mmm. You smell fantastic." He nibbled some more.

She sniffed. "Is sex all you ever think about?"

Why, hell, no. Only this morning he'd been thinking about the great books of the Western world.

"Couldn't we just talk sometimes?"

Swell. He'd shelled out his last twenty for this dump so they could chew the fat. He lay back on the bed and put his hands behind his head, looking like a man with all the time in the world. "Sure. What do you want to talk about?"

She shrugged and didn't turn around. Pouting. He'd rather have a woman yell at him than sit around like a puffed-up toad. He waited her out, knowing she couldn't stand the silence for long.

"It would be nice if we could have a conversation, like *civilized* people."

Was that supposed to mean he was some kind of barbarian? Like she was used to intellectual discussions with that pot-gutted salesman she was married to. He was beginning to wonder if the goal was worth all this aggravation.

"About what, hon?"

She gave an exasperated sigh. "Whatever's going on in our lives. Things in the news. Stuff like that."

Wonderful. The news was all blood and gore and some religious nut holed up in a warehouse with two kids in Oregon. The FBI had sent in a regular army to deal with one whacko and two preschoolers. That was costing the taxpayers a bundle.

As for what was going on in his life, it didn't make for scintillating social chitchat. He couldn't find a job, and his wife suspected he was getting something on the side.

Well, what was a man supposed to do? Dot let him get in her lily-white pants about once a month, if he was lucky. You'd think he was married to the Virgin Mary.

A man had needs. It was Dot's fault he had to get his taken care of somewhere else.

"I talked to a couple of people about a job last week," he said gamely.

She looked around at him. "How'd it go?"

"It didn't. Nobody's hiring right now."

She relented enough to lie down beside him, her head propped in her hand. "Poor baby."

He touched the top button of her dress experimentally.

"I'll find something eventually." Sooner than that if he could get all those buttons undone.

"Sure you will, honey. Is Dot still giving you a hard time?"

"Dot gives everybody a hard time, even herself. I don't pay her any mind. She can't be satisfied unless she has something to gripe about."

"You'd think she'd be more supportive, especially now. It's hard on a man's pride to be out of work."

"Yeah, but Dot's not the most understanding woman in the world. Besides which, she's a worrier. She's not sweet-natured like you."

She gave him a stingy little smile and ran her fingers through his hair. "Why do you stay with her then?"

"You know the answer to that."

"Maggie?"

"What else."

She digested that, then asked coyly, "You really think I'm sweet-natured?" He'd never known a woman who needed so much reassurance.

He had two buttons undone and was working on the third. "You know I do, baby." He'd have sworn she was Mother Teresa if that's what it took.

She wrapped her hand around his fingers before he could get another button loose. "It seems like a year since I saw you."

"Don't I know it."

"You're not getting tired of me, are you?"

Was she reading his mind? The depressing truth was, he was plenty sick and tired of being hassled by both the women in his life. They never did that in the beginning. They waited until they thought they had him hooked.

"Never," he said earnestly.

She studied his face, searching for more reassurance, then decided not to push her luck. "Tell me what else you did last week."

Hell's bells. If she wanted a talk show, why didn't she watch Donahue? "Not much. Worked on my truck—put in a new radiator hose. Built Maggie a bookcase for her room. She's a great reader, Maggie." He kept this up, somebody would nominate him for Conversationalist of the Year. He wondered if it paid anything.

All this talking had made him go limp again. But he was out twenty bucks, and he meant to go along with her till he got what he'd paid for. This bait-and-switch stuff wouldn't deter him.

He searched his memory for a new topic of conversation. Nothing much came to mind. He'd paid a visit to old Zeb Smoke, whom he'd known all his life. Ed had been raised on a farm a mile from Zeb's place, and he'd always liked listening to the old man, even though he'd sounded kind of paranoid during that last visit.

But Susan didn't have a clue where a traditional old Cherokee like Zeb was coming from. That left the job hunting. Okay, if she wanted to hear the boring details, he'd oblige her. "Well, let's see . . . There was this guy I talked to about a job, told him I had experience and said I could get references. I couldn't figure him out, though. He acted like I made him nervous or something.

"Did you know him?"

"Never saw him before in my life. He got sort of flustered when I pitched in to help unload some blocks. Figured it couldn't hurt to show I was willing to work. He said thanks, but no thanks, and they didn't have any openings so

I should leave. Like I was dying to hang around and chat with such a friendly fellow."

She giggled and settled more comfortably beside him.

"I asked if I could fill out an application anyway, in case they had an opening later. He said he didn't do the hiring and, besides, they were out of application blanks, and I should leave my name and phone number, and somebody would get back to me when they got more forms."

"Sounds like he was just having a bad day."

"Maybe, but he was lying through his teeth. I saw a folder labeled Employment Application Blanks and it wasn't empty. For some reason, he didn't want me hanging around long enough to fill one out." He reflected, then added, "It was like I'd walked in on the middle of something—" He paused again, searching for the right word. "—something private."

She giggled again. "Maybe he was hiding a woman on the premises, and they didn't want anybody to know they were together." She released his hand and worry lines appeared between her eyebrows. "Like us."

He hastily loosed another button. "I don't know about that. I didn't see anybody else, it was after five. As I was leaving, another guy showed up and asked what I wanted. I was steamed by then, so I said I was looking for a job but, after sizing things up, I didn't think I wanted to work there."

"That wasn't too smart, Ed."

"I know it, but I was ticked off." Another button out of the way. He was almost home. "You know, baby, you might be right. Maybe they were both just eager to get out of there so they could love their women." He slipped his hand inside her dress and cupped her full, warm breast. "Like me."

She tensed for a moment, but he kissed her until she relaxed.

Evidently she thought she'd made him pay enough for standing her up. "You're a regular pistol, Ed Whitekiller," she murmured, looking up at him with soft, teasing eyes. "What am I going to do with you?"

Shut up and let me get on with emptying my barrel, while it's loaded. He almost said it aloud, but he didn't think she'd appreciate the joke. That was another flaw he'd noticed in his women. Lately, neither Dot nor Susan had much of a sense of humor.

If they had, he might want to spend more time with them than with his buddies. Well, it was their loss. They didn't know what they were missing.

Only his daughter appreciated him. Maggie laughed at all his jokes. She and his mother were the only ones who had ever loved him unconditionally.

Ah, Maggie. He doted on that girl. Dot said he spoiled her, but then Dot was jealous. Sometimes he wondered if he'd made a mistake in his choice of wife, but then he'd think of his daughter and know he'd do it all again just to have Maggie.

Women. A man couldn't please them and he sure couldn't get along without them. There were times when Ed wished that he could, but not right at the moment . . .

Afterward, when his heart quit beating like a snare drum and his thoughts focused on the here and now, he knew he'd lied to Susan.

Sure, Dot wasn't perfect, but he had to admit he wasn't

an ideal husband, either. At least she wasn't a clinger, like Susan. He wished Dot would loosen up, and she wanted him to quit spending so much time away from home. They had their share of problems. What married couple didn't?

On the other hand, he liked a clean house and a hot meal of an evening and other people there to eat it with. Dot was dirt's sworn enemy and she was a great cook. She never threw cold cuts on the table because she'd worked all day and was tired. He knew guys whose wives didn't even know the house had a kitchen. If they wanted a hot meal, they had to go to Burger King.

And he'd heard his divorced buddies talk enough to know that the old bachelor life wasn't all grins, either. They'd conned themselves into believing it would be, but after a few months they were singing the blues.

It was about time to shore up the home front. Susan was history. He was tired of dealing with her insecurities, and she was getting too demanding. He'd concentrate on Dot for a while. Something told him she wasn't bluffing with those ultimatums.

5

From the air, south Tulsa's Woodland Hills Mall must have looked like a sprawling, dun-colored, many-chambered hive with bees swarming to it from all directions.

Dot Whitekiller drove slowly up and down lanes in the huge lot, looking for a car backing out of a parking space. She could have driven right up to the door and paid for valet parking but, with Ed out of work, that was an extravagance she could ill afford.

Thinking of her husband made her feel depressed again. Ed had lost two jobs in three years. Without the skills employers were looking for, he didn't qualify for most positions that paid a living wage. She had begged him to take a vo-tech course in something, anything marketable, but he refused to believe that willingness to work and a line of good-old-boy patter were no longer enough to provide job security. It had been enough for his father, so it should be enough for him.

Every time they discussed it, he pointed out that, with two college degrees, she earned less than he did when he was working. The fact that the oil business had been depressed for several years and construction jobs were scarce and getting scarcer made no impression on him. Nor did the fact that, at least, she had job security and fringe benefits and would draw a pension upon retirement.

Dot had struggled not to resent the straits he'd put the family in, but she was losing the battle. About the time they got on their feet, he was laid off again.

She resented even more his cavalier attitude toward his situation. "Something will come along," he'd say. "Don't worry so much."

In his place, she would be spending all day, every day, looking for work—in Muskogee or Tulsa, even farther afield, if necessary.

Friday evening, she had spotted a newspaper ad for a manager trainee at McDonald's in Muskogee. He would have to start at the bottom, of course, working behind the counter for low pay. But it could lead to something if he proved he was dependable and willing to work hard. For all his faults, Ed wasn't afraid of hard work. And he had such a way with people, he was bound to increase their customer base.

Ed had laughed at her and tossed the paper aside, ending the matter with, "Can you see me working a cash register in one of those silly hats?"

Frankly, she couldn't. He had too much macho pride. One of his buddies might see him.

Later, he'd come out of the bathroom smelling of musk cologne and had the nerve to tell her he had a job interview that night and it might keep him out late. It was the last straw. She'd suspected for some time that he was seeing another woman, and it wasn't the first extracurricular detour he'd taken during their marriage, either.

She'd flown off the handle and mentioned Susan's name.

Ed hadn't reacted to it, though, and she had no real proof that Susan Butler was his latest romantic interest. Dot didn't know the Butler woman, but a friend had told her she'd seen Ed's pickup in Tahlequah one afternoon in George and Susan Butler's driveway.

It was hardly possible the friend had mistaken somebody else's truck for Ed's. But even if she confronted Ed with proof positive that he'd parked his truck in the Butlers' driveway, he would make up some reason why he'd been there to see Susan's husband.

Anyway, Friday night she'd finally said the words she had been keeping down for weeks, words she had always stopped short of before. If he left the house, she didn't want him back.

Even then, she had wanted him to convince her she was wrong. If he'd told her where the interview would take place and with whom, she could probably have managed to believe him. She *wanted* to believe him. Instead, he got huffy and made a phone call canceling the interview. Or pretended to. Then he'd accused her of costing him a job. Ed was good at putting the blame for their problems on her.

So what did he do all day Saturday instead of looking for a job? Built a bookcase for Maggie, who still thought he was as nearly perfect as a man could get. Well, Maggie was fourteen. Give her a few years, and she'd see through her father as Dot did. Unfortunately, Dot had been blind to Ed's flaws until long after they were married. He was so handsome and easy with people. Everybody liked Ed Whitekiller. Dot, on the other hand, was naturally shy and self-conscious in social situations. Ed had drawn her out, helped her to relax and be herself, even with strangers.

She'd never known a man with so much self-confidence. Ed could walk up to anybody anywhere, start a conversation, and they'd be chatting like old friends in no time. She'd have fallen in love with him for that, if for no other reason. In those days, she had thought herself lucky beyond her dreams that a man like Ed Whitekiller wanted to marry her.

The very characteristics that had attracted her to Ed had begun to wear on her nerves as the years passed. Life wasn't one good time after another.

She wanted to feel love and trust for her husband. She wanted to feel compassion for his jobless state. She wanted to feel anything but the recurrence of anger and resentment that had filled her when she first suspected he was having another affair.

Twice before, she had let Ed convince her that she was wrong, that her own insecurities made her see betrayal in the most innocuous things. But she could no longer deny her own senses. Ed was so cocksure of himself that he didn't even bother cleaning up after he'd been with another woman. Several times recently she had smelled sex on him.

He had the nerve to come home after being with *her*, crawl into bed, and cuddle up to Dot. A few times lately she had resorted to sleeping in the spare room, so angry she didn't even want him touching her accidentally in his sleep.

She no longer felt her heart lift at his smile or her body stir at his touch. She felt little these days but cold hard fury.

She had meant what she said to Ed Friday night. When she said it. But, later, when she tentatively broached the subject of a separation with her daughter, Maggie had turned on her in a rage. "If you and daddy get a divorce, don't expect me to stay with you! I'll go with daddy."

Dot should have expected that reaction, but it wounded her nevertheless, because she knew it wasn't just adolescent histrionics. Given the option, Maggie would choose her father.

"Mom!" Maggie shrieked, jolting Dot from her gloomy thoughts. "You drove past a parking space. Back up! Back up! We can still get it."

Dot slammed on the brakes and threw the car into reverse, backing fast and barely beating a Mercedes coming up from behind into the empty slot. The driver of the Mercedes honked and made an obscene hand gesture. Dot ignored him.

"Gosh, Mom, what's wrong with you?" Maggie asked. "You've been on another planet ever since we left home." Did she really have no inkling? Apparently Maggie had decided that Friday night hadn't happened. She glared at Dot in disgust. The big brown eyes that had once shone with love for her mother were more often hostile these days.

Dot said the only thing that she could truthfully say. "Sorry." She managed a smile. "Ready to brave the crowd?"

She put on her jacket but Maggie left hers in the car. The mild weather had held throughout the weekend, but the forecasters were predicting a cold front by midweek and possibly snow.

The mall smelled of pine and bayberry. "I'll Be Home for Christmas" blared from the P.A. system. Dot wondered what *her* home would be like by Christmas.

Would she celebrate the holiday alone?

Maggie and Dot decided to separate immediately so that Maggie could shop for presents for her parents. Dot gave her fifty dollars and told her to try to come back with ten. They still had to buy presents for Dot's parents and Ed's mother, and Dot had to redeem from layaway the expensive sweater Maggie had fallen in love with the last time they were at the mall. She hadn't bought anything for Ed yet, but she certainly wasn't in the mood today.

They arranged to look for each other every half hour in front of Gloria Jean's, the gourmet coffee shop in the food court.

Dot had gone without lunch for weeks in order to save two hundred dollars for Christmas. Ed didn't know about her stash. She'd told him she'd add today's purchases to her Visa card balance, which was beginning to look like the national debt.

It was a necessary deceit. If Ed had known about her Christmas fund, he'd have talked her out of walking-around money, as he called it. Dot wasn't about to give up more than a month of lunches so Ed could spend the money on one of his bimbos.

As soon as Maggie had disappeared into Dillard's, Dot stared at the rack of pay phones near the door by which they'd entered. An empty booth seemed to beckon her. Don't do this to yourself, she lectured silently.

She hesitated for several moments, but she couldn't talk herself out of calling home.

Piped strains of "Jingle Bells" poured relentlessly from the P.A. system as she squeezed into the only available booth to make her call. She let the phone ring a dozen times, but there was no answer. Ed had gone out. No big surprise, but her heart constricted painfully.

She banged the receiver down and fought back angry tears. If she asked him about it, he'd say he fell asleep in front of the TV set and didn't hear the phone.

Unless she could prove otherwise. If they started back right now, maybe they could get home before he did.

And then what? Pack his clothes and set them out on the porch? Oh, right. Maggie would cry and beg her to stop and, if Dot refused, she'd leave with her father. They'd move in with Ed's mother until Ed found a job. She didn't want that woman raising her daughter. She'd spoiled Ed rotten, just as he was spoiling Maggie. Without Dot's balancing influence, the child would be ruined.

What if she told Maggie the truth? That it was her father who had destroyed the marriage with his women and his lies?

Maggie wouldn't believe her. She couldn't. It would tarnish her image of her father beyond restoring, and no fourteen-year-old girl could handle that.

Even if somehow Dot made Maggie understand, she would hate Dot for taking away her father.

Dot gripped the metal shelf beneath the telephone and bowed her head. It was academic, anyway. The trouble in her marriage had nothing to do with Maggie. Whatever Ed was or had done, it was Dot's problem. She would not put her daughter in the middle of the mess she and Ed had made all by themselves.

"Lady, are you finished with the phone?"

Dot jumped as the impatient male voice jerked her from her desperate quandary. "Sorry," she murmured, edging around the harried-looking man who had somehow walked up behind her without her hearing him.

She detoured around a group of laughing teenagers and made her way down the mall, repeatedly weaving left or right around other shoppers. Deep in thought, she was barely aware of the holiday gaiety that surrounded her.

Nothing could be accomplished by dragging Maggie out of Dillard's with some flimsy excuse. She would try not to think about it, get Maggie's sweater out of layaway, and find gifts for her parents.

She had to stop reacting in the heat of anger, as she had Friday evening. She let herself get too overwrought. She had to get herself in hand.

No more confrontations unless she had proof that Ed was lying.

She couldn't afford a private investigator, and she couldn't follow Ed everywhere he went. Even if she could, she didn't think she wanted to lower herself to that level. Besides, her gut knew what was going on, even if she couldn't prove it.

What she had to do was wait, go on as before, and give herself time to come up with a reasoned solution she could live with. She would not give up her daughter. That wasn't even an option. She and Maggie stayed together, or no divorce.

But she wasn't going to deceive herself any longer, either. Ed would not change. If she stayed in the marriage, she would have to live with the resentment and humiliation of his infidelities. She'd done it for years, but she didn't think she could stand it indefinitely. She wanted out—with her daughter.

Mutually exclusive goals, it would seem on the face of it. But there had to be a way. She hadn't found it yet, but she would.

Nothing was impossible when you were desperate.

6

On Choctaw Street in Tahlequah, George Butler unlocked his front door and went inside. Dropping his suitcase on the sofa, he looked around and muttered an oath.

The place was a mess, clothes piled wherever Susan had taken them off. On the floor in front of the chair facing the TV set was a grocery sack half full of cracked pecans from the big native pecan tree in the back yard. Shells were scattered on the carpet around the sack. Susan had been picking out nut meats for holiday cakes and candy, probably stuffing at least half of them in her mouth as she worked.

"Susan!"

The kitchen was worse than the living room—counters and tabletops littered with dirty dishes, Pepsi cans, and fast-food cartons. It didn't look as though she'd cooked since he left Wednesday.

He'd like to believe she'd have cleaned up the mess if she'd known he was coming home early, but it wouldn't have mattered. His wife could live in squalor indefinitely. From what he could tell, she didn't even notice.

George figured he'd find her piled up in bed with a sack

of miniature Baby Ruth bars and a stack of supermarket tabloids.

"Susan!"

He stomped down the hall to check the bathroom and two bedrooms. In the room they shared, the bed was unoccupied and unmade, the sheets tangled. An empty potato-chip sack lay on the bedside table.

What had she been doing while he was gone—besides eating, watching television, and picking out pecan meats? And where the hell was she?

He banged out the back door, kicking furiously at dead leaves as he crossed the yard. He hadn't checked the garage when he drove into the driveway, but he did so now. Her car wasn't there.

Cursing, he went back inside, looked around, and cursed some more. Then he took off his suit jacket and tie and rolled up his shirt-sleeves. He started hot water running in one side of the sink, got out a trash bag, and began cleaning up the kitchen.

The last time he did this, he swore he wouldn't do it again. He'd promised himself he'd make Susan do it, if he had to stand over her until she finished. But he couldn't sit down in the middle of this mess and wait for her. No telling when she'd be back. She hadn't expected him home today.

He squeezed liquid detergent into the dishwater and put the dirty dishes in to soak, then he carried the trash bag full of soft-drink cans, fast-food cartons, and old newspapers out to the alley.

Next, he tossed her discarded clothes into the hamper and attacked the floors with a vengeance, his anger simmering as he wielded broom, mop, and sweeper.

By God, there would be some changes made around here.

He'd tried reasoning with her, shaming her, yelling at her. Somehow he had kept himself under enough control not to strike his wife. Well, he'd shoved her a couple of times, but a man could only take so much. And words sure weren't getting through.

Susan didn't work away from home; they'd agreed on that when they married. He'd expected their home to be a haven after a hard day on the road, a clean house and dinner on the table, the way it had worked with his parents. Susan had all day to take care of four rooms and a bath and to cook dinner. He didn't know *what* she did while he was away.

Before he left, she'd been after him to let her take an aerobics class to lose weight. He knew it would be wasted money. Susan never finished anything. Last year she'd badgered him until he'd given her sixty dollars for a karate class. That had lasted three weeks. She'd said she was going to practice at home. He suspected that had lasted about two days. She claimed she still practiced regularly, but he didn't believe her.

When she brought up the aerobics class, he told her she could walk or jog and it wouldn't cost a cent. Besides, he thought, if she'd move her fat butt and clean up around here, she wouldn't have a weight problem. But he wasn't in a good position to talk to Susan about her weight; he'd put on forty pounds since they married. It was all those restaurant meals he ate while traveling. He always meant to order the diet plate or a salad, but his good intentions vanished when he got hold of a menu.

In an hour, he had everything shipshape. In the process, he'd worked out some of his anger. But Susan still wasn't home and, after fifteen minutes pacing from window to window, looking for her car, he was madder than ever. He was tempted to get in his car and go looking for her.

First, he called a couple of her friends. One didn't answer, the other said she hadn't seen Susan for a week. As a last resort, he called her brother's house and was relieved when Pete's wife answered. George had never gotten along with his brother-in-law.

"Is Susan there?" The sound of his own voice was strange. Bottled up anger gave it a high, tight pitch.

"Is this Ed?"

George opened his mouth to identify himself, but something clicked at the back of his mind, and a suspicion that had crossed his thoughts once or twice came into focus. Suddenly he knew why he hadn't phoned Susan to let her know he'd be home early.

He kept mum.

"Listen," Della said after a pause. "I don't want any part of this thing with you and Susan. I think you're both crazy to jeopardize your marriages like this. So don't call here again looking for her."

She hung up.

Replacing the receiver, George felt all the blood leave his head.

A sudden stillness had gripped him, and for a moment his mind was blank. Then it filled up with rage. He grabbed the phone and threw it across the room.

She came waltzing in half an hour later. He was at the kitchen table, drinking coffee, his fourth cup since he'd cooled off enough to sit down. All the acid had given him a pain in his gut. The ulcer that hadn't bothered him in months was sending out distress signals.

"Georgie?"

She strolled into the kitchen, smiling. She had on a new dress, which she must have charged to a credit card. That little talk they'd had last month about getting the Master-Card paid off had gone in one ear and out the other.

"What are you doing home, honey?"

He rose from his chair.

"You cleaned the house. You didn't have to do that, sweetheart."

He set his chair aside with elaborate care and turned to face her.

"Did some of your customers cancel?" Amazing that she didn't seem to sense the explosion that was coming.

He wondered why he felt so cold inside. On the outside, his skin was on fire and his shirt was wet under the arms.

"You're trembling, honey," she crooned. "Are you sick?" She was halfway across the kitchen, arms out to give him a wifely hug, when he drew back his hand and slapped her, putting the force of his body behind it. He enjoyed the sharp smacking sound and the pain in his palm.

She shrieked and fell sideways and slid down the wall, clutching her jaw. Blood trickled from one corner of her mouth.

"*George?*" she wailed. Her tongue whisked across her lower lip, found the cut, and she swallowed blood.

He stood over her. "Where have you been?"

She started crying jaggedly and looked up at him with wide, terrified eyes. She smelled of fear. He enjoyed that too.

"H-have you g-gone crazy?"

Whore, he thought, and slapped her again. "Where have you been?" His voice was like steel.

She held her hands in front of her face and cringed away from him, sobbing hysterically. She tried to get up and he shoved her back down. Her head banged back against the wall.

"Answer me!"

She shook her head dizzily. "Driving . . ." She scrabbled sideways on the freshly mopped linoleum, still trying to get away from him. "D-driving around. I-I get lonely when you're g-gone."

He reached down and grabbed a handful of her dress beneath her chin, jerked her to her feet, and heard the sound of ripping fabric. He slammed her against the wall and stood, legs spread, between her and the door. "Liar."

She hiccupped and gulped, trying to stop crying, and held both hands out in front of her face. "G-get away from me, George! You've lost your m-mind! If you touch me again, I swear I'll call the police!" The pathetic bitch was trying to sound tough but her words were distorted by the split lip.

"Who is he?" If she gave him any name other than Ed, he'd kill her.

She looked past him wildly, telegraphing her intent, and then made a lunge for the back door. He caught her and slammed her up against the wall again. His hands squeezed her arms. He wanted to break some bones.

She whimpered, "You're hurting me, George."

He pushed his face into hers. "Who is he?"

She couldn't look at him. Blood and snot streamed from her nose into her mouth. She wiped it away with the back of her hand. "I—I don't know what you're talking about."

"Who is he?" he repeated for the third time and hit her with his fist.

She lay as he had left her, crumpled in a heap against the wall, knees drawn up, head resting on the linoleum. Her face throbbed and burned as though the skin had been scraped away. Her new dress—not even paid for yet—was ripped from neck to waist, where he'd grabbed her and jerked her upright so that he could go on hitting her.

She ran the tip of her tongue around the inside of her mouth and over her swollen lips and swallowed the metallic taste of blood.

She stared at the legs of a chair that had been knocked away from the kitchen table and tipped over on its back no more than a foot from where she lay. From her perspective on the floor, the legs looked like the bars of a cell. The click of the refrigerator coming on was the sound of the cell key, locking her in. The low, steady humming of the refrigerator's motor mingled with the thrumming in her head.

She had to get up. She lay there for long minutes while she gathered the strength to move. Then pain shot through her right shoulder. She rolled over on her other side and managed to sit up. She drew her legs up. Her breasts were sore—so sore. She hugged herself, careful not to mash her tender breasts. At the end, when he'd stopped hitting her face, he had pummeled her chest. That had hurt worse than the blows to her face. "Tell me his name, whore," he'd snarled, "or I'll kill you." His contorted face had been the face of a stranger, and she had believed him. She had told. And finally he had stopped hitting her.

Then, mercifully, he was gone, she didn't know where. She was vaguely surprised to be alive. She had been sure he meant to kill her and, briefly, she'd wished he'd do it and get it over with.

She realized slowly that she was cold. A draft moved through the crack beneath the back door where the strip of insulation had come off, and flowed across the kitchen floor. She shivered and tried to pull the torn edges of her dress together and hugged herself tighter, forgetting her breasts, and gasped at the throbbing tenderness.

Had to get up. She crawled to the fallen chair and held onto it as, slowly, she inched herself to her feet. The bathroom. If she could just get to the tub, run water as hot as she could stand it . . . let the heat ease the throbbing of her body.

She crept across the kitchen, down the hall, and into the bathroom. She locked the door.

The face reflected in the mirror was red and puffy, one side of the mouth three times the size of the other, the eyes deep and dull behind the narrow slits made by swollen lids. Blood was smeared over her cheeks and chin. She didn't know the person in the mirror.

She turned away and, bending carefully, turned on the faucet over the tub. The hardest thing was removing her bra. When she bent her arms and reached behind her, pain like the blow of a sledge hammer ripped through her shoulder. She cried out. Tears streamed from her eyes. She waited for the pain to subside, then gritted her teeth and reached back again, tore the bra's hooks loose.

Blackness enveloped her. She caught hold of the wash basin and hung there until she could see again.

Trembling, she turned off the faucet, stepped in the tub, and slid down into the searing hot water. Her muscles contracted, but she welcomed the surface pain. For a few moments, until she got used to the heat, it took her mind off the other pain deep in her body.

Where had he gone? Would he be back? She didn't think he'd return soon, maybe not ever. Did she want him to come back? No, she didn't want him, could not love him now. Had not loved him for some time, she realized. Maybe she had never loved him. She had gotten married because she'd finished high school and had no college plans. The only options open to her were some minimum-wage job or marriage. But she could hardly remember a time in her marriage when she had not felt restless and unfulfilled.

She did not even know what being fulfilled meant. But she was terrified of being alone. She didn't know how she would take care of herself. She had never thought she'd have to. There would always be a man to take care of her.

But if the man she married, the man who said he loved her and promised she'd never want for anything, could do what George had done to her, then there was no comfort or security anywhere.

There was only the illusion of security. There was Ed. She clung to the thought as the water slowly cooled around her.

7

"Ed . . . *Oh, Ed* . . ."

The voice on the phone was muffled and distorted. "Susan, is that you?"

"Ed, you have to come get me!" Her voice shook so badly he could barely understand her.

Had the woman lost what few brain cells she'd had? "I told you never to call here. Dot and Maggie are due home any minute."

"*Listen to me*! George came home early. He knows about us—"

Oh, shit. "Did you tell him?" He wouldn't put it past her. Maybe she had wanted to force his hand. She probably thought he'd leave his family if she kicked her old man out. Stupid woman.

"He made me, but he already knew."

"How?"

"He wouldn't say. He was waiting for me when I got home. He—he hit me."

"Where is he now?"

"I don't know." Her voice was steadier now. "He left—I

don't want to be here when he gets back. Come get me, Ed."

He was going to have to spell it out for her. He hated these messy breakups, but some women wouldn't let go any other way. "I can't come, Susan. I don't think we should see each other again. I know I should have told you this afternoon, but—" He faltered, unable to think of a credible excuse.

There was a long silence. Then she said, her voice trembling, "But you had to get laid first." She swallowed a sob. "Don't do this to me, Ed. You don't understand. He'll kill me! He'll kill both of us!"

Talk about dramatizing. She was hysterical. He spoke slowly, calmly, to get the message across. "I can't help you, Susan. Call the police and get a restraining order."

"Damn you, Ed Whitekiller! You can't throw me away like trash. Do you hear me, Ed?"

He hung up. The phone rang again immediately and he took it off the hook. He paced the house. What if Susan showed up here after Maggie and Dot got home? What if her old man did?

He'd better come up with something believable.

Okay . . . don't panic. Think.

He'd say he didn't know what was going on. Susan Butler had one of those obsession things, like those pathetic women who stalked celebrities.

Yeah, that was good.

Susan Butler had been stalking him. He'd done nothing to encourage her, but she wouldn't leave him alone. He'd been trying to handle it himself, hadn't wanted to worry Dot with it.

Would Dot buy it?

A few months ago, he'd have said sure, no problem. Now he didn't know. Dot had changed.

Maybe he wouldn't have to say anything to Dot. Susan was obviously off her nut. Nobody was coming after him. Still, he went through the house, turning out all the lights and locking doors. Then he sat in his recliner in the living room and watched the street. When, after an hour, neither Susan nor her husband had appeared, he began to relax.

Dot and Maggie got home at seven forty-five. Ed was in the den, leaning back in the recliner in front of the TV, where he'd been when they left. He was still wearing his old gray sweats too.

"Hey," he greeted them cheerily and made a show of consulting his wristwatch. "I was starting to worry about you two. You must have bought out the stores."

Maggie, who was clutching their purchases to her chest, gave him a kiss on the cheek.

He reached for a sack. "Let me see what you bought me."

Maggie laughed and danced away. "No way. I'm going to put these in a safe place, and don't you dare look for them, Daddy."

He put on an expression of innocence. "Would I do that?"

"Yes, you would," Maggie said. "You have to promise me you won't look."

He placed a hand over his heart. "Scout's honor."

She headed for the hall and presumably her bedroom.

Witnessing all of this, Dot felt only her own growing hatred. It was directed at Ed for his destruction of the marriage and his offhand ability to keep Maggie's trust, no matter what he did. It was directed at herself too, for the humiliating feeling that if she'd somehow been a better wife, Ed wouldn't want other women.

"You look tired, hon," he said.

"Shopping wears me out faster than anything." Her voice sounded taut, and he looked up at her questioningly. "The mall was a mob scene," she added. "I hate to shop when it's like that."

"Why do you think I didn't go with you?"

I am a vast sea of calmness, she thought. Nothing he says can make me tell him what I really think. It was the only power she had in her relationship with her husband, hoarding her thoughts to herself, refusing to let him in.

Looking down at him, she saw the deceit and selfishness behind his handsome face and quick smile. She wondered why it had taken her so long to recognize it. How had two such dissimilar people ever gotten together in the first place?

Looking back, she could remember only that she had been dazzled by him, head over heels in love with his beauty and his lovemaking. At the time, she had believed they were soul mates, their union decreed by some higher power.

If that was true, it was a demonic power.

Except for their daughter, they had no common interests. Their backgrounds, outlooks, values, ambitions were all different. No wonder it had fallen apart. The wonder was that the marriage hadn't self-destructed much sooner.

"I'm starved," she said and started for the kitchen.

"So am I."

I'll bet, she thought. Sex always made Ed hungry.

He got up and followed her into the kitchen. "You're too

tired to cook, hon. Why don't you take it easy. Can't we afford to order a pizza?"

She poured a cup of leftover coffee and set it in the microwave to heat. His feigned concern for her made her sick. "I think so. Just one, though." Fifteen dollars remained from her Christmas money. It would pay for a large pizza and the three dollars extra for delivery so far from town.

She bit her tongue to keep from asking what had happened to the twenty she'd given him yesterday.

He went to the phone and ordered a large pepperoni with extra cheese. Dot sat down at the table to drink her coffee. Gripping the cup with both hands stilled their trembling. It wasn't easy to remain calm. She wanted to kick and scratch and scream that she hated him.

"Did anybody call while we were gone?"

"No," he said quickly.

She lifted her eyes from her coffee and fixed them on him. "Were you here all the time?"

"Yes—" He looked at her worriedly and she could see the calculation in his eyes. "Oh, I forgot. I was in the garage for a while, sanding Maggie's bookcase. It probably didn't take more than half an hour, but it could have been longer. I lost track of time." He poured the rest of the coffee and put it in the microwave. "I got bored with the ball game. Don't even know who won."

He was neatly providing cover for more questions. He'd always done that, she realized now, but until recently she hadn't noticed because she hadn't wanted to. What a naive dimwit she'd been.

He brought his coffee to the table and sat down. "There's a Bill Murray movie on tonight. I don't think we've seen it before. Maybe the three of us could watch it and eat our pizza. We haven't done anything as a family in a long time."

The big family man. What a con. "Okay," she said indifferently. "If Maggie wants to."

His brow furrowed. He was clearly troubled by her reactions—or lack of them. Good. She hoped it drove him crazy.

"Guess I'll put the stain on Maggie's bookcase in the morning."

She said nothing.

"Tomorrow afternoon, I thought I might drive over to Muskogee and check into that job at McDonald's."

He was tossing her a bone. A few months ago she would have caught it eagerly. Now, she didn't care if he ever found another job. It wasn't going to affect her and Maggie.

"If you want to," she said.

"I thought that's what *you* wanted."

"Frankly, I don't care whether you go or not." He wasn't going to work at McDonald's. Who did he think he was kidding?

He leaned toward her. "Are you all right?"

She widened her eyes. "I'm fine. Why wouldn't I be?"

He shook his head doubtfully. He started in on some long tale about a fishing trip a couple of his friends had taken recently. Dot sat there, drinking her coffee and nodding occasionally, while her mind dwelt on other things.

Finally, the doorbell rang.

He jumped. "It's probably the pizza," she said, wondering why he seemed edgy all at once.

He got up. "I'll get it."

"You can take the money from my purse. I'm going to change before we eat."

She'd hidden Maggie's sweater in the car trunk and decided to leave it there for the time being. But she needed a little time to get herself together before they sat down to watch a movie.

As she was going through the closet she and Ed shared, she noticed a shirt hanging half off its hanger. It was one she'd ironed and hung up only yesterday. She would never have left it like that. She always buttoned the top button when she hung a freshly ironed shirt.

As she straightened the shirt, she caught the scent of cheap perfume. It was a scent that neither she nor Maggie had ever worn.

Cheap perfume for a cheap bimbo, she thought savagely.

If he'd had another woman in her bed . . .

She jerked back the spread and sniffed the sheets. There was no scent of perfume, not even her own, which she used sparingly. She remade the bed. She was spared that indignity, at least. He'd met her somewhere else, as she'd suspected when he didn't answer the phone.

If Ed had put the shirt back as he'd found it, she might never have noticed the other woman's smell.

Here was one base Ed had failed to cover. He was getting careless. Did he actually think he could talk her out of her suspicions as he always had before? Maybe not. He *had* seemed worried about something just now.

Evidently his damned self-assurance was deserting him. It had finally entered his thick skull that she could actually entertain the idea of living without him. About time, but too late to save the marriage.

She grabbed a pair of jeans and a red knit shirt and shut the closet door on the sickening scent of gardenias.

8

"You're preoccupied tonight," D.J. said Sunday evening as he and Molly left the New Echota House restaurant outside Tahlequah. His words demolished Molly's belief that she had covered her unsettled mood with a spate of meaningless chatter.

He opened the car door for her and went around to the driver's side. The restaurant was on a bank overlooking the Illinois River. Molly looked out at the slow-moving water. At night, it looked like black glass streaked with silver, its surface reflecting a shimmering white moon.

As D.J. got in, he said, "I gather you haven't turned up any promising job leads."

"Not really. I doubt that anything will develop until after the holidays." The words were out before she remembered that she had pleaded the urgent necessity of employment interviews as an unarguable reason for not going to Colorado with D.J.

"You can still change your mind and go with me."

She couldn't deal with this again tonight, and she resented him for bringing it up. She had told him all along that she wasn't going.

"I don't want to talk about it," she said wearily. "For one thing, I have to find a dress this week for Moira's wedding." Her best friend might actually get married this time, although Molly wasn't sure she would believe it until she heard Moira and Chuck say their vows. Four weeks remained until the wedding. A lot could happen in four weeks, particularly when Moira Pack was involved.

As they drove toward town, Molly put her head back on the seat and closed her eyes. The silence grew until she broke it. "I spent the afternoon with my grandmother, but I still couldn't tell her I'm probably going to be unemployed by the new year." She lifted her head and glanced over at him. His eyes were on the road. "She wanted to clean up my grandfather's and mother's graves while the weather was nice. If I hadn't helped her, she'd have gone without me, and she's getting too old to be tottering around the cemetery alone."

"So," he said quietly, "that's why you're so down."

"It's not the way I'd choose to spend a Sunday afternoon, if that's what you mean."

"It's more than that. You don't like visiting Josephine's grave."

She sighed and rubbed her eyes. "I think it's pointless, that's all. Do you know grandmother still puts sprays out on Memorial Day and birthdays?"

"Lots of folks do that. It's their way of paying homage to their dead."

"Nobody's *there*, D.J. Sometimes I think people do it to relieve guilt feelings for things they didn't do or say when their relatives were alive."

He ran his fingers along the smooth curve of the steering wheel. "That's a pretty harsh assessment, don't you think?"

She didn't reply.

"If it makes her feel better," he said, "what's the harm in it?"

"No harm. But I wish she'd leave me out of it."

He braked at a four-way stop, taking the opportunity to examine her face in the gloom. "Did she ask you to go with her?"

"No, she merely happened to mention that a neighbor would drop her off at the cemetery and pick her up later. I couldn't let her be out there alone." She turned on the car radio and restlessly ran through the stations. Country. Easy listening. Rock. A couple of preachers begging for money.

He waited until she'd given up on the radio and flipped it off. "If she goes alone, you feel guilty."

She sat slightly bent forward, her arms crossed. It was a particularly self-protective position. "Don't start up with me, D.J. Please."

He appeared to consider the request before rejecting it. "Can't you see what you're doing? You've fashioned an impossible quandary for yourself. You hate going but you can't let your grandmother go without you."

The air in the car seemed suddenly too close. It felt oppressive. She leaned over and rolled the window down a crack and let the cool night air wash over her cheeks. They'd entered Tahlequah via Downing Street, where the lights of fast-food restaurants created warm havens in the darkness.

"What if she was out there by herself and fell?" Molly said finally. "That road's not well traveled. It might be a day or two before somebody found her."

"She could fall in her own house," D.J. pointd out.

"I've tried to get her to move in with me, and you know how far I've gotten with that."

"Why don't you try not to borrow trouble," he suggested.

She sighed. "One of these days, I know she's going to ask me to keep up the graveyard visits after she's gone. Like a deathbed promise or something."

"You can tell her no." When, after several moments, she hadn't responded, he said half to himself, "No, I guess you can't."

"You're darned right. Now *that* would really make me feel guilty."

"It looks like you'll have to forgive her then."

Molly glanced his way briefly before turning back to the window. "There's nothing to forgive. Grandmother has no idea how I feel."

"I'm talking about Josephine," he said.

It was after midnight when D.J. went home. She had come very close to asking him, for the first time, to spend the night. It had been a drearily depressing day, and even the time spent with D.J. hadn't lifted her gloom.

He was leaving for Colorado tomorrow. She wouldn't see him for ten days, and she was going to miss him—far more than she would have believed possible a few months ago.

In the end, though, she hadn't suggested he stay over. If she ever took that step, it wouldn't be because she didn't want to be alone.

Instead, she'd let Homer, her golden retriever, in for the night. Now he was curled up in front of the sofa, watching her wander restlessly around the room.

She got an Oreo cookie for Homer, who loved them. "Here you go, old man."

He perked up and trotted over to the kitchenette, which could be hidden from the living room by folding wood doors.

While he chomped on the treat, she unfolded the sofa bed and turned on the TV, still thinking about D.J.

Two months ago, he had told her he was in love with her. He hadn't said the "L" word since, but she knew he was only waiting for some hint that she wanted to hear it. And sometimes she did want to, she admitted. She thought she loved D.J. too, though she had never told him in so many words.

She wished they could acknowledge their feelings without having to do something about it. To D.J., the next logical step would be marriage.

She wondered how long he would wait for her to overcome her fear of commitment. Not indefintely; even D.J.'s patience had limits.

She didn't want to think about the limits of D.J.'s patience tonight.

Homer came back and sprawled on the floor beside the sofa bed. She was bone tired, but too wired to fall asleep. She got into bed anyway, reaching down to scratch behind Homer's ears. He groaned with pleasure.

Molly stared at a black-and-white rerun of *The Fugitive*, hoping the mesmerizing drone of television voices would put her to sleep.

Instead, her mind wandered to another field.

Was D.J. right? After twenty-two years, had she still not dealt with Josephine's suicide?

She was willing to admit the possibility.

Why else did she resist visiting the grave? Even if it held little meaning for Molly, it was a small thing to do for her grandmother.

Eva had given of herself all her life and asked for little in return. It would be pure ingratitude to refuse when, two or three times a year, Eva wanted Molly to accompany her to the cemetery.

D.J. had been right about something else too. She *did* have a tendency to argue herself into corners and then waffle endlessly over which of the undesirable exits to take.

Enough of this stupid agonizing. There was really no question about what she must do. She would suck it up and go to the cemetery whenever Eva asked.

Although it was a foregone conclusion, spelling it out seemed to give her relief.

After *The Fugitive*, a rerun of *The Andy Griffith Show* came on, the one where Barney arrested Gomer, and Gomer reciprocated by making a citizen's arrest. Molly had seen it before, but Barney could always get a chuckle out of her.

Finally, as the show ended, she drifted into a deep, dreamless sleep.

9

Monday

"What's he doing out there?"

Cecil Kelly looked up from the tub of cement he was mixing. Franklin Soap had grabbed hold of two steel roof supports and was leaning out between them, staring toward the field behind the construction site.

They'd started work at 7:00 A.M., before the sun was up. The foreman wanted the concrete-block walls in place by the end of the week. The blocks would be concealed in the finished building by bricks outside and wallboard inside. They were behind schedule because they'd had to wait three days for the inspector to arrive and approve the blocks as meeting the architect's specifications before they could lay them.

Out in the field where Franklin was looking, a figure moved in a circle against the gray-white sky.

The figure was too far away to be recognizable if they hadn't already become so familiar with the sight of the old man. "More mumbo jumbo," Cecil said and added some cement to the mixture in the tub. Zeb Smoke hanging around the site wasn't anything new. Last week they'd caught him hiding behind the portable john, spying on them. Moss said he thought Smoke had been scattering tobacco around. It was enough to give a man the willies, Cecil thought, but Moss said to ignore the old man, he was harmless.

Horace Wilson came over to where Franklin was leaning out and squinting hard. The sight of the two men standing side by side was almost comical. Franklin was built like a sand crane, tall, with a scrawny neck, a long jaw, and the longest legs this side of the Arkansas line. He had enough white blood to grow a scraggly little beard. Trying to hide that pointed chin, Cecil thought. But the beard wasn't thick enough; consequently, it only called attention to his chin.

The top of Horace's head hit Franklin at shoulder level, though he outweighed the other man. With his bull neck, blocky shoulders, and squat build, he was nearly as wide as he was tall.

"It's a medicine ceremony," Horace said. "Listen."

Cecil stopped scraping the sides of the tub with the trowel he was using for mixing and cocked his head. In the stillness, the faint, gutteral sound of chanting drifted to them. "Maybe he's putting a hex on us," Cecil said jokingly.

As they watched, the old man lifted a pipe, then seemed to blow smoke out his mouth. He did this four times, each time blowing the smoke in a different direction.

"More likely," Horace said, "he's building a wall of protection between the construction site and his house." Everyone knew that Zeb Smoke had been forecasting doom and destruction on the whole Cherokee Nation because of the bingo halls.

It made sense that Smoke would try to protect himself from the disaster he thought was coming. What worried Cecil was Horace's serious tone and anxious look.

Come to think of it, Cecil had never heard Horace crack jokes about the old Indian the way some of the men did. "You don't believe that stuff, do you, Horace?" Cecil asked. Cecil himself wasn't sure what he believed. He made jokes about the old man to cover his uncertainty.

"Maybe I do and maybe I don't, but it ain't right to belittle other people's beliefs." Horace frowned.

Franklin scratched his crotch and spat on the ground. "Hell, Horace, you know Cecil ain't got no respect." He stopped scratching and squinted again. He was nearsighted, but after breaking two pairs of eyeglasses, he no longer wore them when working. Now he tripped over small objects and cursed a lot.

The old man had stopped blowing smoke and squatted on the ground. "What's he doing now, Horace?" Franklin asked.

Horace shook his head. "How should I know? I ain't no authority on medicine ceremonies."

Horace knew more about the old ways than many Cherokees, Cecil thought, but evidently Cecil's making light of Smoke's medicine hurt his feelings, so he wasn't going to talk about it. That suited Cecil just fine. He'd really rather not hear any more about medicine.

"Looks like he's poking at the ground with a stick or something," Franklin said.

"Mebbe he's digging a grave, mebbe his dog died," Cecil suggested.

"He ain't got a dog," Horace said.

A black GMC pickup drove up to the site, and Moss Greenleigh, the construction foreman, swung out and strode toward the three men. Moss was a big, rugged-looking man, well known and well liked in Tahlequah. He was active in civic affairs and a deacon in the Baptist church. At the moment, though, his scowl seemed to indicate a preoccupation with something other than town affairs or religion.

"Uh-oh," Franklin said. "Moss's got another splinter up his ass."

"It's the same one," Cecil said. "He can't stand it 'cause we're three days behind schedule."

"Maybe he's gonna get docked if we don't finish on time," Horace said.

"Naw," Cecil contradicted. "I think he's got another project supposed to start as soon as we finish here."

"Then why don't he come out here at seven o'clock and lay some blocks," Franklin muttered, turning to stare at Zeb Smoke again.

"He ain't above it," Horace said mildly. "I seen him outwork a whole crew once."

"Will you guys quit gawking at that old man and haul some blocks up here?" Cecil said. "This cement's ready."

Franklin and Horace hurried outside, stopping to speak to Moss on the way.

"How's it going?" Moss asked.

"We'll have the walls up by the end of the week, if the weather holds," Horace said, because it was what Moss wanted to hear.

Franklin jerked a thumb toward the field behind the site. "And if Zeb Smoke don't bring a plague down on us."

The foreman gazed at Zeb Smoke, who was moving around in circles again. "I can't help worrying about the old codger," Moss muttered. "He's isolated out here. He ought to be in town where people could look in on him once in a while. You think I should talk to the sheriff about it?"

"The sheriff can't do nothing," Franklin said. "Smoke's different, but I don't think he's crazy."

"Maybe," Moss murmured. "I wouldn't want him mad at me." He looked once more toward the field, then went over to Cecil, said something, grabbed the trowel, and stirred it around in the tub. Cecil watched him expressionlessly.

Seeing this over his shoulder, Franklin said, "He's probably eating Cecil out because we ain't put up a whole wall since we got here."

"Better Cecil than us." Moss hardly ever lost his temper except when a job was behind schedule. Horace snagged a wheelbarrow and pushed it over to the stack of concrete blocks.

The two men began hoisting blocks and setting them in the wheelbarrow. "Does it seem like to you these blocks been moved?" Franklin asked.

Horace picked up a block in each hand. No problem. Those exercises he'd been doing had strengthened his arms. "What do you mean, moved?"

"Moved. Don't you know what *moved* means? It seems like to me they was closer to the building when those guys from the lumber yard unloaded them."

"What you think, Zeb Smoke moved 'em over the weekend? What'd he want to do that for?"

"He couldn't move 'em if he had a year," Franklin snorted. "He ain't strong enough."

"Maybe he used magic. Just to drive you nuts."

Franklin looked at him to see if he was serious. "They're not where they was," he said stubbornly.

Horace picked up two more blocks and tossed them on the pile in the wheelbarrow. "Whyn't you wear your glasses, Franklin? You can't see shit without 'em."

"I ain't so blind I can't see a whole damn pile of concrete blocks," Franklin snapped.

"Whyn't you get you some of them goggles like ball players wear to protect their glasses."

"Look here. There was some blocks stacked here before. See the way the ground's mashed down?"

"Where?"

"Right here."

Franklin was bent over and Horace peered over his shoulder. "You're having visions or something. I don't see a thing."

"Then you're the one that's blind." Franklin stooped lower and stared at the spot. "Maybe they all ain't been moved. Maybe somebody stole the ones that was stacked in this spot over the weekend. We oughta count 'em."

"You count 'em," Horace said. "I got better things to do."

Franklin straightened up. "I'm gonna tell Moss some of these blocks been moved."

Horace cackled. "Franklin, you wouldn't admit you're wrong if it harelipped Chief Mankiller." He tossed two more blocks in the wheelbarrow. "We got a load. Let's go."

They headed for the building. "The old man's gone," Franklin said, craning his neck. "When we take a break, I'm going out there and see if I can tell what he was doing when he squatted down like that."

Horace whipped his head around and glared at him. "Wouldn't do that if I was you."

"Don't you want to know what he was doing?"

"Ain't none of my business."

"Well, I'm gonna do it."

"You're messing with something you don't understand."

"I just want to know what he's up to. I'm a curious fellow. I won't bother nothing."

Horace scowled and cast a troubled look at the field where, minutes earlier, Zeb Smoke had made medicine.

Dot Whitekiller was arranging her and Ed's breakfast dishes in the dishwasher when Maggie shuffled into the kitchen in her Mickey Mouse nightshirt.

Ed greeted her as usual. "Mornin', glory."

Dot looked at her wristwatch. Her nerves jangled. She'd been sitting at the kitchen table for half an hour, making cozy conversation with Ed. A stranger looking on would think they were clones of Ward and June Cleaver. Dot couldn't keep it up much longer.

"I'm leaving in ten minutes, Maggie," she said. It was twelve miles into Tahlequah, where Maggie attended school and Dot taught. They'd built their house in the country when Maggie was seven so that she could ride and run free over five acres. Maggie had had a horse then, but they'd sold it last spring, when she'd lost interest in riding, preferring to spend the time with her friends.

The school bus passed their front gate, but since she'd entered high school this year, Maggie was humiliated if her friends saw her getting off the school bus. She insisted that only dweebs rode the bus.

Yawning, Maggie opened the refrigerator to get the milk and fixed herself a bowl of corn flakes. She was making no noticeable effort to hurry. "Just because you have to be at school half an hour early, I don't see why I have to," Maggie complained.

"Because that's when the car is going," Dot said with taut patience. "Of course, you could always ride the bus."

Maggie rolled her eyes. "Daddy will take me later, won't you, Daddy?"

"There's no need to burn up gasoline by driving two cars to town," Dot snapped. "In case you haven't noticed, Maggie, we're down to one salary around here."

"Dot, sweetheart . . ." Ed put in. "I know you don't like being late, but you don't have to make such a big deal out of every little thing."

God knew he wouldn't worry about a few gallons of gasoline, Dot thought. Whether or not he took Maggie to school, she knew he would drive to town later, if the notion struck him. As he'd driven somewhere yesterday afternoon to rendezvous with a woman. When he needed gasoline, he'd charge it to a credit card, with no thought for how they would pay the bill when it came due. Dot knew all that, knew, too, that she was taking out her frustration on Maggie, instead of the rightful target. If she ever got started on Ed, she'd lose the tenuous control she had on herself.

"I need to pick up some stain for Maggie's bookcase, anyway," Ed said, continuing to take his daughter's side, as usual. And making Dot look like the mean ogre. Also as usual. "I might as well drop her at school while I'm at it." He grinned at Maggie. "I hated to ride the school bus when I was a kid too."

And look how great you turned out, Dot thought. "I could pick up the stain after school," Dot said, "or you could get it this afternoon in Muskogee. Unless you've decided not to apply for that job at McDonald's, after all."

"I've got another contact to make first."

"What contact?"

"I don't want to get your hopes up," he said, "but I got a

feeling I'll have a job soon. If nothing comes of that, I'll check on the Muskogee job later. Anyway, I want to get the stain on this morning. Lighten up, honey. It's only twelve miles."

"Twenty-four, round trip." Dot couldn't resist underscoring the obvious. "And that pickup guzzles gas."

She checked her watch again. Five minutes until she had to leave, so she might as well shut up and go now. Maggie would never be ready in time. She could insist that Maggie take the bus, but then Maggie would be snappy with her for days. And Ed would end up driving her to school, anyway. Dot always fought a losing battle when she took a stand against the two of them.

Resentment crowded into her throat, but she kept her mouth tightly closed.

She had decided yesterday to pick her battles judiciously, and this one wasn't worth the hassle. One way or another, Ed wouldn't be around much longer to undermine Dot's every attempt to make Maggie more responsible.

"I'd better get on the road," she said. She desperately wanted to remind Ed of the time Maggie was due at school, but somehow she restrained herself. If Maggie was late, she'd have to stay after school in detention hall, which might teach her a lesson.

"I'll see you two later," she said and left the kitchen.

By early that afternoon, Ed decided it was safe to turn the telephone ringer back on. After an uninterrupted night, a pleasant breakfast with his wife, and a trip to town, his equanimity had returned. Susan had merely been blowing off steam when she'd warned he couldn't get rid of her easily. He'd made his position clear enough for even Susan to understand, and she had to accept it. What choice did she have? She and George the salesman would work things out. Or not. He didn't care which, as long as they left him out of it.

He took a big thermal mug of coffee and the fruitwood stain out to the garage. Maggie had messed with her hair until they were late, and they'd arrived at school that morning ten minutes after the final bell. He'd let her talk him into going to the principal and making an excuse for her tardiness.

He knew he shouldn't have, but he didn't see what difference ten minutes would make to his daughter's education. And he thought that thirty minutes in detention, after all day in school, was pretty harsh punishment for a few minutes' tardiness. Maggie had probably missed roll call. Big deal. Besides, he had a hard time saying no to Maggie, and the little minx knew it.

He'd told the principal his truck wouldn't start that morning, which was why Maggie was late. The tardiness was excused, and Maggie wouldn't have to go to detention hall.

He hoped Dot didn't find out about it, though. She'd throw a fit. She was about due for one, anyway. She'd been much too quiet Saturday and Sunday. It made Ed uneasy.

But she was bound to revert to type by this evening. She'd be on him again about Maggie needing to suffer the consequences of her own actions and other psychological garbage. Personally, he thought the kid would learn that lesson soon enough. Let her have a good time first.

Meanwhile, the old man was around to smooth the way for his little girl.

After talking to Maggie's principal, he'd picked up a can

of stain, then made another stop, setting into motion the scheme he'd thought of during the night. He'd come home feeling optimistic about his job prospects. The atmosphere could be tense for a while, but once he had the job he'd work harder than anybody, and they wouldn't regret that they'd hired him.

He stood in the garage, sipping his coffee, and looked down the driveway. A row of tall, shortleaf pines grew at the edge of his acreage next to the road. Their straight trunks were so evenly spaced they might have been planted, though they hadn't been. The species was plentiful in this part of the state. When Maggie was younger, she had loved gathering the cones and spray painting them for Christmas decorations.

Above the trees, a few clouds drifted, but they were too wispy and white to portend rain. It was going to be another mild day. Hard to believe it was December.

He whistled a tune as he turned, walked to the back of the garage, and set his coffee on a shelf. He switched on the portable radio he kept there, found a country-western station, then got a screwdriver to pry the lid off the can of wood stain. Humming along with the tune on the radio, he carried the bookcase closer to the open garage door to take advantage of the morning sunlight.

His pickup sat on the east side of the double garage. He positioned the bookcase in the center of Dot's vacant parking space, on the west side.

That done, he got his coffee, the stain, and a stool to sit on. Still humming, he settled down, facing the rear of the garage so the sunlight could warm his back through his denim shirt while he worked. He began to mix the stain with the wood spatula he'd picked up at the paint store.

As he stirred, he admired his handiwork. He'd done a perfect job of putting the bookcase together, and he'd sanded it until it was as smooth as glass. He inhaled the pleasant smell of new lumber. He didn't even mind the odor of wood stain. He enjoyed working with wood, and he was good at it. It wasn't fair that he couldn't get a decent job because he didn't have some rinky-dink vo-tech credentials.

After mixing the stain, he ran his palm over the sanded surface, enjoying the feel of it, just as he'd taken pleasure in the smoothness of Susan's skin yesterday afternoon. But, unlike the warm softness of female flesh, this was cool and hard. Still, he could almost see her flushed face and half-closed eyes and feel the tightening of her thighs against his flanks.

But that was over now and, frankly, he was relieved.

Once they'd finished yesterday, he'd wanted to say good-bye immediately and get back home. She'd had other ideas, preferring to linger in bed. No more complaints about the accommodations then. He'd felt tense and impatient with her clinging. You might say the honeymoon had been over long before that frantic phone call yesterday.

As they left the motel, she'd wanted to know when she'd see him again. He'd said he had to be careful now, Dot was getting suspicious. Any other woman would have gotten the picture. *Don't call me. I'll call you.*

Knowing Susan, he should have had the courage then to tell her flat out that it was over. If he had, he told himself, she wouldn't have phoned him, expecting him to drop everything and run over there because she'd had a knock-down drag-out with her old man.

Well, it was behind him now. He didn't think Susan was going to be a problem.

He picked up the brush and dipped it into the stain, drawing it up and back against the rim of the can as he pulled it out.

The next half hour passed without notice, as he applied the stain evenly to the bookcase.

He stood and stretched and reached for his coffee. He'd let the stain penetrate for a few more minutes. After finishing the coffee, he used a piece of cheesecloth to wipe the excess stain off a spot on a back corner of the bookcase. The color looked about right. He went over the bookcase, wiping away the stain that hadn't penetrated. Then he stood back to admire his handiwork. Nice job, if he did say so himself.

He could probably apply the varnish that afternoon. He thought he had enough left over from previous projects. He'd look for it in a while. Right now, he wanted to catch a weather report.

He walked back to the radio again and ran the dial until he picked up a station that gave frequent news and weather updates. As he let his hand drop, he thought he heard the telephone ringing inside the house. He tensed. Maybe Susan hadn't given up after all. He shook off the thought.

It was probably his imagination. He couldn't hear the phone ring over the noise of the radio. The announcer promised a news and weather update after the next song, which was one of Ed's favorites.

He hummed a few bars with Garth Brooks. Now, there was a guy who didn't have to worry about being out of a job. Ed spent a few minutes fantasizing about making as much money as a country-music star. A couple of good years and he'd never have to worry about money again. All those women throwing themselves at him wouldn't be bad duty, either.

The fact that he couldn't carry a tune in a bucket didn't interfere with his daydream. He was really getting into the country-music-star fantasy when he thought he heard footsteps. He whirled around, expecting to see somebody— Susan?—walking down the driveway toward the garage.

Nobody there. Frowning, he turned off the radio and listened. He heard no more footsteps. Why was he so jumpy today? He was letting Susan's hysteria get to him, make him imagine things.

Taking a breath, he reached out and flipped the radio back on. As he did so, he caught, from the corner of his eye, a movement in the shadows between his pickup and the garage wall.

His heart lurched. "Who's there?" He had an irrational urge to run. Instead, he took a step toward the pickup. "Is anybody there?"

A figure moved out of the shadows and came toward him.

"Hey—" In confusion, he saw who it was. "What are you doing here?" He took a moment to compose himself. "I didn't hear you come in. I—"

He took another step and banged into the lawn mower. He'd forgotten it was there. Pain shot up his leg. He muttered an oath and grabbed his shin. Bending down, he saw that he'd ripped a hole in his jeans. Blood oozed from a cut beneath his knee.

He bit back another oath and straightened up. The figure had disappeared.

What in the hell was going on?

Suddenly he was aware of a movement, a presence, behind him. A split second too late, he pivoted, tried to turn around. As he did so, a movement flashed on his left.

A blow fell.

It struck solidly at the base of his skull. Colored lights flashed in front of his eyes and white pain shot through his head. He went down and the lights faded and darkness closed in.

He was dragged across the garage floor, but he didn't feel it.

He did not hear the engine start or the garage door closing or footsteps fading away.

10

It was after five that afternoon when Dot and Maggie drove into their driveway. Dot left the car in the drive because she had to go to a PTA meeting later.

Maggie jumped out of the car as soon as it stopped. She was furious with her mother. Dot had had a conference with a parent after school and hadn't reached the high school until an hour after the last class was dismissed.

The least she could have done was phone Maggie at the high school to let her know she'd be late. But, no. Maggie was supposed to stand around outside the building, like a dork, waiting until her mother decided to show up. After all, she had nothing more important to do.

In fact, Maggie suspected that Dot had dawdled in order to be as late as possible. What kind of parent conference took an hour? She thought Dot was punishing her because she hadn't been ready in time to ride with her that morning.

After half an hour, Maggie had grown tired of waiting and phoned home, confident she could talk her father into coming for her. Unlike her mother, Ed would do just about anything she asked. But Ed hadn't answered the phone. Dot had nagged him so much that he'd probably gone to Muskogee to apply for that dumb job. She'd simply *die* if he went to work at McDonald's.

"Daddy," Maggie called. There was no answer. Her father wasn't at home. Had he really gone to Muskogee to see about the McDonald's job? Not necessarily, she told herself. He'd mentioned something about another job that morning, hadn't he?

Maggie dropped her books on the couch and went to the kitchen for graham crackers and a glass of milk. By the time Dot had gathered up her papers and purse and come inside, Maggie was heading for the back bedroom with the food.

"Maggie, don't leave your books in the living room," Dot called.

Why couldn't her mother get off her back! Maggie set her snack on her bedside table and went back for the books. Hugging them to her chest, she stalked past Dot, who was standing in the dining room, arms folded.

"And you can just get over your little snit too," Dot snapped. "I'm sorry I was late. I couldn't walk out in the middle of a parent conference, and you know it."

Maggie dropped the books on one of the twin beds in her room and slammed the door. Silently cursing her mother, she threw herself on the other bed and reached for a graham cracker.

She almost wished her parents *would* separate, so she could get away from her mother. But that was probably because she was mad at Dot at the moment. Her mother was strict and demanding, but Maggie doubted that her grandmother would be much easier to live with, and if she and her father left, that's where they'd go.

Her grandmother was old-fashioned. She often remarked that Maggie wore too much makeup and that her skirts were too short. All of grandma's dresses were long-sleeved and almost reached the floor. She ought to see some of the girls at school. She'd probably faint. At least her mother didn't hassle her because she wanted to dress like her friends.

Even if her father had a job, she didn't think she could talk him into getting an apartment for the two of them. He wouldn't want her to be alone when he had to work late or go somewhere in the evening. Maggie sighed and reached for another graham cracker. What a bummer. Everybody thought she was such a baby.

She finished the graham crackers and sat up to drink the milk. Her bedroom looked out on the back yard. The dog-wood trees that shaded her bedroom in the summertime lifted barren, black branches against the hazy sky. Daylight was fading fast, and the dark branches bent and swayed in the rising wind.

Beyond the back-yard fence was the pasture where, until last year, they'd kept her mare, Tilly. Last summer, with Tilly gone, weeds and Johnson grass had grown as high as the fence. The autumn rains had been heavy and now the beaten-down vegetation was brown and rotting.

When she was younger, Maggie had loved looking out at Tilly grazing in the pasture. Before entering high school, she'd been a member of 4-H and gone on trail rides with the group. But she'd outgrown that kid stuff. If only they could move to town so that she could be with her friends after school.

Since that probably wasn't going to happen, she'd have to bear the isolation until she could drive. She'd already started working on her father—when her mother wasn't around—to buy her a car for her sixteenth birthday.

She set down her empty glass. Might as well do the algebra homework before dinner and get it over with.

Just then a rabbit ran into the back yard and stopped to nibble at the dead grass. Glad to be diverted from homework for a few more minutes, Maggie got up. She jammed her fingers in the hip pockets of her jeans and leaned her forehead against the cold windowpane. Wind groaned at the window as if begging to be let in.

As though sensing her presence, the rabbit lifted his head and seemed to look right at her. She tapped on the glass and watched him hop through an opening in the chain-link fence and across the driveway in front of the garage.

That was the moment when the big light over the garage came on. The light was equipped with an electric eye and turned itself on when it grew dark enough.

Through the small glass panes at the top of the garage door, Maggie saw what looked like the roof of her father's pickup truck.

Had he been in the garage all this time? He could work on that old truck for hours without knowing how much time had passed. But if he was working on the truck, the light inside the garage would be on, and she didn't think it was. She would have noticed the light behind the glass panes before the yard light came on outside.

Maybe the truck wouldn't start and a friend had come by to take him somewhere. Her father had hordes of friends he could call on. Maggie knew it got on Dot's nerves when Ed's buddies came over to watch a ball game on TV and drink beer, but Maggie thought it was neat that they enjoyed each other's company so much.

She grabbed a jacket from her closet and went back down the hall and through the living room to the front door.

Dot heard her and came to the kitchen doorway. "Where are you going?"

"Be back in a sec," Maggie said and shut the front door behind her. She ran across the porch and down the driveway to the garage.

She heard music. The old radio her father kept in the garage must be on. She frowned. She wasn't worried, exactly, she just wanted to see if her father was in the garage. If he was, he should have heard her mother's car and come out to greet them. If he wasn't, why had he left the radio on?

She bent over to grab the garage-door handle and pulled on it. The door slid up smoothly on its runners beneath the roof of the garage.

The pickup sat in its accustomed place.

"Daddy?"

No answer.

The yard light illuminated enough of the garage for her to find the switch and turn on the interior light. Her father wasn't there.

Sometime during the day he'd stained her bookcase. The scent hung in the air and the bookcase had been moved. It sat in the vacant half of the garage. Admiring the color, Maggie touched it gingerly. The stain was dry enough for her to move it out of the way. If her mother had to move it later to drive her car in, it would give her another reason to criticize Ed.

She set the bookcase against the wall on her mother's side of the garage.

Her father had left the lid off the can of stain with the

uncleaned brush resting on the lid. The bristles were dry and stiff.

It wasn't like him not to clean up after himself. Maggie put the lid on the stain and stuck the brush down in an open jar of paint thinner that her father must have readied earlier. Evidently he'd left the garage in a big hurry.

She turned off the radio. Now she was beginning to feel worried, and an eerie shiver snaked down her spine. She remembered something she'd seen on television. An entire family had disappeared from their home, leaving food on the table and the television set on. No trace of them had ever been found.

She shivered again and looked around before turning off the light, to make sure she hadn't missed something her mother's car could hit.

The space was clear. As she reached for the light switch, she saw a shadow in the cab of the pickup. It looked like something was leaning against the steering wheel. Cautiously, she walked closer.

Somebody was slumped over the wheel.

She had already reached out to grab the door handle before the thought fully registered. She opened the door. It swung back.

She watched, frozen, as her father's body fell sideways out of the truck and landed at her feet. His head hit the concrete floor with a loud crack.

Maggie felt her stomach heave. *He's sick. He passed out!*

"Daddy?"

She reached down to touch him. His face was cold.

She jerked her hand back.

And screamed.

11

By the time Dave Highsmith arrived, the woman had taken the girl into the house. The paramedics had come, declared the man dead, and were waiting impatiently for Highsmith in the driveway when he got there.

Highsmith had taken time to finish his dinner before leaving home. The woman had said the guy was cold and stiff, so what was the hurry? Highsmith didn't get in a hurry about much of anything. Which was probably the reason he had a reputation in some quarters for being lazy. He wasn't lazy. He thought things through before acting, looked before he leaped, which was a whole different thing.

In his six years as sheriff of Adair County, he'd had three previous suicides in his jurisdiction. Two had done it with guns, and one woman had crawled into her bathtub and slashed her wrists.

Carbon-monoxide poisoning wasn't as messy, but Highsmith wished this guy had done it where somebody besides his daughter could have discovered the body. There was no doubt in his mind that Ed Whitekiller had died of carbon-monoxide poisoning. The girl had found him in his pickup, the windows rolled down and the garage door closed. The

key was still in the ignition and it was turned on. The gasoline tank was empty. Ed Whitekiller had probably been
dead long before the engine burned up all the fuel in the
tank.

Unfortunately, the girl had opened the truck door and
the body had fallen right at her feet. Naturally, the kid
had spazzed out. From her mother's description, she'd had
to use physical force to get her daughter out of the garage
and away from her father, who she kept insisting was not
dead.

As a routine procedure, Highsmith took a few pictures of
the corpse and the interior of the pickup cab, including a
close-up of the ignition with the key in it, as he'd found it.
There was nothing in the cab now but a few black stones on
the passenger seat. Odd, but people carried all kinds of
weird stuff in their cars. Maybe Ed Whitekiller had col-
lected rocks.

Dutifully, Highsmith snapped a shot of the stones and
made a rough sketch of the scene.

Then he shut the cab door and instructed the paramedics
to transport the body to the Cherokee County Morgue in
Tahlequah. In all cases of unattended death, the law required an official ruling as to cause of death, and the medical examiner in Tahlequah serviced both Cherokee and
Adair counties.

When the ambulance left, Highsmith went around to the
front door of the house. It was a ranch-style brick with
dark-turquoise shutters, neat and well-kept. Low-growing
holly bushes created a hedge beneath the shuttered windows.

Ed Whitekiller's wife let him in. The daughter wasn't in
evidence. He hoped her mother had gotten her to sleep. A

bachelor, Highsmith dreaded, above all else, having to deal with hysterical females.

The inside of the house was as clean and tidy as the exterior. Highsmith took off his jacket and laid it over the back of a chair.

The living room was floored with wide oak planks, the center section covered with a multicolored floral-design carpet. On it sat a hunter-green camel-backed sofa, a gray leather recliner, two red and hunter-green chairs, and dark wood tables. The prints and watercolors on the neutral-gray walls picked up some of the bright colors in the furniture and carpet. He saw a discerning touch, probably Dot Whitekiller's, everywhere he looked. It made Highsmith think a little sadly of his own barren quarters.

"I apologize for disturbing you at a time like this, ma'am, but if I could ask a few questions, for my report."

She nodded numbly and indicated the leather recliner which faced a tall, cherry entertainment center. Probably her husband's chair, Highsmith thought a bit uncomfortably as he sat.

After a moment's hesitation, she lowered herself to the edge of the sofa, her hands clasped tightly in her lap. Dot Whitekiller was a nice-looking woman, tall and slender in a crisp white shirt and straight navy skirt. She had dark hair and eyes, but she didn't look Indian, though he guessed her husband had been at least half.

The woman was pale and tense. He was clearly an unwelcome intruder, not an unfamiliar situation in which to find himself. She didn't appear to have been crying. She seemed more apprehensive than struck by grief. Probably still in shock, as you'd expect from the wife of a suicide whose body had been discovered an hour ago.

"I don't want my daughter subjected to questioning," she said. "She's resting, and I don't want to disturb her."

"I understand. This kind of thing is tough on everybody, especially a child. She'll need help to get through it."

Unaccountably, she bristled. "I can take care of my daughter, Sheriff."

"I didn't mean to imply otherwise, ma'am. I may have to ask the girl a question or two later, but I'm sure you can tell me all I need to know right now."

She gazed at him without blinking.

"I'm very sorry for your loss, Mrs. Whitekiller."

"Thank you," she murmured.

Remembering the stones in the pickup, he asked, "Was your husband a rock hound?"

Confusion filled her eyes. "A what?"

"A rock collector."

"No." She almost sounded amused, but she didn't smile. Highsmith wasn't sure she could; her face looked stiff enough to crack. "Why would you need to know that for your report?"

"There were some rocks in the pickup cab, ma'am."

"Rocks?" She shrugged helplessly.

He moved on. "If you'll bear with me a few more minutes, I'll be out of your way."

She nodded. "Good. I'd like to get this over with as quickly as possible."

That made two of them. He'd much rather be kicked back in his favorite chair at home, reading the *Outdoor Life* that had come in the day's mail.

He fumbled for his pen and notebook. "Did you have any idea that your husband was contemplating taking his own life?"

She lowered her eyes and stared at the pale, blue-veined hands in her lap. "Not really."

"He didn't make a will recently or give away cherished belongings?"

She looked up, clearly amazed by the question. "Ed?" A single breath eased from her. "My husband never thought about the future, Sheriff. He spent money like we were printing it in the back bedroom, but he didn't give away belongings."

"He didn't have a will?"

"He wouldn't even talk about it. Ed preferred to go on as though unpleasant things like death didn't exist. He was like a child in that way." She fixed her eyes on a print of bright-red poppies on the wall opposite the sofa.

"I guess there are a lot of people like that."

"I suppose. It's not easy to live with somebody who refuses to face reality or plan for the future. In my opinion, it's irresponsible and self-centered."

Highsmith cast her a querying look. Shock made people say and do strange things, but he'd never run into such undisguised bitterness before. She didn't stir. "So, as far as you knew, your husband had no reason or thought of committing suicide?"

She looked at him. She took some time to think it over. "It never crossed my mind before—" She chewed the inside of her cheek.

"You've thought of something?"

She lifted one hand, then let it flutter back to her lap. "Ed had been out of a job for about five months and was having trouble finding something."

"Did he seemed worried or depressed over that?"

"Depressed?" She paused to think it over. "Until recently,

I'd have said absolutely not. He was too sure of himself. I always thought depression was brought on by self-doubt." She looked at him, her eyes questioning.

He nodded encouragingly. "What happened recently to make you change your mind?"

"I didn't change my mind, exactly, but lately I realized I couldn't always tell what was going on with him."

Now, what did that mean? "He wasn't one to express feelings then."

"Oh, he expressed feelings all the time, but not necessarily the ones he was experiencing. Not with me, anyway."

Was she calling her husband a liar? In Highsmith's experience, recent widows tended to paint their late husbands as saints, or the next thing to it. Perhaps the Whitekillers' marriage had been in trouble. *Something* was off here. She wasn't acting like a grieving widow, even one suffering from shock.

Highsmith leaned forward to ask, "What did you think when you realized he was dead?"

A moment's hesitation. "I thought—well, I thought he might have been trying to scare me—thinking somebody would find him before—well, in time to save him."

Highsmith stared at her. Had he heard correctly? The man had clearly been dead for hours when he was discovered and, from what he had gathered, the wife and daughter weren't expected home until four o'clock, at the earliest. As it happened, they hadn't arrived until after five. Who did she think her husband expected to rescue him? And why would Ed Whitekiller have taken such a dangerous risk just to scare his wife?

She must have seen the bafflement on his face. "It was only a brief flash," she amended. She lowered her eyes and clasped her hands in her lap. "The next instant, I realized I wasn't thinking clearly. It was the shock and dealing with my daughter. She was hysterical . . . kept begging me to help her carry him into the house and put him to bed." Suddenly her eyes filled with tears.

Frankly, Highsmith was glad to see something that looked like grief. "So, you knew immediately that he had committed suicide?"

She wiped her eyes with her fingertips. "It was obvious, Sheriff. I mean, the garage door was closed when Maggie found him in the pickup, and the ignition key was turned on. I don't know why I happened to notice that in the middle of trying to calm Maggie down, but I did. The motor must have run until the truck was out of gasoline."

"That appears to be what happened." Odd, he thought. Families of suicide victims usually denied it at first, no matter how plain the evidence was. "Then, Mrs. White-killer," Highsmith said, "you must have asked yourself why your husband had killed himself. Did you come up with any answers?"

She took a deep breath. "I think he may have suffered something like temporary insanity. It's the only explanation I can think of. In his right mind, Ed would never have killed himself at home, where Maggie might find him."

He noticed that she didn't say, where *she* might find him. "If he wasn't worried or depressed, why would he suddenly go crazy?"

She shrugged faintly. "He only had another month left of his unemployment benefits and no real job leads. So maybe he was depressed, after all, but covered it well."

They both heard the muffled sob at the same time and looked up to find the girl standing in the doorway. She was as tall as her mother, thin and shapeless as a young boy. But she had good bones, and when she filled out she might turn into a real beauty.

At the moment, her thick brown hair was in disarray, her eyes swollen from weeping.

She stared incredulously at her mother. "Don't you dare talk about him like that!" she cried. "My daddy was not crazy! And he didn't kill himself!"

12

Tuesday

Winter returned Monday night and forecasters warned that the temperature could drop below freezing Tuesday afternoon or evening.

Horace's car wouldn't start, not an uncommon occurrence. He'd called Cecil to get a ride to work. When the two men drove up to the construction site at 7:00 A.M. that morning, Franklin was standing in front of the stack of concrete blocks. He had his glasses on and an envelope and the stub of a pencil in his hands.

Moss drove up right behind them.

"What's Moss doing here so early?" Horace asked.

"I think he's gotta go to Tulsa later," Cecil said.

All three men got out, looked at each other, then at Franklin as he walked around a stack of blocks, his lips moving silently, and wrote something on the envelope.

"What're you doing, Franklin?" Moss asked.

Franklin didn't look up, but he flapped the envelope to show he'd heard and didn't want to be interrupted. He walked and scribbled on the envelope again.

"What's he doing?" Moss asked Cecil and Horace.

"My guess is he's being his usual hard-headed self," Horace said.

"What's that mean?" Moss asked.

"When Franklin gets something in his head, it takes brain surgery to get it out," Horace told him. "He's still got that bee in his bonnet, the one he kept going on about yesterday."

"Which one?" Cecil asked sarcastically. "He's got a whole damned hive in there. That wouldn't be so bad, but he has to tell everybody else about it."

Yesterday, when Franklin hadn't been going on about the concrete blocks being moved, he'd been badgering Horace about the rocks Zeb Smoke had left on the ground, or that Franklin thought he'd left. Nervous about going alone, he'd finally talked Cecil and Moss into going out to the field with him to look around.

Seven rocks, Franklin kept saying to Horace, seven *black* rocks. What did it mean? *Come on, Horace, I know you know. Why won't you tell me?*

All Horace would say was, "I told you not to mess with that—keep away from me." Of course, Franklin wouldn't. He'd dogged Horace's footsteps all afternoon, asking the same questions, until Horace had finally had enough and threatened to jerk his scraggly beard out by the roots, one hair at a time, if he didn't shut up.

Hunching his shoulders up against the early-morning cold, Cecil laughed. "By God, he's counting them blocks."

Franklin was wearing snug blue jeans that made his skinny legs look at least six feet long. He finished writing, stuck the pencil stub behind his ear, and ambled toward them.

"Looks like he's finished," Horace said. "He must have got here at six-thirty."

Moss planted his hands on his hips. "Franklin, what in hell is wrong with you?"

"Had to know, boss," Franklin said, handing him the envelope on which he'd written a column of figures and the total. Couldn't stand not knowing."

"Someday you're gonna have to know one thing too many," Cecil said.

Franklin looked blank. "Huh?"

"Somebody's gonna break your long nose for sticking it where it don't belong."

Moss glanced at the column of figures and scratched his chin. "I can't believe you got here early to count blocks."

"Had to satisfy my curiosity," Franklin said.

"You wanted to prove you were right, you mean," Horace said and spat on the ground.

"What's the verdict, Franklin?" Cecil drawled. "Is Zeb Smoke carrying off our blocks in the middle of the night? Gonna add a room on his house, maybe?"

Franklin scuffed the toe of his boot in the dirt. "I never said it was him. Anyway, there ain't no blocks missing." The admission was made grudgingly.

Cecil hit the side of his head with the heel of his hand, as though to clear his ear canals. "Am I hearing things? Did Franklin just admit he was wrong about something?"

"Sort of," Horace responded.

Moss wadded the envelope and flung it away. "Maybe you can keep your mind on your work today instead of worrying everybody else with conjured-up mysteries."

Franklin bristled. "I always do my share of the work. You can't say I don't."

Moss heaved a sigh. "What I'm saying is you run your mouth too much," he said, not unkindly.

Franklin stuck out his jaw, removed the pencil stub, and took off his glasses, which he put in a case and stuck in his shirt pocket with the pencil. Then he stalked back to the concrete blocks and began throwing them, two at a time, into the wheelbarrow.

"Aw, now you hurt his feelings, boss," Cecil snickered.

"You think?" Moss queried.

"He needed it," Cecil said. "Maybe he'll give us a little peace and quiet around here."

As Moss and Cecil walked toward the building, Moss said, "I've decided to talk to the sheriff about Zeb Smoke, see if we can get the old man some help."

Overhearing, Horace thought the old man would not appreciate Moss's help. He started to tell him so but changed his mind because he doubted he could make Moss understand. His boss was something of a do-gooder, the kind that thought they knew what people needed better than the people themselves. Sometimes he was right. Almost singlehandedly, Moss had established a homeless shelter in Tahlequah in an unused building behind the Baptist church. He'd gotten the women of the town involved and the shelter was run with volunteer help. Moss meant well, but he could get carried away, like he was about to do with old Zeb Smoke.

Horace joined Franklin and began piling bricks in the wheelbarrow. "Moss didn't mean nothing," he said.

Franklin threw him a dark look. "Sometimes I think he likes to throw his weight around. Thinks he's some hotshot since his wife's family put him in charge of the construction company."

"Moss is okay," Horace insisted.

"What if I'd been right?" Franklin asked. "What if there had been some blocks missing? He'd have thanked me then."

Horace sighed inwardly. Franklin was worse than a pit bulldog. When he locked his teeth on something, you couldn't pry him loose.

Molly hadn't fully shaken her weekend gloom when she reached her office Tuesday morning. D.J. had left before daylight on Monday and already it felt as though he'd been gone a month.

The lowering gray sky outside her office window threatened rain or snow. Since the mild weather had been blown away during the night, she was dressed in a bulky yellow sweater, brown corduroy jeans, and boots to ward off the drafts in the old building.

She started to phone tribal headquarters to ask if the chief had any further news on the grant that paid her salary, but she changed her mind before she finished dialing. If the chief heard anything, she'd contact Molly. She knew Molly was in an agonizing limbo, waiting to hear. That was the worst, the waiting. Even if the news was bad, once Molly knew, she at least would know what she had to deal with.

She felt angry and frustrated, but there was no one to blame. It certainly wasn't the chief's fault. The new administration in Washington was keeping the president's campaign promise to cut costs by eliminating jobs. The Bureau of Indian Affairs, which administered federal grant funds to the tribes, was only one of the agencies to be affected. All offices of the Native American Advocacy League would probably be slimmed down or closed altogether.

That didn't make it any easier for Molly to accept the probable end of her tenure.

Disconsolate, she rummaged through a desk drawer until she found a Snickers bar—her favorite comfort food. With the mingled tastes of chocolate and caramel melting on her tongue, she gloomily surveyed her small office in the old Cherokee Capitol Building, which sat in the center of Cherokee Square facing Muskogee Avenue, Tahlequah's main street.

This job fitted her to a T. Not that the salary was all that generous, but it met her needs. Every day was different, depending on the cases under investigation, and she liked being virtually her own boss and being back home in Cherokee County, five minutes from Park Hill and the grandmother who had raised her. She even liked her one-room garage apartment behind the home of retired university professor Conrad Swope.

It wasn't a good time to be looking for a job. For months, she'd heard television commentators say that the economy was in recovery. If so, Molly's corner of Oklahoma hadn't gotten the word. She wanted to stay in Tahlequah, but her chances of finding another job here were virtually nonexistent.

She finished the Snickers and tossed the wrapper into the wastebasket beside her battered old desk. In addition to the desk, the office contained just enough room for two metal file cabinets and two wood chairs for visitors. The furnishings consisted of castoffs from the tribal office complex south of town. The plaster walls were covered with hairline cracks, which Molly thought gave the place character. The ceiling was high, the tile floor faded. She liked to imagine she was surrounded by the ghosts of long-dead chiefs of the Cherokee Nation.

Unfortunately, with Christmas approaching, business was at a standstill. She would have welcomed an involved investigation to take her mind off her troubles, but apparently people didn't worry about civil-rights violations when they were in the holiday spirit. After the first of the year, she'd get some new cases. If she was still there.

She gazed out the window, across the square. A bare-branched sugar-maple tree marked the edge of the sidewalk. Beyond that, across Delaware Street, the second-floor windows of an old red-brick hotel had been boarded up and the ground floor converted to businesses—the Oklahoma State Employment Service, an abstract company, and Kelly's Deli. Next to the deli, the Tahlequah Chamber of Commerce, formerly across the hall from Molly's office, now occupied the old post-office building.

She sighed and tapped her foot restlessly. She might as well think about shopping for a bridesmaid's dress. She reached for the phone and dialed the attorney's offices where Moira worked.

Moira herself answered. "Benson and Hilldebrand." Bruce Hilldebrand, a young Native American (Cherokee and Choctaw) attorney, had recently joined the partnership after an intensely ambitious female attorney, who had driven Moira crazy, had moved to a large Oklahoma City firm.

"It's Molly."

"Hi. What's up?"

"I've got some time on my hands, so I thought I'd shop for a bridesmaid's dress today. Can you join me? We could go during your lunch break."

"I'm busy today. Besides, what's your hurry? If you wait till after Christmas, you can get something on sale."

That would be less than two weeks before the wedding. It would be cutting it pretty close if alterations were needed.

"Uh-oh," Molly said.

"What?"

"You're getting cold feet." It had happened three times before, each time with a different fiancé. But Moira had sworn that this time she was sure, Chuck was the one. "You've decided not to get married."

"I have *not* decided not to get married. I'm dying to get married."

"Uh-huh."

"Honestly. I'm just trying to save you money on the dress."

"Does Chuck know you have a pathological fear of walking down the aisle?"

"No! And I do not!"

"Okay, okay." Scratch the shopping trip. Molly didn't particularly enjoy shopping, anyway, but it would have been something to do, a way to keep busy and occupy her mind for an hour or two. She should have known it was too soon to think about a bridesmaid's dress.

"Let's have lunch this week," Molly suggested.

"Hmmm. I'm snowed under with work. I'll probably be eating at my desk all week. But I'll see you Thursday night."

"Thursday night?" Molly repeated blankly.

"I've enrolled in that weaving class you told me about."

Molly turned her desk calendar to Thursday and saw her reminder that the first class would meet at 7:00 P.M. at the library. It had been a month since she signed up and she'd forgotten all about it. She'd wanted to learn Cherokee finger weaving for a long time, but Moira's interest was a surprise. Starting the class practically on the eve of her wedding didn't seem like the best idea in the world to Molly.

"Since when are you interested in Cherokee finger weaving?" Molly asked.

"You kept talking about it and that got me thinking. I'm living right in the middle of the Cherokee Nation and I know zilch about the culture. I decided it was time I learned something."

All of which made sense. It just didn't sound like Moira.

"I have to go," Moira said. "Felix is buzzing me."

"I'll see you Thursday night." As Molly hung up, there was a hesitant knock at the office door. People usually didn't knock.

"Come in," she called.

The door opened. A girl thrust her head around the door facing. "Are you Molly Bearpaw?"

"Yes. What can I do for you?"

Still the girl hesitated. "I can come back later, if you're busy."

"I'm not occupied at the moment." She motioned for the girl to enter. "Come in and sit down."

As the girl lowered herself into the nearest chair, Molly saw how painfully thin she was. Her body seemed to be lost in an oversized navy-and-green plaid flannel shirt that fell to the knees of faded jeans. Looking at her, Molly thought of some poor orphan waif who'd escaped from the cruel mistress of a children's home.

She was in her early teens, Molly judged, and already five-eight or nine. Her body had used all its nourishment to grow taller, leaving none to pad the bones with a little fat. But time would take care of that. Right now, though, she seemed all arms and legs. And she ought to be in school. But—Molly had just noticed the dark circles under her eyes—maybe she was sick. Even more reason she shouldn't be running around without a coat.

The girl was studying Molly. "Yes?" Molly prompted.

"I thought you'd be older."

Molly smiled. "I'm twenty-eight. Is that old enough?"

The girl did not return her smile. She wadded the tail of her shirt in one hand. "I read about you in the *Cherokee Advocate*. About that murder you solved at the Cherokee Museum."

Where was this going? "I didn't solve it all by myself," Molly said. "I had help."

"It sounded like you did the hard part. I mean, you got shot and all."

"I spent one night in the hospital. It was only a flesh wound." Which had been pure luck. She hadn't solved the case with brain power; the truth was she'd just kept poking around until she'd stumbled on the solution. If she'd figured out sooner who the murderer was, she would never have put herself in the way of that bullet.

The girl looked at her hand twisting the tail of her shirt. She was finding it difficult to say what she'd come there to say.

"So—what brings you to my office?"

She looked up and, to Molly's dismay, her eyes were full of tears. She used her shirt to wipe them away. "I don't know where to start. You see, it's so important that you believe me."

Molly leaned back in her chair and laced her hands behind her head. "Why don't you start with your name?"

"Oh, I'm sorry. I didn't say, did I? I'm Maggie White-killer. My father is—was Ed Whitekiller."

Molly nodded, though she didn't recognize the name. She'd picked up on the change of verb tense, though. "Did your father pass away recently?"

Maggie Whitekiller nodded and wiped more tears. "Yesterday."

Yesterday? Good Lord. No wonder the child was in a state. Molly dropped her hands and sat forward, leaning her elbows on the desk. "I'm so sorry. I know what it's like to lose a parent when you're young."

"You do?"

"Yes. I know it doesn't seem possible now, but it gets easier with time."

Maggie stared at her. She clearly didn't believe a word of it.

"Do you live in Tahlequah?" Molly asked.

She shook her head. "Twelve miles out, but I go to school here. I didn't go today. My mother didn't go to work, either."

Molly wondered how the girl had gotten to town. "Where is your mother?"

"At the funeral home, making arrangements. I said I'd wait in the car, because I wanted to come here and talk to you. If I'd told her that, she wouldn't have let me."

She had mentioned reading about Molly's last murder investigation in the tribal newspaper. Had her father been murdered? "How did your father die?"

A fierce determination flickered through the girl's tears. "My mother thinks he killed himself, but he didn't. I know he didn't!"

Molly pictured a man with a noose around his neck.

"Why does your mother think he committed suicide?" she asked gently.

"Because he couldn't find a job."

"Did he give her some indication he might take that way out?"

"No, no. It's just, he—he was in the garage, in his truck with the garage doors closed. The sheriff said the motor had been running, and it burned up all the gasoline before I—" She took a deep, shuddering breath. "Before I found him."

Dear God, this vulnerable waif had found her father's corpse. Molly couldn't imagine anything more traumatic. But it sounded like carbon-monoxide poisoning, pure and simple.

Maggie hugged herself. "You would have to know my father to know why I'm so sure he would not kill himself. He had fun, enjoyed life. He was *happy*. He was always happy. And he loved me. He would never leave me alone."

That was an odd way of putting it. She still had her mother.

Maggie swallowed hard and went on. "The sheriff thinks it was suicide too."

"Do you know the sheriff's name?"

"Highsmith. I don't know his first name."

Dave Highsmith. The death had occurred in Adair County, then. Twelve miles from Tahlequah. It must be just over the county line.

"My mother won't listen to me," Maggie said, "and neither will the sheriff. I called him this morning." Her brown eyes darkened in despair. "He said I should rest and talk to my mother, and he'd take care of everything else."

Which sounded like good advice to Molly.

"Nobody will listen to me."

"The medical examiner will determine the cause of death," Molly said, wondering if the girl understood about autopsies. "If it was carbon-monoxide poisoning . . ."

"I don't care! That still won't prove he killed himself! They'll never make me believe it!"

"Maggie, perhaps the sheriff was right. You should talk to your mother." The girl needed help to deal with her grief, but surely the mother would realize that.

Maggie shook her head violently. "I don't want to talk to her. It wouldn't do any good. Please, you have to help me."

"Well—" Molly said doubtfully.

"That's what you do, isn't it?" she demanded. "Help people?"

"Yes, but I don't understand exactly what you think I can do for you."

"Investigate! Like you did in that museum murder case. Nobody else is going to. Please, will you find out how my father really died?"

For some time after Maggie Whitekiller left, Molly gazed out her office window at the gloomy gray day. She felt as if she were bleeding. Maggie's plea had pierced her heart.

Because she knew what the girl was feeling. If Maggie let herself believe that her father had chosen to die, it followed that he hadn't loved her enough, after all, to stay with her. From there it was a mere step to thinking that Maggie herself was lacking in some essential ingredient. If she'd been a better daughter, her father would not have left her.

Molly knew all about that kind of thinking. Even though she'd dealt with her own self-doubt long ago, knew that Josephine had killed herself because there was something lacking in Josephine and her father had run away because he was weak, it hadn't been easy. As it wouldn't be easy for Maggie Whitekiller.

It did seem to ease Maggie's mind a little when Molly said she'd look into Ed Whitekiller's death. She had a strong feeling she'd be wasting her time, but what else could she have said to that pathetic, lost child?

There was no suspicion of a civil-rights violation, which, after all, was what Molly was charged with investigating, according to her job description. Beside the fact that it was almost certainly suicide, she had a perfectly legitimate reason for not getting involved. But how was she supposed to explain that to a grieving teenaged girl?

As it happened, she had time on her hands. And she'd rather be sniffing around the corners of a suicide victim's life than sitting in her office, waiting for the days to pass until, finally, it was her office no longer.

She took a new folder from a drawer, labeled it "Whitekiller," and dropped it in the file cabinet in front of her current case files, the investigations of which were at a standstill. She was waiting for official documents in two cases—birth certificates, driving records and so forth—which might or might not give her new angles to pursue.

She shut the file drawer, grabbed her jacket and purse, and left the office. The first thing to do was talk to Dave Highsmith. If she left now, she'd arrive in Stilwell about noon. She'd find that barbecue place where she and D.J. had eaten once and have lunch before calling to the sheriff.

13

When Molly entered the sheriff's office, Dave Highsmith was running his hands over his face as though trying to rub away cobwebs.

Molly cleared her throat and he looked up. "Molly Bearpaw," she said. "Remember me?" They had met at the ground-breaking ceremony for the Cherokee Nation's new bingo outpost in Adair County.

"Sure do." Highsmith half stood behind his desk and extended his hand. The amenities taken care of, he flopped back in his chair. He was about forty, Molly guessed, on the tall side, and getting a little thick around the waist. His red hair was mussed on the left side. She suspected she'd interrupted a nap. He'd been asleep in his chair, that side of his head resting against the back.

"Sit down, sit down. How are things over in Tahlequah?"

Molly wobbled a hand in midair. "So-so." She sat in a green plastic chair with steel arms which was placed at right angles to Highsmith's metal desk. The sheriff's department occupied space in the Adair County Courthouse, a four-story, tan-brick building surrounded by a square block of lawn, typical of Oklahoma courthouses built in the early twentieth century. A low, one-story wing, added more recently, housed the Adair County Welfare Department.

The sheriff's department consisted of a reception area, a couple of rooms used by the deputies, and the sheriff's office, which was large and appeared to have been recently carpeted and painted. There was a parakeet in a cage near the window. Its feathers were bright blue, its tail long and pointed.

Molly dropped her purse on the floor beside the chair and shrugged off her jacket. "It's getting colder."

"Yeah." Highsmith stifled a yawn. "The weather the past week has been too good to last." He settled back in his chair. He had a slow, unhurried manner and a long, freckled face.

The parakeet chirped and Molly looked over at the bird.

"That's Hazel," Highsmith said.

"Does she talk?"

He shook his head sadly. "Not a word. I worked with her for months, but she won't—or can't—do it. I'm kind of attached to her, anyway."

"I've heard male birds are easier to teach," Molly said.

"Really? Imagine that."

The bird hopped up on the side of the cage and pecked at one of the metal bars.

Highsmith extended both arms toward the ceiling, stretching. "So, what can I do you for?"

Molly turned back to him. "I'd better say up front that this is sort of unofficial."

He nodded and waited patiently, his hands laced across the beginning of a little pot belly.

"I had a visit this morning from a girl named Maggie Whitekiller."

His sandy eyebrows scrunched together and he gave a grim shake of his head. "Poor kid. She called me this morning too. I guess she told you the same thing she keeps telling me. Her daddy didn't commit suicide. It's not uncommon for relatives to deny suicide at first, but Maggie's even more adamant than most. She may never accept it."

Molly had had the same impression. "She begged me to conduct an investigation. The case isn't the type I'd ordinarily get involved in, but . . ." She crossed her ankles and curled her fingers around the arms of the chair. "I couldn't bring myself to turn her down flat. She's going through a tough time."

He bent his linked hands backwards as far as they would go, cracking knuckles. "No doubt about that. The kid's devastated. I talked to the mother, Dot Whitekiller, Monday night. She's taking it a lot better than the girl."

"How old is Maggie, do you know?"

"Fourteen."

"A hard age in the best of circumstances." Maggie hesitated, wanting to couch what she had to say in nonjudgmental terms. "For some reason, Maggie doesn't feel she can talk to her mother about her father's death."

"That's probably because the mother accepts that it was suicide." He unlinked his hands and rubbed his palms together. They sounded dry, like paper. "And, between you and me, Dot Whitekiller didn't come across as a warm person. I guess Maggie told you how it happened?"

"She told me she found him in his truck in the garage with the door closed, and that you said the gas tank was empty."

"That's right. Plus, there was no blood, nothing to indicate a struggle. Obviously carbon-monoxide poisoning,"

Highsmith said. "The key was in the ignition in the *on* position. What else could it be but suicide? Maggie just won't believe it."

"Has the medical examiner made his report?"

"No. I expect to hear from him tomorrow." He fingered a metal cylinder on his desk. Its top was covered with holes for pencils and pens, and most of them were filled. "Maybe if Maggie saw it in black and white . . ." He looked up from the pencils and pens. "I can show her the M.E.'s report, if you think that'll help."

"I don't," Molly said. "She insists that even if it was carbon monoxide, it wasn't suicide because her father wasn't the kind of man who'd kill himself."

The parakeet left the side of the cage and hopped up on a swinging bar. Her bright eyes seemed to be taking Molly's measure. Suddenly, she did a somersault on the bar and trilled loudly.

"Put a sock in it, Hazel," Highsmith said fondly and the bird stopped mid-trill, as if she understood what he'd said.

Highsmith looked at Molly. "Whitekiller's wife said something about her husband not being the suicidal type too. Said she'd always thought he was too self-confident to kill himself. She also said he'd been out of a job for five months and might have been depressed without showing it." He frowned. "I didn't quite know how to take her, to tell you the truth. She seemed like a cold fish. Said her husband was . . . wait, I have it right here." He opened a manila folder lying on his desk and picked up a handwritten report. "Irresponsible and selfish." He glanced down the page. "Said when she realized he had killed himself, her first thought was that he'd done it to scare her. Hadn't meant to kill himself at all."

"That's bizarre. No sane person would take a chance like that."

He smiled wryly. "Well, her second thought was that he'd snapped. Had a case of temporary insanity. Said if he'd been in his right mind he wouldn't have done it where the girl could find him. I guess she didn't think he'd mind if *she* found him."

"You're right. A cold fish."

He looked as if he was relieved that she agreed with him. He evidently didn't want to come across as lacking compassion. Highsmith was a true politician. "Sure didn't seem to be any love lost on the wife's part. I figure they must have been having marital problems. Maybe she was going to divorce him and he couldn't take it."

"Did she mention divorce?"

"No. I was about to ask about that, but the girl heard us saying her father had committed suicide—we thought she was in the bedroom. I looked up and there she was in the doorway, shaking like a leaf. She jumped all over her mother. She was still yelling when I left."

Outside on the square, a truck was backing toward the building to unload a desk and chair at the side entrance, and Highsmith fixed his gaze on it for moment. Turning back to Molly, he said, "Between you and me, I think the kid could have handled the loss of her mother a lot better."

"I got the impression Maggie and her father were very close," Molly agreed. "She said he'd left her alone, almost as if she thought of herself as parentless now." Molly stood restlessly and went over to the parakeet's cage. She touched the cage and the bird pecked the tip of her finger. She pulled back.

"You have to watch Hazel," Highsmith said. "Did she hurt you?"

"Not really. She just surprised me." Molly turned to face the desk. She hadn't learned anything that would make Maggie feel better, but still she was reluctant to leave. "There's no doubt in your mind, then, that Ed Whitekiller killed himself?"

"None at all." He shuffled through the folder that still lay open on his desk. "Here, take a look at these." He tossed several snapshots across the desk.

Molly lined them up along the edge of the desk and studied them. They were shots of the death scene. Two of the dead man lying on his side, knees drawn up, on a concrete floor; an automobile tire could be seen at the right edge of one of them. A close-up of the pickup's ignition with a key in it, turned to the right in the *on* position. Then a step-back shot of the interior of the pickup cab.

Molly picked up the last snapshot for a closer look. "What's this on the pickup seat?"

"Black rocks," Highsmith said.

She looked at him, puzzled.

"Small black rocks," he repeated. "Seven of them. Except for that, the interior of the cab was as clean as a whistle. I thought maybe Whitekiller was a rockhound, but his wife said no. She had no idea why he had rocks in his pickup." He chuckled blackly. "As opposed to in his head."

"Odd," Molly said, gathering up the snapshots and handing them back to Highsmith. Something stirred at the back of her mind. She tucked it away to think about later.

"Do you mind if I give Ken Pohl a call?" Molly had dealt with the medical examiner for Cherokee and Adair counties before. "I'd like to know if he found anything unexpected on autopsy."

"No need. I'll call you as soon as I hear from him, tell you what he said." Highsmith sounded a little proprietary.

Molly backed off. "I'd appreciate that. I'd also like to talk to Ed Whitekiller's wife."

He hesitated, then said, "Be my guest. Don't know what you hope to accomplish by talking to Dot Whitekiller, though."

"Neither do I," Molly admitted. "I guess I'm looking for something I can give Maggie, some small detail that makes accidental death an outside possibility. It would give her something to hang on to."

He studied her thoughtfully. "You're a nice lady, Molly Bearpaw. But I think you're wasting your time."

"Maggie got to me."

"I know what you mean. I had the feeling she could come apart at the seams if the mother doesn't get her some help."

"Can you tell me how to get to the Whitekiller house?"

He did, and she put on her jacket and picked up her purse. "Thanks, Sheriff. I'll keep in touch."

"You do that," Highsmith said.

As she turned to go, a man strolled into the office. "Oops, sorry, Dave. Your door was open, so I assumed you were alone."

"Hey, Moss," Highsmith said heartily. "Come on in. Have you met Molly Bearpaw?"

Molly recognized him from the Chamber of Commerce banquet she'd attended last spring. Moss Greenleigh had been named Tahlequah Citizen of the Year for his work with the community's homeless. Under Greenleigh's leadership, the Baptist church had taken on the project and established a second town shelter on church property; the first shelter was overflowing.

"I know who you are," Moss said, shaking Molly's hand. "You work for the Cherokee Nation, got an office in the old capitol."

"Pleased to meet you," Molly said.

"I'll wait in the other room," Greenleigh offered.

"No, I was leaving, anyway," Molly said, buttoning her jacket.

"If you have a minute, could you stay?" Greenleigh asked. "I'd like you to hear what I came to tell Dave."

Molly sat back down, and Greenleigh pulled over another chair. "My company's building the new bingo hall in Adair County," he began. "There's an old Cherokee man who lives next door. I've been worried about him all along, so I finally decided to see if the county"— He looked at Molly—"or maybe the Cherokee Nation could help."

"What's the problem?" Highsmith asked.

"He's very old, and he lives alone in a little shedlike place you wouldn't want your elderly relative living in."

"What's his name?" Molly interjected.

"Zeb Smoke. Do you know him?"

She shook her head.

"Where he lives doesn't worry me as much as the way he's been acting." Greenleigh looked truly concerned. "He wanders all over the countryside—this is a man way up in his eighties, mind you. We found him hiding in the portable john one day, and he seemed kind of confused. I just don't think he's got all his faculties."

"Hmmm," Highsmith said. "I guess you and I could go out and talk to him, Moss."

Greenleigh shook his head unhappily. "He wouldn't let

me on his place. He's got it in his mind that the bingo hall
is cursed, or some such thing, and everybody working on it
is evil. He's kind of irrational on the subject. Always doing
medicine ceremonies around the site, scattering around tobacco and other stuff."

"Doesn't he have relatives who look out for him?" Molly
asked.

"Just a nephew, as far as I can find out," Greenleigh said.
"A teacher at the university. Name's Fishinghawk."

"Will Fishinghawk," Molly said. "I know who he is."

"Anyway," Greenleigh went on, "I'm not sure the
nephew knows how bad off the old man is. I'm afraid he's
going to wander off and get lost, fall and break a hip or
something."

"He's probably on welfare," Molly said, "so his social
worker should be keeping tabs on him."

"I'll check with the county welfare department," Highsmith offered.

"If they don't have his case, I'll see if one of the Nation's
social workers can check on him," Molly said.

"Good." Greenleigh smiled. "Meantime, do you think
it'd be okay if the missionary ladies at my church called on
him, maybe took him out some food?"

"Sounds good to me," Highsmith said, looking at Molly
for a reaction.

"It can't hurt for them to visit him, I guess." But she
couldn't help wondering if Zeb Smoke was as proud as her
grandmother. Eva would be insulted if strangers carried
food to her house. Of course, she didn't need it and perhaps
Zeb Smoke did.

14

A late-model blue Pontiac sat in the driveway next to the Whitekiller house. Molly pulled in behind it and got out.

A dark-haired woman in her late thirties opened the door to the house. She wore a bright-orange shirtwaist dress which looked garish beneath her pale face.

"Mrs. Whitekiller?"

"Yes."

"I'm Molly Bearpaw. I'm employed by the Cherokee Nation as an investigator—"

Dot Whitekiller cut her off. "I know who you are. What do you want?"

"Your daughter came to my office this morning. She asked me to investigate her father's death."

"That's impossible. My daughter has been with me all day." She spoke in a brisk tone that was at once summation and dismissal.

Molly spoke hastily, before the door was closed in her face. "Maggie was in my office while you were at the funeral home."

Her eyebrows went up and she drew in a sharp breath.

"Oh, dear." She shook her head. "I don't know what I'm going to do with Maggie. She won't listen to reason."

"I understand," Molly said. She hugged herself. The porch created a wind tunnel. It felt ten degrees colder there than in the yard. "All I want to do is let her down gently. I don't want to cause her any more pain, if that's possible." She tucked her chin into the neck of her jacket. Her teeth were starting to chatter. "May I come in for a few minutes? It's awfully cold out here."

Dot hesitated, and Molly was sure she was going to turn her away. But she relented. "All right. Come in, but keep your voice down. Maggie's in her bedroom. I hope she's finally gone to sleep—she's hardly slept at all since her father died."

Molly stepped into a warm, cozy room. A wood fire crackled in the brick fireplace. Two chairs were angled toward each other next to the hearth. On the floral carpet beside one of them sat a basket containing balls of red and blue yarn and a strip of knitted red worsted on a needle. It appeared that Dot Whitekiller had been sitting there before she got up to answer the door. The mental picture was incongruous. Dot Whitekiller did not seem like the knitting-by-the-fire type. Evidently there was more to her than the cool facade she presented to the world.

"Sit by the fire," Dot said, indicating the other chair. "May I get you something hot to drink? Coffee? Tea?"

"Coffee sounds wonderful. Black, please."

"It'll have to be instant," she said with a little grimace. "I'm out of ground."

"Instant's fine," Molly said, reluctant to change her order now. She was very particular about coffee, and she never drank instant.

Dot went into the kitchen. Molly took off her jacket and held her hands toward the fire to warm them. The room was lovely without being off-putting; it looked as if people really lived in it.

A room for a family. Not a very happy one, if High-smith's instincts were accurate. And, after all, there was strong evidence that the man of the family, at least, had been extremely unhappy. What had happened to Ed Whitekiller to bring him to such despair? People did not kill themselves over a minor disappointment. In spite of Dot Whitekiller's suggestion that her husband must have been temporarily deranged, Molly's impression from talk-ing to Maggie was that Ed seemed normal. Whatever that meant. Actually, Maggie had said he'd been happy, that he'd always been happy.

On the other hand, if his wife had asked for a divorce . . .

The kettle in the kitchen began to whistle and was set off the fire. Moments later, Dot Whitekiller returned with two gold-banded white cups in saucers. She handed one to Molly. "Black, no sugar, right?"

"Yes, thank you." Molly sniffed the pleasant coffee aroma and decided she could manage a sip or two, after all. It was at least hot. "I've been admiring this room," she added.

"I'm glad you like it. I decorated the entire house my-self," Dot said with a touch of pride. "Ed had no notion of what should go with what."

"Are you a professional decorator?" Molly asked.

"Self-trained," Dot replied. "I'm an elementary-school teacher by profession. I teach at Sequoyah in Tahlequah."

Molly took a sip of her coffee and set the cup on the hearth. "I didn't know your husband, Mrs. Whitekiller, but I have some idea of what you and Maggie must be going through. I wouldn't be here now if Maggie hadn't seemed so desperate to have me investigate."

"There's nothing to investigate, really. Ed killed himself."

"The question seems to be, why."

"I've already gone through this with Sheriff Highsmith. Ed was out of a job. He was a very prideful man. I guess it finally got too much for him."

"Maggie doesn't believe that. In fact, she says he was happy."

Her gaze did not waver. "Then why did he kill himself?"

"I thought it might help us figure that out," Molly said, "if we could come up with a list of places your husband went, people he talked to, during the last few days of his life. Do you think you could help me with that?"

Dot Whitekiller shrugged, a nominal assent. Molly got a small note pad and ballpoint pen from her purse. "Let's start with last Thursday."

"I was at work, of course, but Thursday night, Ed said he'd filled out a job application somewhere, and the same on Friday. I'm sorry I don't know where and I don't think he said who he talked to."

Molly looked up. "What about Thursday and Friday evenings?"

A nerve at the corner of her eye twitched. "He was at home both nights."

"And the weekend?"

"Again, he stayed at home. Maggie and I went to Tulsa to shop Sunday afternoon." The nerve twitched again. "Ed was here when we got back. He said he hadn't been anywhere else, except out to the garage to work on a bookcase."

Molly's instincts told her Dot Whitekiller was leaving

something out. He *said* he hadn't been anywhere else. Did Mrs. Whitekiller think he'd lied?

"Monday?"

"He drove Maggie to school in Tahlequah and picked up some stain for the bookcase he was working on. Before I left for work, he said something about a job contact he was going to make that day." She swallowed and thought for a moment. "He seemed optimistic about it. For whatever reason, I can't say. Evidently the contact didn't pan out or—"

Or he wouldn't have come home and killed himself, Molly finished to herself. "He didn't tell you anything about this job contact or why he felt optimistic?"

She shook her head. "All he said was, he didn't want to get my hopes up but he had a good feeling about it."

Molly kept her eyes on the note pad. "I spoke to Sheriff Highsmith earlier today. He seems to think that you and your husband were having problems."

She lifted a dark brow. "It's not easy living on my teacher's salary. Now that it's going to be permanent, I'll probably have to sell this house and find a rental in town."

"I didn't mean that kind of problem. The sheriff thinks you'd discussed divorce. If that's true, it's possible your husband's suicide had nothing to do with being unemployed. Perhaps he couldn't face living apart from you and Maggie."

"Are you suggesting that I'm the cause of Ed's suicide?" The thin face held no expression, but the tone had hardened.

"No, of course not. I—"

"In the first place, Ed didn't think I'd ever leave him." She stared into the fire. "It was Maggie who was afraid I might. I suppose she mentioned that when she came to see you."

Instinctively, Molly did not deny it. She merely looked at the fire and waited.

"She must have told you," Dot said, "that she intended to go with her father if there was a divorce. Ed would have assumed she would. It would never have occurred to him that he'd have to give up Maggie."

"So you did ask him for a divorce."

"Not in those words, no. But . . . well, it can't do any harm to tell you. I was seriously considering a separation."

"You were willing to leave Maggie with her father?"

She didn't answer immediately. Finally, the reply she made was enigmatic. "That was a problem I thought I could deal with."

Now that would not be necessary. Her husband's suicide had conveniently removed the problem. It occurred to Molly that Dot Whitekiller might view Ed's death as a solution to at least one dilemma. "I take it your husband didn't want a separation."

She smiled faintly. "Oh, no. Ed wanted it both ways."

"I don't understand."

"He wanted a wife at home to keep his house clean, do his laundry, cook his meals, and take care of his daughter. So he could spend his time chasing other women."

So that's what she thought her husband was doing while she and Maggie were in Tulsa. Still, Molly was surprised by the woman's bluntness. "I'm sorry. I didn't know."

She gave a small defensive cough. "Then you're one of the few who didn't. All of his friends knew, I'm sure. He probably bragged about his women to them."

"Any particular friend?"

She took a drink of her coffee. "Garth Reynolds and Tobin Ward, for two. They both live in Tahlequah. There were others, but Garth and Tobin may be willing to talk to you about Ed and his extracurricular activities, if you don't believe me." Her upper lip curled slightly. "Ed was having an affair, Miss Bearpaw. And it wasn't the first one, either. I—I wasn't completely truthful with you before. I believe he was with the woman Sunday afternoon, while Maggie and I were in Tulsa. Of course, he said he was here the whole time, so I could be wrong. But I don't think so." For some reason, it seemed important to her that Molly understand her husband wasn't a nice person.

Her words were as sharp and cold as icicles. Molly almost shivered. "I'm sure you'd know, if anybody does, Mrs. Whitekiller."

She seemed to sense criticism in Molly's words. "Are you married?" The tone was superior.

"No."

"Then you'll have to take my word for it. When the husband is carrying on with another woman, the wife always knows. It may take a while for her to admit it to herself, but she knows. Besides, in this case I had more to go on than my instincts. I know who the woman was. I don't know her personally, nor do I care to. She's married also, by the way. A friend of mine saw Ed's pickup parked in her driveway in Tahlequah."

Molly waited, hoping she would name the woman. Instead, Dot took another sip of coffee and looked at Molly over the rim of her cup.

Hoping to prod her into revealing the name, Molly asked, "How can you be so sure if you don't even know the woman?"

"I am, that's all."

"There could be any number of reasons for your husband's truck to have been parked there."

She waved a negligent hand. "You needn't try to make me feel better, Miss Bearpaw. The woman isn't even important. If it hadn't been this woman, it would have been some other. I know what I know."

It was almost as if she needed to believe it. Maybe it made it possible for her to further believe that her husband had deserved to die. If she could believe that, then she wouldn't feel so guilty about being relieved that he was out of her daughter's life permanently, no longer a problem to be dealt with. And maybe she was right. Maybe the wife always knew.

"I see," Molly said. "You've been very frank, Mrs. Whitekiller, and I appreciate it. But I guess I was hoping you'd confirm what Maggie told me, that your husband wasn't suicidal." It would mean so much to Maggie, Molly added to herself, if she could find something pointing to accidental death.

"The way he died would seem to exclude that."

Molly nodded. "I know. I'm grasping at straws. It seems he went out to the garage fully intending to take his own life."

"I'm not sure I'd go that far."

"What do you mean?"

"Ed was already in the garage."

"Pardon?"

"As I said, he'd built a bookcase, for Maggie. Monday he was out in the garage putting on the stain. When Maggie found him, the stain had been applied and the excess wiped off. I can't really picture someone who's decided to kill himself taking time first to stain a bookcase, can you?"

Molly gave a negative shake of her head.

"I don't think Ed *was* planning suicide when he went out to the garage. But the can of stain was still open, with the brush he'd used left as he'd laid it down. He hadn't cleaned it, which wasn't like Ed. He was always very particular about taking care of his tools."

"So, leaving the brush uncleaned was out of character?"

She picked at a tiny chip in the rim of her cup. "Yes, and I've given that a lot of thought. It's possible he was thinking about his situation while he was working on the bookcase, and he got depressed. Monday morning he told me if the job he was optimistic about didn't come through, he would go to Muskogee that afternoon to apply for a manager-trainee job at McDonald's. He'd rather have taken a beating than do it. He thought serving hamburgers was demeaning. Frankly, I didn't believe he'd really go. In fact, I called there this morning and talked to the manager. Ed never showed up there."

"But he definitely told you he planned to apply for the job?"

"Yes. But he didn't think he'd have to, you see. He thought he had a line on another job. When that fell through, as I assume it did, he began to feel desperate. He'd given up on finding another job. Apparently, as he thought about it, he just decided he'd rather die than go to Muskogee as he'd promised he would. The pickup was right there and—" Molly's perplexity must have shown on her face. "I know it doesn't sound like a reason for suicide," Dot said, "but you didn't know my husband."

"No," Molly admitted. "I didn't."

She seemed to have come to the end of what she was willing to say, for she set her cup down, sat back in her chair, and crossed her arms.

"Is there anything else you can tell me?" Molly asked.

"No, and I'm very tired."

Molly put on her jacket. "I'm sorry to have bothered you."

"It's all right, but I need to lie down now and try to nap." She stood.

"Thanks for your time."

"It's kind of you to want to help, Miss Bearpaw, but Maggie would be better served if you'd tell her the truth about her father's death. The sooner she faces it, the sooner she'll be able to accept that her father opted out of his life and left us to pick up the pieces."

Dot headed down the hall the moment after she closed and locked the front door. She paused to look in on Maggie, who was sleeping.

After quietly closing Maggie's door, she continued to her bedroom where she drew the draperies, shrouding the room in shadow.

Sighing, she kicked off her shoes, lay down on top of the comforter, and closed her eyes.

Her frankness had shocked Molly Bearpaw. Dot had seen the same uneasiness in her eyes that had been in the sheriff's when she'd spoken the truth about Ed.

It may have been wiser to play the role of the grief-stricken wife of a suicide victim, but she was finished with roles. Thank God, pretending to be content in her marriage until she could find an acceptable way out was no longer necessary. She was simply incapable of following that performance with another.

She didn't really care what the sheriff or Molly Bearpaw thought of her. The sheriff had a job to do, but the Bearpaw woman had no official capacity to investigate Ed's death. When she'd opened the front door to her, she'd thought Molly was lost and had stopped to ask directions. It seemed the only reasonable explanation for the appearance of the woman she'd seen only in newspaper photographs before today.

She'd been so taken aback to learn that Maggie had gone to Molly Bearpaw's office while Dot was in the funeral home that she'd let her in. Had she been better prepared, she'd have turned her away at the door.

She knew she'd sounded cold and unfeeling. What had possessed her to name Ed's friends? Clearly the Bearpaw woman intended to question them too, trying to verify Dot's story about the affair. What business was it of hers, anyway? She should have threatened the woman with a lawsuit if she didn't butt out, she thought with sudden anger.

Well, Molly Bearpaw could have found out who Ed's friends were from somebody else, if she was determined. Let her talk to them. Let the whole world say that Ed wouldn't have killed himself. There was no real evidence to support that opinion, and the autopsy would show what he'd died of. Then she could get through the funeral and start over with her daughter.

15

True to his word, Dave Highsmith phoned Molly the next day.

"I just talked to Dr. Pohl," Highsmith said. "It's official. Ed Whitekiller died of carbon-monoxide poisoning. Full rigor had set in, so he'd been dead several hours when he was found. Pohl estimates between four and seven."

It was exactly what they'd expected, but Molly dreaded having to break the news to Maggie.

"No surprises, then?"

He hesitated. "Nothing serious."

Molly felt a flicker of irritation. "Tell me about the unserious surprises, Dave."

"Wait a minute—" Highsmith paused to find something on his desk. "Here it is. The M.E. found a fresh wound on the right shin, and a bruise at the back of the head which was inflicted shortly before death. Pohl almost missed that one, it was up under the hairline."

What would it take for Highsmith to consider it serious? Dismemberment? "How about that." A bruise at the base of the skull was highly suspicious and Highsmith must know it. At the very least, it had to be investigated, if he'd be objective about it. But Molly didn't think Highsmith could be pushed. "What do you make of it?" she asked.

"Been mulling it over, and I've got a theory that'll still fit with suicide."

"I'm listening." And what she was hearing was that Highsmith had dug in his heels on the suicide verdict. Possibly he was right, but a closed mind made you overlook conflicting evidence.

"Can you meet me at the Whitekiller place this afternoon about two?" Highsmith asked. "The family will be at the funeral, and Mrs. Whitekiller said she'd leave the garage unlocked for me."

Wild horses couldn't keep Molly away. "I think I can make it."

"My theory's not quite as neat as I thought," Highsmith said in greeting Molly that afternoon, "but I believe it'll still work." He was standing at the back of the garage next to a gasoline-powered lawn mower.

She pushed the hood of her down jacket off her head but kept her hands buried in the deep pockets. A few spits of snow had struck her windshield on the drive from Tahlequah, and it was frigid in the garage with the wind whistling down the driveway and buffeting them from behind.

"I hate this weather," Molly groused.

"Me too. I'm ready for spring already." He wore a fleece-lined denim car coat and was warming his hands in his armpits. His nose and the tips of his ears were red. "Sometimes I think I'll move to south Florida when I retire."

"With all the foreigners? Not me. A neighbor of mine visited her granddaughter there recently. Nobody could understand Florina—that's my neighbor. Nobody speaks English." Florina Fensten had been outraged by this turn of events. She'd only been home a few days when she decided to visit a son in Oklahoma City, "where people still speak the language."

Highsmith was looking faintly confused, as though the influx of non–English-speaking immigrants into south Florida was news to him. "Maybe I'll move down to the Texas hill country."

"Don't rush into anything," Molly advised, although she couldn't imagine Highsmith rushing for any reason. "It's hard to meet new people when you're not going to a job every day."

He nodded. "Something to think about."

Molly joined him beside the lawn mower. "So what's your theory?"

"Whitekiller ran into the mower and cut his shin. See this?" He bent and touched the corner of a black metal chute-shaped attachment to the mower. On it in white letters was painted: *3.5 Reserve Power. Solid State.*

"That's a toe guard," Highsmith said. "I already checked, and it's the right distance from the floor to have hit him about where the wound on his shin was. Look at this." He pointed to a brown stain on the sharp corner. "I'll wager that's dried blood."

It looked like blood to Molly too.

He straightened up and pointed to a portable radio on a shelf running across the back of the garage. "When the girl found him, the radio was playing. I figure Whitekiller came back here to turn on the radio, turned around, took a step, and hit the toe guard." He demonstrated.

"Sounds good to me," Molly said, "but I'm more concerned about the bruise on the back of his head."

He held up a hand to indicate she should wait, then cupped the other hand over his nose and mouth and blew into his palm to warm his nose. Then he folded his arms and stuck his hands in his armpits again. "What I think happened, Whitekiller turned on the radio, ran into the lawn mower, drew blood, jumped or staggered back because of the pain, fell, and hit his head on the edge of the shelf as he went down." He seemed pleased with these deductions.

Molly thought about it and shook her head.

"What's wrong?"

"I'm not sure." She looked at the shelf and back at the lawn mower. "Move away and let me try something." He complied and she took his place, her shin touching the corner of the mower's toe guard. Pivoting, she took several steps and let herself fall toward the shelf, arms outstretched to catch herself with both hands. She straightened up and shook her head again. "It's too far from the lawn mower to the shelf to have happened the way you theorize."

Highsmith was reluctant to give up such a convenient theory. "He was taller than you by four or five inches." He blew into his hand again. "Damn, I've gotta buy some new gloves." He dropped his hand. "Whitekiller was about my height. Let me try it."

They changed places and Highsmith went through the pantomine of falling. The distance to the shelf was still too great. "Well, look." He did it again, this time taking three long steps away from the lawn mower. "He took three or four steps before he lost his footing and fell."

"Backwards?"

"It's possible."

The trouble with you, my friend, Molly thought, is that you make up your mind first and try to make the evidence fit afterward.

Her ears stung and she hunched her shoulders in an effort to cover them. "You didn't mention any blood on the back of his head."

"There wasn't any."

"Shouldn't there have been, if he hit his head on the sharp edge of that shelf?"

He stared at the shelf as though he could change the sharp angle to a smoother edge if he stared hard enough.

"Did Dr. Pohl have any suggestions about what might have caused the bruise?" Molly asked.

"Maybe a karate chop, but I think he was kidding about that. He did say it was something more blunt than sharp. That's as far as he wanted to go. Remember, though— damnation, my feet are getting numb." He stamped his booted feet. "Remember, Whitekiller's hair padded the blow, which could be why the skin wasn't broken.

Molly's ears were losing feeling. She pulled her hood up. "Okay, I'll go along with that for now." She glanced at the pickup. Judging from the snapshots Highsmith had shown her of the death scene, it hadn't been moved since White-killer died. "But there's another problem. The pickup is twelve or fifteen feet from where he would have had to hit his head if he ran into the lawn mower first. I don't know . . ."

"Let's get in my car," Highsmith said. "I've got a ther-mos of coffee."

Molly expelled a long breath. "Great. Let's go."

They climbed into Highsmith's patrol car, a tan Ford with a shield on the side. It was parked in the driveway near the open garage door. He started the engine to get the heater going. He turned on the wipers long enough to clear the windshield of the wet snowflakes that fell steadily now. Then he filled the thermos's screw-on plastic cap and handed it to Molly. He rummaged around on the floor in front of the back seat and found a thermal mug for himself.

Molly lifted the plastic cup in both hands and let the steam warm her face. She blew on the coffee and chanced a sip. It was strong enough to stand a spoon upright and so hot it burned the tip of her tongue. She jerked back. "Great thermos you've got there."

He blew on his coffee and said, "Should've warned you. Sorry. Now, go ahead with what you were saying."

She cleared the fog off her half of the windshield with a gloved hand. From where they sat, they could see the interior of the garage. "Say for the moment that Whitekiller got the cut on his shin and the bruise at the base of his skull as you think."

"For the moment?"

"I'm trying to keep an open mind. You also said both wounds were inflicted shortly before death. Which means he had to walk twelve or fifteen feet, get in his pickup, and—" She looked over at him sharply. "I just thought of something. Was the garage door open or closed when Maggie found him?"

"Closed. It was just luck—if you can call it that—that Maggie saw the roof of the pickup from her bedroom window. Otherwise, they might not have found him until the next day."

She imagined Maggie seeing the pickup and running out to the garage to check on her father, perhaps wanting to look at the bookcase he was working on or to talk to him about something that had happened at school.

"Okay," she said finally, "let's play it like this. He turned on the radio, barked his shin, fell, and hit his head. Then he got up, walked the length of the garage, closed the garage door, walked back to the pickup, got in, and started the motor."

"How do you know the garage door wasn't closed all along?"

"He was staining a bookcase, and it was close to sixty degrees out that day. He'd have left the door open because of the fumes. And closed it when he decided to commit suicide. Forgetting the logistics problem with that fall, why turn on the radio if he meant to kill himself? Does that make sense to you?"

"Why not?" he asked sharply, evidently sensing unspoken ridicule of his deductive powers. "Maybe he wanted the radio to drown out the sound of the engine, didn't want somebody coming into the garage to check on him."

"Nobody else was home."

Highsmith took a loud swig from his mug and shook his head. "It's a simple suicide, Molly."

Molly blew on her coffee and tested it again with her tongue. It had cooled enough to drink. "It still doesn't sound right to me."

Highsmith averted his eyes. She sensed he was irritated with what he probably thought was obstinacy. "All right," he muttered. "Let's try it another way. Maybe he felt dizzy after that fall. Doc said it was a pretty good blow. He has to sit down. The pickup's right there, so he gets in and passes out."

It was a small concession for Highsmith, a willingness to

consider something besides suicide. Molly gave it serious thought. If it had happened like that, she could tell Maggie her father's death was accidental. She really wanted to believe it, but there were too many problems still. "Why close the garage door—or leave it closed if it already was—and start the motor?"

He pointed his mug in Molly's direction with an unspoken *ah-ha*. "I got the answer to that one. There's an automatic garage-door opener clipped to the pickup's sun visor. Let's say the garage door was already closed—who knows? Maybe he liked the smell of paint fumes. Anyway, he got in the pickup, meaning to start the motor, open the garage door and back out, but he passed out before he could open the door."

"You're saying he was woozy enough to pass out, yet he intended to drive?"

Highsmith set his mug on the dashboard harder than was necessary. The steam from the coffee added more fog to the already foggy windshield. "He obviously didn't realize how close to fainting he was." He hesitated. "Hell, I don't know. To be frank, I think I was right the first time. He planned to kill himself all along. He didn't mean to hit his head, but it happened. Yet it didn't keep him from carrying out his original plan. Whitekiller committed suicide. The gash and the bruise are incidental, something to mess up the picture for us." For him, he meant.

It was even possible, Molly supposed, that the sheriff was right—Whitekiller intended to commit suicide when he went to the garage, and staining the bookcase was one last thing he could do for his daughter.

"There is another possibility," she said.

He looked over at her warily.

"Somebody caught him in the garage working on Maggie's bookcase, knocked him unconscious with—something, a board, that old baseball bat I saw in the garage—whatever, he cut his shin as he fell—then they put him in the pickup, started the engine, closed the garage door, and left."

He slumped down in the seat and dropped his head back against the headrest. "I had a feeling that's what you were getting around to."

"You must have given it a passing thought," she said charitably. "Now that I consider it, it's as likely as the other theories we've come up with."

"Maybe it did cross my mind once or twice. What kind of law officer would I be if I didn't think of every angle? But I dismissed it as too improbable."

Molly had heard enough about Highsmith to know he wasn't exactly obsessive when it came to his job. He took care of business adequately, but she guessed that left plenty of time in the normal course of things to enjoy coffee breaks and leisurely lunches in various places around Stilwell and maybe catch a nap at his desk after lunch.

A suicide wouldn't upset his schedule much. It required little leg work and was far easier to wrap up than a murder, particularly when you didn't even know if it *was* murder and had no criminal types handy to serve as suspects.

"Murder's so unlikely, Molly, it's hardly in the picture," he said. "If you're going to kill someone, you'd make sure he dies. A gun, a knife. What if Whitekiller gained consciousness and got out of the garage?"

"How long does it take to die of carbon-monoxide poisoning?"

"A few minutes, according to Doc Pohl."

She finished her coffee and screwed the cap back on the thermos. "The murderer hit him hard enough to be sure he wouldn't come to in time to escape. He or she wanted it to look like suicide."

Highsmith sighed.

"No matter how remote it is," Molly went on, "we're going to have to pursue the possibility of murder."

He said nothing. Clearly, he didn't believe they had to do any such thing.

"You can't let it go down as a suicide until you're sure, any more than I can," she insisted, not really certain it was true; but he couldn't afford to let her pursue a murder investigation on her own, either. If it turned out it *was* murder, and he'd been sitting on his hands, the voters might decide to replace him.

He sighed again. "Okay, dammit. We'll go ahead and look for suspects. Hound people, ask a lot of nosy questions, rattle all the skeletons in closets."

"Comes with the territory."

He grumbled an assent.

"I even have an idea where to start," Molly said. "Whitekiller's wife thinks he was having an affair with a married woman."

He arched his brows. "Is that a fact? She tell you who?"

"No, but it shouldn't be too hard to find out. I'll work on it and check the woman out. Her husband too."

He nodded. "Okay. I'll stop and talk to the Whitekillers' neighbors, see if they noticed anybody at the Whitekiller house Monday. Drive all over hell and gone, using up the county's gasoline."

"That's what you get paid for, isn't it?"

He snorted.

"Let's give it our best for a few days. The more I know about this thing, the more I feel something's just not right."

"You're as bad as Maggie."

Molly didn't deny it.

Nobody answered at Tobin Ward's number, but Molly reached Garth Reynolds's wife at home later that evening. "You'll probably find him at the New Moon Lounge. He practically lives there." The woman banged the phone down before Molly could thank her.

She turned on her answering machine, in case D.J. called, and dressed in warm sweats and her down jacket before leaving the apartment. She ran down the outside stairs and Homer met her at the bottom.

He nuzzled her leg. She stroked his head and he leaned against her. His fur was wet. It had snowed a little off and on since early that afternoon, the flakes melting as soon as they landed. The snow that was falling now was still melting, but it would start to stick before long if it continued.

"Want to go for a ride, boy?"

Homer barked and tried to shake his tail off.

Conrad opened his back door. "Molly, that you?"

"I'm going out for a bit," she told him. "I'm taking Homer with me."

"Be careful." Conrad waved and she opened the Civic's passenger door. Homer jumped in, and she went around and slid into the driver's seat. Immediately the car smelled like wet dog. Still, she was a little uneasy about hanging around the New Moon Lounge alone. The start of most of the drunken brawls and the occasional shooting or knifing that occurred in Tahlequah could be traced to the New

Moon. Homer was too friendly to be a good guard dog, but his bark could sound fierce.

Backing into the street, she rolled her window down a few inches to let the cold air dilute the wet Homer smell. The draft carried flakes of snow that stung her cheeks.

The New Moon was a small stone structure surrounded on three sides by a graveled parking area. In its former life it had been a gas station. About a dozen pickups and cars ringed the front and sides of the building.

The interior was so dim Molly could barely make out the bar and the hunched backs of several men lined up on stools. It was even darker on the opposite wall, though she could see shadowy figures in the four booths. The place smelled of beer and male sweat.

She gave her eyes a few moments to adjust, during which time every head in the place turned toward her. She went to the end of the bar. As she leaned an elbow on the laminated surface, the bartender slid a mug of draft beer in her direction. The man on the last stool reached out and grabbed it deftly without ever taking his eyes off Molly.

"Hey, Molly."

For the first time, she looked closely at the man who'd snagged the beer. It was a guy she'd gone to high school with. She'd only seen him two or three times since, but she'd know that ferrety face anywhere. "Hi, Billy."

He took a swig of beer. "You lost or something? Never saw you in here before."

"Never been here."

"Decided to go slumming, huh?"

"Business."

"Yeah, sure. I won't ask what kind of business." He grinned, exposing crooked teeth. "Can I buy you a brew?"

"No, thanks. I'm looking for Garth Reynolds."

Billy spun around on his stool and pointed. "Over there. In the last booth. It's got his name on it, he spends so much time there."

Molly squinted. "Is he facing front or back?"

"Back." Billy spun around to the bar and brought his ferret face close to hers. "Speaking of back, better watch yours, Molly. Garth's old lady's hell on wheels." His boozy breath almost knocked her down. The man next to Billy laughed and leered at Molly.

"I've got no quarrel with Mrs. Reynolds. This really is business," Molly said and headed for the back booth.

"I'll be sure to tell Donna that when she comes looking for ol' Garth," Billy called after her. Laughter rippled up and down the bar.

Reynolds and his companion, a fat, greasy-looking man in a leather jacket, watched Molly approach.

"Garth Reynolds?"

He looked up at her with sleepy eyes. "Who wants to know?"

"Molly Bearpaw." She stuck a hand in his face. He looked at it a moment, then let go of his beer mug long enough to shake it. His hand was wet and cold.

Molly wiped her hand on her jeans. "Could I have a few minutes of your time?"

He squinted narrowly at her over the rim of his mug in what she suspected was an effort to be flirtatious. "You can have all night, lady, far as I'm concerned." He winked at his friend. "Go use the head, Dub, then get us another round and take your time about it." He looked up at Molly. "You want a beer?"

"No, thanks."

Dub didn't move. "I paid for the last round," he grumbled.

Reynolds fished out a five and handed it to him and Dub lumbered off. Molly took the seat he'd vacated. The vinyl was warm from his fat rump; it made Molly want to squirm. She sat straight, trying to touch as few things as possible. Since her eyes had adjusted to the gloom, she'd noticed that the whole place, including the customers, looked as though it hadn't had a good cleaning in a while.

Reynolds shoved his empty mug to one side and leaned on the table. "Have we met before?" he inquired, focusing on her with half-closed eyes.

"I haven't had the pleasure," Molly said, straight-faced. "I'm conducting an investigation and your name came up."

He frowned. "Now I know where I heard your name. You work for the Cherokees. Some kind of detective or something."

Molly didn't bother clarifying her status. "I called your house and your wife told me where I could find you."

"I'll bet that's not all she said."

"Just about. She said you spend a lot of time here, then hung up on me."

He grinned. "That's Donna, all right."

Molly realized her hand was resting on the scarred, dirty tabletop and stuck both hands in her jacket pockets. "I understand you were a friend of Ed Whitekiller."

He propped his chin in his hand and looked as though he might burst into tears. "They made The Killer and threw away the mold. That was my nickname for him on account of his name." Molly wondered how Ed Whitekiller had reacted to the nickname. Chief Mankiller had a standard answer when people asked how she'd gotten a name like that.

She said she'd earned it, and that usually shut people up. "The Killer," Reynolds was saying, "never met a stranger. No matter how bad things got, he could cheer you up."

"I've been trying to reach another friend of Whitekiller's too. Tobin Ward."

"Toby's up in Nebraska on a job. Might be home for Christmas, might not." He rubbed his watery eyes and looked at Molly. "Wait a minute. You said something about an investigation. Don't tell me the law finally worked it out it can't be suicide."

"They're looking into the possibility," Molly said. "I'm working with the Adair County Sheriff's Department on it."

He planted both hands on the table and leaned closer to her. "You keep after it, hear?" he said earnestly. " 'Cause Ed Whitekiller didn't frigging kill himself." He moved his head back and forth, shaking lank brown hair into his eyes, like Homer climbing out of water. He raked the hair back with his hand. "No way on God's green earth did The Killer do that."

"That's what his daughter says. His wife disagrees."

"Oh, Dot." He waved Dot's opinion aside. "I wouldn't put a lot of stock in what Dot says. The woman didn't have a clue what Ed was up to—not till lately, anyway."

"What was different lately?"

"The last month or two she'd been giving him a hard time." He grinned and got a faraway look in his eyes. "Not that old Ed didn't deserve it." His voice had taken on an edge of envy. "I'd killed that Injun with my bare hands, I'd been married to him."

"Because of the other women?"

"You know about them?"

"A lot of people seem to."

He grinned. "Yeah, they hung around Ed like bitch dogs in heat," he said in an admiring tone. "Don't know how he did it. Musta seemed mysterious and kinda exotic, you know, him being an Injun." He blinked at Molly. "Oh, hey, I didn't mean nothing disrespectful by that."

"Don't worry about it."

He looked relieved in a sloppy sort of way. "Yeah, old Killer always had a woman on the side, ever since I knew him, and that's been eleven, twelve years." He shook his head wonderingly. "This last one, though, Dot found out about. Started watching him, wanting to know where he'd been all the time, who he'd been with. Me and Toby had standing orders to say Ed was with us if Dot ever asked."

"Do you know who the woman was?"

"Sure I know. Me and Toby always knew. Ed liked to give us all the details. Kind of bragging, you know, but you couldn't get mad at him for that. There was this one gal a year or two back, lived way over at Sand Springs . . ."

Molly thought it was time to nudge him back on track. "Can you give me the name of the woman Ed was seeing when he died?"

He looked at her blearily, then shrugged. "Why not? Her name's Susan. Married to a guy named George Butler. It sure ain't no secret. Half the town knows what was going on. I think Ed was getting ready to dump her, though. You could always tell when he was getting tired of a woman. He'd stop giving me and Toby a blow-by-blow, like the fun had gone out of it for him."

"She lives in Tahlequah?"

"Sure. On Choctaw Street. She's one of those women you can just tell has got a roving eye, know what I mean? I took a karate class with her last spring. She was making up to the instructor like you wouldn't believe. Then she met Ed and that's all she wrote for the instructor. Her husband's away from home a lot. Real convenient." He winked at Molly. "She's probably already got somebody else in mind to take The Killer's place." He looked sad for a moment and muttered, "Slut."

Ed, he admired. The women were sluts. Typical redneck chauvinistic attitude. This guy was a fugitive from the fifties.

"How well do you know this Susan Butler?"

"I feel like we're intimately acquainted." He gave Molly a sly grin. "After listening to Ed go on for the past few months."

"What I mean is, was she in love with him?"

"Hell, they all loved him, to hear Ed tell it." He was getting restless, looking around for Dub and the beer.

"I was thinking," Molly said, "if he ditched her and she really cared for him, it must have hurt her, maybe angered her." She remembered that Dr. Pohl said the bruise at the base of Ed Whitekiller's skull could have been made by a karate chop. And Garth Reynolds said that Susan Butler had taken karate lessons.

She had his full attention now. "You mean, maybe she snapped and killed him? Set it up so it looked like suicide?"

"If it was murder," she said, "somebody set the stage very well."

He gave it some thought, as well as he could, that is, with a brain that was foggy from too much beer. "Aw, I don't know."

"Did Ed have any enemies?"

"Huh, lots of men in this town have to hate his guts—the ones whose wives or girlfriends made it with Ed."

"Can you give me any names?"

His gaze went to the bar where Dub was talking to another man. "Don't think so. That's old news. He wasn't seeing anybody but Susan Butler since last summer."

"What about Susan's husband?"

"Ed said he didn't know what was going on. Big bas—er, guy, kind of dumb. That's what Susan told him, anyway. Said he was so fat he disgusted her."

"Maybe her husband found out."

"All I know is, I knew Ed, and he didn't kill himself. I'd bet on that all day long. I was thinking more along the lines of an accident, though."

"We're looking into that too."

He saw Dub coming with two beers and slapped the table happily. "If somebody killed Ed, my money's on Dot. That's one sly woman. Quiet, you know, but always thinking. Never did like her, myself. The feeling is mutual. She let me and Toby know she thought we were a bad influence on The Killer." He laughed. "Shoot, it was the other way around."

Dub set the beer on the table, slopping it out of the glasses. Molly watched a stream trickling toward her side of the table and slid quickly out of the booth. She'd gotten all she would get out of Garth Reynolds.

"Thanks for your help," she said to Reynolds and nodded in Dub's general direction as she left.

"Hey, Molly, don't run off mad," Billy called as she reached the exit.

She waved at him and shoved open the door. Outside, she

lifted her face and let snowflakes wash the grimy feeling off her skin and the stink from her nostrils.

Homer was sound asleep. As she turned the key in the lock, his head came up and he gave a warning bark.

"You old fraud," she said as she got in. He stood up in the seat, his plumey tail flopping. She rubbed his head. "If I'd been in the parking lot fighting off a Crips gang, you'd have slept through the whole thing."

He licked her face to show her his heart was in the right place. It was impossible to insult Homer.

The red message light on Molly's answering machine was blinking when she got home. She punched the *play* button and started undressing.

"Sorry I missed you, Molly," D.J.'s voice said. "If you're out with another guy, you're both dead meat." He paused and she could hear a child's voice in the background. Courtney. "We got here this afternoon and headed straight for the slopes. The lodge is great. Snow cover's good. The situation's almost perfect, only I wish you were here. I miss you." Another pause. "We're going down to dinner now. I'll call again tomorrow night. Be there." He gave the number of the ski lodge and signed off. "Take care. Love ya."

Suddenly, missing him was a physical pain. She rewound the tape, wishing she'd been there for his call, and turned away from the phone.

Homer was barking outside. He wanted in, but she couldn't take the wet-dog smell all night. Conrad might let him in the house, if he wasn't already in bed. Otherwise, Homer would crawl into his doghouse once he was convinced nobody was going to take pity on him.

Fortunately, she needn't worry about Florina Fenston—

Conrad's neighbor to the east who complained when Homer barked, since Florina was visiting her son's family in Oklahoma City and wouldn't be back until after Christmas.

She showered and got ready for bed, thinking about her conversation with Garth Reynolds, wondering why Dot Whitekiller was so willing to accept a finding of suicide when Ed's friends and his daughter were convinced it wasn't true, wondering most of all why Reynolds thought Dot could have killed her husband. Was it just drunken rambling? Or petty spite because Dot hadn't tried to hide her dislike of Reynolds?

Regardless, it was worth investigation. Was there sufficient time during Dot's lunch period for her to have left school, gone home, murdered her husband, and returned to school without being late for her next class?

She would talk with Dot's principal tomorrow. If nothing else, it would give her an idea what Dot's boss thought of her.

16

Wednesday

Molly's telephone woke her the next morning shortly after seven. It was her landlord.

"Time to get up," Conrad greeted her cheerily. "Come over for breakfast. I'm making biscuits and gravy. You'll need the fuel today. It's twenty degrees outside."

"Give me ten minutes," Molly mumbled and hung up.

She was there in eleven. Close enough. Conrad's big, old-fashioned kitchen smelled heavenly. Fresh-brewed coffee, fried sausage, and baking bread.

He handed her a mug of hot coffee as soon as she arrived. "Sit down and talk to me while I cook these hash browns."

The aroma suggested the coffee was chocolate almond. Molly sank into a chair at the table and shrugged off her coat. Winter sunlight slanted through the window over the sink. Streets would be slick with yesterday's snow and overnight freeze, but if the sun stayed out, the snow would melt quickly.

"I needed this, Conrad."

"Thought you might. We haven't had an opportunity for a good talk in a while," Conrad said from the stove. "Are you avoiding me?"

Molly smiled. Conrad knew better than that. He was one of her favorite people. "Trying to spare you. I haven't been very good company lately."

He glanced at her over his shoulder, his bushy white brows raised in question. "Your grandmother's all right?"

"She's fine."

"D.J.?"

"Fine too. He's in Colorado with Courtney at the moment."

"Ah." Whatever that meant.

"I've been a little down because of job problems." She didn't want to go into the details with Conrad until she had to. "Nothing I can talk about yet. But I've got a new case now, and I always feel better when I'm busy."

He lifted the skillet and scraped the hash browns into a bowl, which he set on the table with a plate of link sausages. Then he took a pan of fat, golden-brown biscuits from the oven.

"We're not a bit worried about fat grams this morning, are we?" Molly inquired.

He waved the question away. "You have to take a break from the constant food warnings once in a while. If you listened to all those low-fat, low-calorie, low-cholesterol, no-caffeine alarmists, you'd be eating nothing but rice cakes and bottled water."

"Horrible thought."

"Isn't it?" Conrad shuddered. "What I don't understand is how my parents ate whatever they wanted and lived in good health to a ripe old age without knowing about any of that stuff." Molly had wondered the same thing about her grandmother.

They served themselves and Conrad asked, "This new case . . . can you talk about it?"

Molly spread a generous scoop of butter on a biscuit. "Did you know Ed Whitekiller?"

"Knew of him." He looked up from peppering his potatoes. "He committed suicide, didn't he?"

"Probably." Molly had been so busy trying to track down Ed Whitekiller's friends the evening before that she'd forgotten to eat dinner. Now she was ravenous. At home alone, she would have made do with toast or cereal. This was indescribably better. Bless Conrad.

He looked at her thoughtfully. "Why are you involved, then?"

"Because his fourteen-year-old daughter asked me to investigate," Molly said. She split a second biscuit and ladled sausage gravy over it. "The girl is devastated and won't believe her father killed himself."

"I get the picture. You couldn't say no."

"True, but Whitekiller's friends agree with his daughter. I think the least I can do is leave no stone unturned." She paused with a forkful of potatoes in her hand. The thought she'd tucked away when she looked at the snapshots in Dave Highsmith's office popped to the surface of her mind. Speaking of stones, she'd heard or read something about seven black stones recently. She couldn't remember what, but it had something to do with Cherokee mythology.

"That reminds me," she said. "There were seven stones in the pickup where Ed Whitekiller died. Black ones." She watched Conrad's face. He had a library shelf devoted to books about the Cherokees and was something of an authority on the subject. "Does that ring any bells with you?"

He frowned. "Sure does. Remember that article the

Tahlequah newspaper ran a couple of months back, about the Cherokee oral-history project I'm working on?"

Molly nodded vaguely.

"They used an excerpt from one of the interviews I taped, the one with Wanda Weems. They used the part where Wanda tells of an ancient death curse she remembered her grandmother talking about. It involved a medicine ceremony and seven black stones that Wanda thought were supposed to be hidden with something belonging to the intended victim. Wanda couldn't remember the details."

Molly recalled the article now. She hadn't known about the ancient death curse before reading it. Perhaps the curse had not been practiced by the Oklahoma Cherokees after their separation from the Eastern Band.

"Seven and black often recur in the mythology," Conrad said as he got up to get a jar of blackberry jam from the refrigerator. "There may be something about the curse in one of my research sources." He dipped out a spoonful of jam and transferred it to half a biscuit.

"It probably goes back to the Eastern Cherokees," Molly said. "I've never heard the old people around here talk about it." But then a death curse, black magic, wasn't something a Cherokee would discuss openly.

"If it was practiced by the Eastern Cherokees before the removal, it's probably in Strickland or Mooney. I'll research it for you."

The irony of the situation made Molly smile. Here she was, a Cherokee, questioning an elderly white man about a Cherokee death curse. The lives of most Oklahoma Cherokees, unlike reservation Indians, were barely distinguishable from those of their neighbors of other races. Molly's grandmother, like many of the older Cherokees, was still apt to call in a medicine man when she was ill, but she visited a medical doctor too. The medicine man was added insurance, and only to be used in a good cause. Eva would have nothing to do with death curses.

"If you have time," Molly said. "Aren't you still working on that oral-history project?"

"I've run into a roadblock. I finally tracked down that old full-blood, Zeb Smoke—didn't I mention him to you?"

Molly shook her head. "But his name came up just yesterday. The foreman on the new bingo hall under construction in Adair County mentioned it. Moss Greenleigh. He's worried about the old man."

"So's his great-nephew, Will Fishinghawk. Will and I have gone out to Smoke's place twice now, but so far he won't let me tape him. But, boy, did we hear about that bingo hall. He's in a real dither over it."

"Greenleigh says he wanders off by himself and sometimes seems confused."

Molly took a bite of biscuit and gravy while Conrad reflected. Finally, he said, "When I was there, he didn't seem confused, exactly. Maybe a little paranoid. And he was contrary as a mule. I gather it's a way of life with him." He paused. "If anybody around here knows about that old curse, it'd be Zeb Smoke." He looked into his coffee and hesitated. "I've remembered something." He looked at Molly. "Those stones—it's eerie."

"The ones found in Ed Whitekiller's pickup?"

He nodded. "The last time I saw Zeb Smoke, he talked about a destruction that was coming on the Cherokees because of the bingo halls, said people were going to die—but he won't leave his home, even though he's in his late eighties. Ed has tried repeatedly to get him to."

As Eva wouldn't leave her home. It might be much nicer than Zeb Smoke's house, but the principle applied. Elderly people clung to familiar surroundings as long as possible.

"My grandmother doesn't feel too good about the bingo, either," Molly said. "Gambling is against her religion."

"Zeb Smoke's been performing medicine ceremonies to protect himself, apparently in view of the construction workers, for Will said they were all uneasy about it."

"Greenleigh mentioned the ceremonies too."

Conrad got up to replenish their coffee. "Smoke claims the construction workers set fire to his yard, intending to burn down his house and force him out."

"I doubt that," Molly said, helping herself to more eggs and sausage.

"So does Will, but the point is, Smoke kept talking about the coming destruction and people dying."

She looked up from her food. "What are you saying, Conrad?"

He forked up a generous portion of potatoes and sausage, chewed on it thoughtfully before replying. "This is a big leap, but do you think he'd take action to make his prophecy come true?"

Molly lowered her fork, rested it on the edge of her plate. "Go so far as to commit murder, you mean? I don't know Zeb Smoke, but if he's getting senile . . ." She shook her head. "No, Whitekiller was a good-sized man, in his prime. How could a man in his eighties kill him? For one thing—if it turns out to be murder—Whitekiller was hit from behind with enough force to knock him unconscious and dragged to his pickup truck. And how would Zeb Smoke have gotten to Whitekiller's house? It's a mile, at least. Does he drive?"

"He doesn't have a car, but he could probably walk it, if he took his time. Physically, he seems fit for a man of his age. Or he could have an accomplice."

Molly didn't know. Nor did she know anything about Zeb Smoke. It was as likely that the stones found beside Whitekiller's body following on the heels of Smoke's dire prophecy were an improbable coincidence.

"Did Will Fishinghawk seem bothered about Zeb Smoke's warnings of doom?"

He nodded. "He accused him of trying to put a curse on the construction workers. Smoke denied it, but Will's worried about him and what he might do—or what might be done to him out there all alone."

"The sheriff is going to see if a county social worker can visit him and make a determination about his ability to take care of himself," Molly said.

"Good."

"I wonder if Zeb Smoke knew Ed Whitekiller."

"I can't say."

"It would be interesting to find out," Molly mused.

"Why don't you go to his house with me," Conrad suggested. "The two of us, without Will. The old man's got a bone to pick with Will . . . with me too, for that matter, because I'm white. You, he doesn't know. You can ask him about the curse and get him talking."

Molly was intrigued by Smoke's prophecy. "I'd like to. When?"

He looked out the kitchen window. Mounded snow covered the outside ledge. They must have gotten two or three inches last night. "When the roads are clearer. Zeb lives on a graveled road. But the sun's out, and with construction vehicles traveling that road, the snow will be slush by this afternoon."

"How about three o'clock?"

"Good. He likes beer. I'll pick up a six-pack to take with us. Maybe it'll get us in the door."

It was eight-thirty before Molly left Conrad's. As she backed cautiously out of the driveway, Conrad was calling Homer inside to give him the remains of breakfast. He'd probably allow the dog to stay in all day. In spite of his insistence, when Molly took in the stray golden retriever, that he wasn't a pet person, Conrad had let Homer worm his way into his heart—and house.

Tapping the brake to keep her speed to a crawl, Molly drove her aging Honda Civic down Chickasha Street which led to Sequoyah Elementary School, where Dot Whitekiller taught. Sequoyah was one of three elementary schools in Tahlequah, the oldest, faced with dark-red brick like most of the town's early buildings.

Dot probably hadn't returned to the classroom yet, since the funeral had been only yesterday. Which could work in Molly's favor. The principal, and anybody else Molly was allowed to talk to, might speak more freely if Dot wasn't around.

Molly found the office, where a fortyish woman in a purple-velour pantsuit was on the telephone. A pair of plastic-framed eyeglasses hung from a chain around her neck. She motioned for Molly to sit down while she finished her conversation. The door to the inner office was closed.

The secretary patted her short, dyed-black hair and looked impatient. "I understand all that, Mrs. Stringfellow, but the state requires a child to be in class for a certain number of days or we can't pass him." She stuck her glasses on her nose and consulted the notes written on the yellow legal pad in front of her. "Kenny has used up all but two of the absences the state will allow, and it's only December. I wanted to bring it to your attention." She removed the glasses and glanced at Molly. She picked up a pencil, tapped the eraser end on the desk, then stuck it in her hair over her ear and rolled her eyes while listening to the woman on the other end of the line.

Mrs. Stringfellow had raised her voice. Molly could hear the strident tone but couldn't distinguish the words.

The secretary held the phone a few inches from her ear until the voice stopped. "Yes, I understand that Kenny is delicate. The problem is, I don't have the authority to change the rules and regulations." She waited. "No, he isn't here right now. But he can't change the rules, either. If you'll bring us a note from Kenny's doctor saying he isn't well enough to come to school, I can request a homebound teacher for him."

She listened again, then said with a glacial smile, "I'm not suggesting anything, ma'am. I'm merely informing you of the situation." She paused, then nodded. "You do that, Mrs. Stringfellow. Good-bye."

She put the phone down and pinched the bridge of her nose between thumb and forefinger. "Why do people think their children are exceptions to the rules?"

"Probably because they think their situation is unique."

The secretary chuckled. "If they only knew how boringly familiar their excuses are. Fortunately, we have only a few parents who keep their children out of school for trivial reasons. They want company. They want help with younger children. Or they want to sleep till noon, can't be bothered getting the kids up and off to school." She shrugged. "But it's not your problem. What can I do for you?"

They introduced themselves. The secretary's name was Abby Doherty, and she said the principal wouldn't be in until after noon. "Is there anything I can help you with?"

"I don't know. I'm working with the Adair County Sheriff's Department on the investigation into Ed Whitekiller's death."

"Investigation?" She looked at Molly alertly. "It was suicide, wasn't it?"

"All cases of unnatural death are investigated," Molly said glibly.

The secretary considered and finally said, "What a tragedy that was." She moved a paperweight on her desk. "Is this about the life insurance?"

Her words dropped into the room like gems falling from the sky, a gift from heaven. "That's one of the things I wanted to ask about," Molly said noncommittally.

"I'm afraid Dot hasn't returned to work yet. She'll be back in a couple of days. You can probably reach her at home."

"Oh, I've already spoken to Mrs. Whitekiller. We need to corroborate the details."

The jarring noise of the school bell prevented the secretary's immediate response. When silence returned, she said, "Well, if you've already talked to Dot, I guess it's okay." She went to a file cabinet, opened a drawer, and flipped through folders. Removing a thick file, she brought it to the desk, where she opened it and scanned its contents.

Molly looked out the window. A car crunched down the street, the driver's blue-stocking-capped head bent anxiously over the wheel.

The secretary looked up. "I thought I was right, but I wanted to make sure. Dot and Ed both took out term life-insurance policies five years ago, naming each other as beneficiaries."

"Wasn't there a suicide clause?"

"Yes, but it was only binding for two years."

So Dot Whitekiller had some money coming to her. "How much?"

"Both policies were for a hundred thousand dollars." She returned the folder to the file cabinet. "I remember at the time that Dot considered making the policies higher, but the premiums were more than she could afford. They're deducted from the teachers' salaries. Still, a hundred thousand will help."

It will indeed, Molly thought.

Abby Doherty touched her hair. "Is there anything else?" Perhaps she was beginning to think she'd said too much.

"A couple of minor points I need to clear up." Abby Doherty gazed at her, waiting. "Can you give me a rundown on the teachers' work schedules? When they get here, when they leave . . ."

She considered the request, then seemed to decide it was harmless information. "They come to work at eight-fifteen. Classes start at eight forty-five, and school's out at three. The teachers are required to stay until three-thirty. If there's a teachers' meeting, of course, they usually stay longer."

"Does everybody have the same lunch period?"

She nodded. "Eleven-thirty to twelve-fifteen."

"Do the teachers eat on campus?"

"Usually. They bring a sack lunch or eat in the cafeteria. They're not required to stay at school unless they have cafeteria duty, but there isn't really time to go anywhere else for lunch."

And there would hardly have been time for Dot White-killer to drive home, kill her husband, and return to school before the lunch period ended.

Molly was about to stand and take her leave when the secretary said, "Fortunately, Dot is supervising a student teacher this semester. He has taken over the class in Dot's absence. We sometimes have trouble getting substitutes to come out in bad weather."

Molly subsided back into her chair. "The substitute's handling things, then?"

"Wonderfully well." Her voice was suddenly animated, as if she'd grown quite fond of the student teacher. "He's great with the children. One of the best students we've ever had at this school. All the other teachers are jealous that Dot got him. They fight over the student teachers, so we have to pass them around. It happened to be Dot's turn this semester."

"I'm surprised," Molly said. "I mean, doesn't it make more work for the teachers to supervise students?"

"Only a little. They have to fill out weekly reports. But on the plus side, they can leave the student in charge of the class and get caught up on paperwork, run errands, hang out in the teachers' lounge."

"Does Dot do that a lot? Leave the student in charge of the class, I mean."

She suddenly looked uneasy. "They all do it. It's good for the students too. They need the experience of being in charge before they go out on their own. It's perfectly acceptable, I assure you."

"I can see where it would be good experience for the students." Molly smiled at her. "Did Dot Whitekiller often leave the building while the student had charge of the class?"

A long moment passed before she replied. It appeared she didn't like the direction Molly's questions had taken.

"I wouldn't know about that," she said. "I'm too busy here to run around checking up on the teachers." Something in her tone gave Molly the impression that Abby Doherty didn't like Dot Whitekiller.

A computer monitor sat on the table beside her desk. She swung her chair around and turned it on, signaling a desire to end the conversation. Then the telephone rang and she reached for it with the air of being glad of the interruption.

Molly thanked her and left. She turned the corner in the hall leading to the school entrance. The hall smelled of chalk dust. A janitor was swishing a rag mop desultorily over the gray tile floor.

"Hi," Molly said. "Can you tell me which room is Dot Whitekiller's?"

He leaned on the mop handle, a little, dried-up man in his sixties. "She's not here today."

"I know. I'm looking for the student teacher."

"Oh, Mr. Sandusky. Adam." He pointed farther down the hall. "One-fifteen."

Room 115 was at the end of the hallway, next to a door marked Emergency Exit. Through the glass pane in the classroom door, she saw a young blond man writing on the chalk board. Molly waited for him to finish. He asked if there were any questions, then set the children to working math problems from their books. Molly tapped on the door. He looked up, saw her, and came out into the hall. He wore a pair of navy slacks and a paisley-print shirt with brown loafers. His blond hair was trimmed neatly over his ears, a wave sweeping down over his forehead. He had sincere gray eyes. In fact, that was the overall impression Adam Sandusky gave. Sincerity. Molly thought he'd probably make a good teacher.

She introduced herself and told him why she was visiting the school. "Mrs. Doherty answered most of my questions," she said. "There are one or two things I'd like to check out with you, though, if that's all right."

"Sure. Any way I can help. Mrs. Whitekiller's been real good to me."

"It's fortunate you're here. She may not feel much like teaching all day long the first few days she's back."

"She'd already turned most of the teaching over to me before—before it happened."

"Does she stay in the classroom?"

"Part of the time. Sometimes—usually in the afternoon—she leaves and just checks back in on me every now and then. I haven't had any problems." He smiled sincerely. "The kids seem to like me."

"Can you remember if she left you in charge of the classroom for any length of time Monday?"

"Most of the afternoon. She had tests to make out and papers to grade." A frown marred the All-American-boy face for a moment. "Why do you want to know that?"

"Just trying to figure out exactly when Mrs. Whitekiller got home Monday afternoon. She didn't hear her husband's pickup running when she got there, you see, which means it had already burned up all the gas in the tank before that. We're trying to establish the time of death."

He didn't seem to recognize this for the nonsense it was.

"Well, I know she had a conference with a parent after school, so she was probably here until after four." But there had been plenty of time between lunch and three o'clock, when school was out, for Dot Whitekiller to have gone home and killed her husband.

"Why don't you ask her?" he said.

"She hasn't been able to recall exactly. Shock, you know."

He nodded sincerely.

"I'll let you get back to your class," Molly said. "Thanks for your help." She got out of there before he could think up any more sensible questions.

17

Having left the school feeling that, at last, the investigation was going somewhere (exactly where remained to be seen), Molly checked her answering machine at the office and found no messages requiring immediate attention.

Still riding on a small cloud of optimism, she looked up George and Susan Butler's address in the phone book and drove to Choctaw Street. Maybe she was on a roll.

The house was in an area of modest but neat frame dwellings, whose streets and driveways held Fords and Chevrolets and an occasional Japanese import. Cream-colored with teal-green shutters and a brown door, the Butler house sat at an angle on a corner lot and was smaller than most of its neighbors.

Somehow Molly had expected flamboyance, more in line with Garth Reynolds's assessment of Susan Butler. Perhaps a bold-colored paint job or lots of gingerbread. But the house could have been a first home for any young couple, Anywhere, USA.

She didn't see a car in the Butlers' driveway, but there was an attached garage with the door closed.

Molly parked in the narrow drive and rang the front doorbell several times and heard it reverberating inside the house. She stepped back and, from the corner of her eye, caught the slight movement of a front window curtain. She waited, but no one came to the door.

She returned to her car and sat for a moment with the heater running. Someone was inside the house, Susan Butler probably. If Dot Whitekiller was right, Susan had been with Ed the afternoon before his death. She was in as good a position as Dot to know what kind of mood Ed had been in and what might or might not have been troubling him. Perhaps more so. She assumed men confided in their mistresses.

Susan Butler—or whoever—had peeked out and seen Molly on the porch. Why wouldn't she come to the door? She didn't know Molly, so it couldn't be anything personal. Molly stared at the heavy curtain, but it hung now, undisturbed. She hated to leave, knowing it must be Susan Butler in there.

She turned off the heater and went back to the front door. Knocking, she called, "Mrs. Butler, I have to talk to you."

She heard a movement inside the house and punched the bell. Moments later the door opened a few inches, with the security chain still engaged.

"What do you want?" asked a husky female voice.

The lights weren't on in the house, and all Molly could see was part of a shadowy form. "It's imperative that I talk to you."

"What about?"

"Ed Whitekiller."

"Who?"

"Please, Mrs. Butler. I know you were a close friend of Ed's."

The door edged back another fraction of an inch, stretching the chain to its limit. Molly still could not see the woman clearly. Most of her was behind the door.

"Who are you?"

"An investigator for the Adair County Sheriff's Department." A small white lie, but in a good cause.

The security chain slid from its slot and the door opened another few inches. The woman who stood there wore a pink-velour robe with blue piping around the collar and the wide cuffs of the long sleeves. The right side of her mouth was swollen where a scabbed-over cut angled toward the center of her upper lip. She had two black eyes several days old, as the fading purple bruises were turning jaundice-yellow around the edges. Her blond hair hung loose and uncombed around her face.

If the house was a surprise, this woman was a shock, and not only because of the state of her face. She was on the plump side, and her robe wouldn't be allowed through the door of Victoria's Secret. Could this possibly be the woman who had broken up Ed Whitekiller's marriage—or would have, had he lived?

"Susan Butler?"

The woman sighed, looked past Molly, perhaps to see if she'd brought reinforcements. "What makes you think I was a friend of Ed Whitekiller?"

"Another friend of Ed's told me. So did Ed's wife. What they said was that you and Ed were lovers."

"Wonderful. They'll run it in the newspaper next." She ran a hand back through her hair, which immediately slid forward again in a limp tangle. "Would you care for a megaphone so you can broadcast it to the neighborhood?" Her voice trembled.

Molly said nothing, fearing to upset the fragile balance between permitted entry and a door in her face.

"What business is it of yours, anyway?" the woman asked, but it was more disgruntlement than outrage. Molly got the feeling she was dealing with some other strong emotion at the moment and couldn't be bothered to be insulted.

Susan Butler didn't wait for an answer. Instead, she turned from the door and walked across the living room toward the rear of the house. Molly followed her and found Susan Butler in the kitchen, pouring the last of the Pepsi from a two-liter bottle into a clear plastic glass. One side of the double sink was full of dirty dishes, and several unwashed glasses and a plate covered with hardened egg yolk and toast crusts sat on the table.

Looking over her shoulder, Susan Butler said, "I wasn't expecting company," in incredible understatement. She tossed the Pepsi bottle into the empty side of the sink. "What do you want with me?"

"I have to talk to you."

She shrugged. "Sorry I can't offer you any Pepsi. I'm running out of everything." She raised the glass and took a sip. Then she moved past Molly and returned to the living room. Slowly, she lowered herself into a lounge chair facing the blank TV screen, as if she hurt all over. And she must, if her body looked anything like her face.

Molly moved a pile of *National Inquirer*s off an armchair and sat down. The chair gave off the odor of heavy dust, and the carpet in front of the lounge chair, where Susan Butler's fuzzy pink mules rested, was dingy, as though somebody regularly sat there to eat and habitually dropped food.

Susan Butler leaned back in her chair and looked at Molly, her face a purple-and-yellow collage of swelling and bruises.

"I'm sorry to have to disturb you when you're feeling unwell," Molly said.

Susan swallowed some Pepsi. "Unwell, huh?" She took another swallow. "I ran into a wall."

With a fist attached, Molly thought. "I'm trying to clear up some problems we've encountered in the investigation of Ed Whitekiller's death."

Susan held her glass balanced against the chair arm. She looked lethargic, overcome with world-weariness or defeat. "What kind of problems?"

"He may not have committed suicide."

Her expression grew more attentive. "He's dead, isn't he? Whether it was accidental or on purpose, he's still dead."

"It may not have been an accident, either."

She took a moment to work this out. "The paper said it was suicide. But I wasn't there, so I wouldn't know."

"I thought you could tell me what he was feeling the last day or two before his death. Who he talked to. If he had any disagreements with anyone."

"His wife would know a lot more about that than I."

"I don't think so. Weren't you with him last Sunday afternoon?"

Susan's fingers tightened their grip on her glass. "I don't know where you got your information, but it's still none of your business."

"He died the next day under suspicious circumstances. That makes it the business of the sheriff's department."

She raked tangled hair out of her bruised eyes. "What did you say your name was?" The tremble was back in her voice.

"Molly Bearpaw. If you'd like to call Sheriff Highsmith and check on my credentials . . ."

She seemed to consider it, then deemed it not worth the effort, much to Molly's relief. So far, Susan evidently assumed Molly was employed by the sheriff's department. It would be easier to get her to talk if she kept on thinking that.

Susan looked dully at the damp circle her glass had made on the chair arm.

"Did Ed seem depressed Sunday when you were with him?" Molly asked.

"Not exactly. I think he was worried that his wife would find out about us." She looked up at Molly. "He wasn't in love with her, you know. But he didn't want to lose his daughter."

"And he thought he'd lose Maggie if Dot divorced him?"

"Of course. He didn't even have a job," Susan muttered. "And I don't think Dot's an unfit mother or anything."

According to Dot, Molly recalled, Ed assumed he'd get custody of Maggie if there was a divorce, but he'd apparently told Susan otherwise.

"If he was so worried, why was he involved in an affair?" Molly asked.

A muscle pulled at the corner of Susan's swollen mouth. "He was in love." It was as if she needed to believe it. "Is that so hard to comprehend?"

"No, but from what I've learned, you weren't the first lover Ed had had outside his marriage."

She stared at Molly, then lifted her glass and took her

time about draining it. "He was just stringing me along, is that what you think?"

"I don't know, Mrs. Butler," Molly said. "What about you? Were you in love with Ed?"

She studied Molly. "Frankly, I was having second thoughts. In fact, on Sunday we decided not to see each other for a while."

"Whose idea was that?"

"We both agreed it was best," Susan said a little too quickly. "We needed space and time to think."

"You didn't argue about it?"

"No," Susan said sharply. Her eyes dropped. She fingered a button of her robe, loosing it and rebuttoning it, once, then twice. "If Ed's death wasn't suicide or an accident, that only leaves—" She seemed incapable of completing the thought.

"Murder," Molly finished for her.

She looked up, her blue eyes growing dark to match the surrounding bruised flesh.

Molly looked around the cluttered room "Were you and Ed here Sunday?"

She drew herself up. "No."

"You met somewhere?"

Susan stiffened. "I don't have to answer that."

"No, you don't. But if you know nothing about Ed's death, you'll answer my questions Surely you want to help us get to the bottom of this."

Susan twisted a lank strand of hair around her finger. "We went to a motel, in Stilwell."

Molly traced a dingy rose in the fabric on the arm of her chair. "Did your husband know about you and Ed?"

She waited too long before answering. Leaning her head

against the chair back, she finally said, "You'll have to ask George about that."

"If you'll tell me where I can reach him—"

"I don't know."

"He's a salesman, isn't he?"

She sighed. "Yes. He sells storm windows and vinyl siding for Sears."

"Is he out of town?"

She brushed a hand across her eyes. "I don't know."

"Well, when do you expect him back?"

"I don't." She lifted her head. "George doesn't live here anymore." There were tears in her eyes. She sounded quite hopeless.

"I—I'm sorry."

Susan shrugged helplessly. "I don't know what I'm going to do. I talked to a lawyer. He says I should be able to get alimony, but who knows how long it will take." After a moment, she added, "Maybe George will come to his senses."

Garth Reynolds was wrong about Susan having another man lined up. She sounded desperately afraid and wanted her husband to return. "You must excuse me now."

Molly stood and went to the door. Susan Butler followed, opened the door, and stood back, waiting for Molly to leave.

In the doorway, Molly turned back. "By the way, where were you Monday between nine in the morning and two in the afternoon?"

A pulse throbbed in Susan's temple. Her hand pushed the door wider. "Right here. I didn't leave the house Monday. I was barely able to get out of bed."

"Molly stepped outside and Susan Butler closed the door. Molly heard the sound of the door chain sliding into place.

She drove away, thinking of the two women with whom Ed Whitekiller had been involved when he died, his mistress and his wife. She thought of the tastefully decorated, spit-and-polish clean house where Ed and Dot had lived, comparing it to the Butlers' cluttered, downright dirty house with its neutral carpet, walls, and curtains.

The women seemed to match their houses. Dot, neatly groomed and attractively dressed, efficient. Susan, uncombed and still in her pajamas at mid-morning. But perhaps it was unfair to Susan to label her lazy and unkempt, after the beating she'd suffered recently.

When had the beating occurred and who had done it?

The *when* wasn't too hard to figure out. It must have happened Sunday, if Susan had been barely able to get out of bed on Monday. But not before she met Ed in Stilwell in the early afternoon. Susan probably hadn't left the house since the beating. She wouldn't want to be seen in her present condition. She certainly wouldn't have driven to Stilwell to meet Ed if she'd just suffered a beating.

So, it had happened at the motel or later, after she got home. If Ed had inflicted the damage, then Susan had lied about their amicable parting of the ways. Indeed, Molly had sensed that Susan was rearranging the facts quite a bit. It was more likely Ed who had wanted to stop the affair. Had she refused, threatened Ed?

Did Ed beat Susan to keep her quiet? It would certainly give Susan a motive for murder.

Or was it Susan's husband? Maybe he made a habit of beating his wife. Or maybe he found out about the affair, possibly while Susan was in Stilwell with Ed. Maybe that's why he was no longer living with his wife. After giving his wife a beating as a good-bye present on Sunday, did George

Butler go to Ed Whitekiller's house on Monday and kill him?

Molly couldn't even make a good guess at the answers to those questions until she or Dave Highsmith talked to George Butler.

When she got back to the office, she called the Adair County Sheriff's Office and briefed Highsmith on her morning's interviews. Highsmith's calls on the White-killer's neighbors had drawn a blank. Nobody had seen anyone at the Whitekiller house Monday.

"My guess is that Susan Butler was beaten by either Whitekiller or her husband," Molly said. "We need to talk to Butler, but she wouldn't tell me where he's staying, if she knows. Do you have time to do some checking?"

"I'll talk to the Tahlequah police," Highsmith said. "They can track him down easier than I can."

18

"Better leave your car here. All kinds of sharp objects lying about," Conrad said as Molly turned off the road on the lane leading to Zeb Smoke's house. It looked like the crooked man's crooked house in the storybook that had been Molly's favorite as a preschooler. Eva probably still had that book around somewhere, since she never threw anything away.

Nor, it appeared, did Zeb Smoke, Molly thought, as she and Conrad picked their way through partially snow-covered mounds of junk.

"Molly, don't say anything about the tape recorder. I'll bring it up if he seems cooperative." Conrad had slipped the small recorder into his coat pocket, leaving his briefcase in the car.

Zeb Smoke took his time coming to the door. When he did, he looked Conrad up and down wordlessly, but accepted the six-pack of Budweiser when it was offered.

Zeb didn't seem inclined to ask them in, however. Instead, he asked, "Where's Will?"

"Working," Conrad said.

"He's always working to hear him tell it," grumbled the old man.

"I brought you another visitor." Conrad nudged Molly forward.

"You ain't one of them church women, are you?" Zeb asked, squinting at Molly. "A couple of 'em showed up here this morning, asking nosy questions. I run 'em off."

Molly wasn't surprised to hear of Smoke's reaction to Moss Greenleigh's efforts to be helpful. "I'm Molly Bearpaw. You may know my grandmother, Eva Adair."

"I know Eva," he said. "Knew your Granddad Echols too." He waited, looking stolidly at Molly as though further comment was beneath his dignity.

"I work for the Cherokee Nation."

"Huh," he snorted. "Ain't nothing to brag about. You see what they're doing over there?" He jerked a thumb in the general direction of the construction site.

"Yes. I can understand you not wanting that on your doorstep."

He didn't reply and barely nodded, as though it went without saying that any sensible person would feel the same.

Molly tried again. "I'm investigating a suspicious death. Could I come in and talk to you about it?"

He thought it over. "I don't know nothing about no suspicious death."

"He was a Cherokee and he didn't live too far from here," Molly said quickly.

"That don't mean I know anything about it. I don't get out much."

"There was something odd about the death scene. I was hoping you could help me understand it." He had reached out to close the door but stopped when Molly said this. His interest was piqued.

"Huh," he said finally and walked away from the door, grunting, "Come in, if you've a mind to." Molly and Conrad stepped inside.

"Shut the door," Zeb grumbled, without looking around. "You're letting in the cold." He set the six-pack on a shelf running along the back wall. Then he sat in a cane-bottomed chair pulled up to a cast-iron stove.

Eyeing them expressionlessly, he took a corncob pipe and a small cloth sack of tobacco from the bib pocket of his overalls. From a bench against the wall next to him, he picked up a piece of cast iron a little bigger around and longer than a pencil, fitted it into a slot in a plate-sized lid on top of the stove, moved it to one side, then stuck a twisted piece of newspaper into the hole. When it caught he used it to light his pipe, then dropped the paper, still flaming, into the stove, and replaced the lid.

The roaring wood fire heated the room comfortably. While Zeb was occupied with lighting his pipe, Molly and Conrad removed their coats and sat on the sagging couch.

Zeb tipped the front legs of his chair off the floor, sucked on his pipe, and watched Molly. "This suspicious death you're looking into. Reckon you're talking about Ed White-killer."

Molly exchanged a glance with Conrad. "Did you know Ed, Mr. Smoke?"

"Yep."

"When was the last time you saw him?"

He thought it over. "Ed came by to see me a few days before he died."

Conrad threw Molly an encouraging look and kept quiet. Zeb didn't seem to take offense at Molly's questions, not much, anyway.

She asked, "Do you remember what day that was?"

He closed his eyes and deep ridges appeared on his forehead. "I lose track of the days. Can't say for sure when Ed was here."

"Why did he come?"

"To visit," Zeb said. He jerked his head toward the bingo hall. "He'd been over next door trying to get a job. They turned him away. I told him he was lucky they did."

"Why?"

He slid a look toward Conrad. "Like I told him and Will, something bad's gonna come out of what's going on over there. When it does, nobody will be able to hold it back. Maybe it's already started. Maybe Ed got infected with the evil."

"What have you heard about Ed's death?"

He shrugged. "He killed hisself. That's what they were saying at the store yesterday when the welfare lady took me to Stilwell to get groceries. She's the one told me about Ed dying." Molly hadn't expected Highsmith to get someone from the county to come out so quickly. "Maybe the evil got in his head." Zeb tapped the stem of his pipe against his temple. "Made him lose his mind."

"Mr. Smoke," Molly said, "have you heard anything about some objects that were found with Ed's body?"

"Ob-jecks?" He pronounced the word as though it were foreign to him.

"Black rocks. Seven of them."

He eased the front legs of his chair to the floor. He stared at her, his body tense.

"According to a Cherokee woman who was interviewed by Professor Swope," Molly said, "there was an ancient death curse involving seven black stones."

He gave her another hard stare and puffed on his pipe. It seemed a long time before he answered. "I heard of something like that when I was a boy, but I never knew anyone to use it. Never messed with any death curses, myself. I don't use my medicine to kill people. It might turn back on me."

Molly had no way of knowing if his disclaimer was true. He couldn't remember what day it was and he was fixated on the bingo hall, both of which seemed not quite normal. His wrinkled face was expressionless. Only the black eyes had any life, and they seemed to be trying to bore straight through Molly. But she had seen senile old people with that same look, as if they didn't fully understand what was going on.

In one way, the old man was pathetic. Aged and alone, smoking beside a wood fire in a hovel, spewing out invectives and prophecies of doom against the Cherokee Nation and their white man's bingo halls.

But he had the manner of a religious fanatic, and that unsettled Molly. Would a hyped-up zealot, even one as old as Zeb Smoke, have enough strength from pure adrenaline to walk a mile and hit a much younger, stronger man in the back of the head hard enough to knock him unconscious, then leave him to die?

But why? Ed Whitekiller had stopped to talk to Zeb, so the relationship had been friendly, at least from Ed's viewpoint.

If Zeb was in full control of his faculties, what possible reason could he have to kill Ed? To give credence to his prophecy that death and destruction were coming on the Cherokee Nation?

Conrad was asking Zeb if he'd given any more thought

to letting Conrad tape his memories of his childhood, and Molly tried to shake her troubled thoughts away.

"I been studying on what you said," Zeb was saying. "About leaving something behind for the young folks to hear when I'm gone. How is that supposed to work?"

"The tapes will be left at the Tribal Studies Institute, on the university campus in Tahlequah," Conrad told him, "to be used by students and researchers, or anybody who's interested in listening to them. Written transcripts will be made, too—somebody will type what you say, and that, along with the other typed interviews, will be bound in books. The books will be sent out to libraries all over the country."

"Will my name be there with my words?"

"Yes."

While Conrad continued to explain, Molly watched the old man. Zeb had at least heard something about a death curse. If he had killed Ed, he might have left seven black stones behind as a warning to other Cherokees. Once word got out that the stones had been found beside Ed Whitekiller's body, Cherokees were bound to make a connection between the stones and something they'd heard or read of an ancient curse.

Zeb seemed to be truly considering Conrad's request for a taped interview now. "I can say anything I want to say on that tape?" he asked.

"Anything," Conrad assured him.

"I can talk about how the Cherokees need to get back the old ways?"

"Absolutely. I'd like to ask you some questions too, but if you don't want to answer them, you can talk about whatever you want."

Zeb nodded slowly. "I'll give it a try, then, but if I say stop, you better do it."

"I'll turn it off anytime you say." Conrad removed the tape recorder from his pocket and looked around for an electrical outlet, seeming unsurprised not to find one. Then he reached in his pocket again and brought out a two-plug connection designed to be screwed into a light-bulb socket. The only light bulb in the shack was the one dangling on a cord from the ceiling.

Conrad explained that he wanted to remove the bulb and replace it with the connection so he'd have a place to hook up his tape recorder. Zeb agreed. Behind Zeb's back, Conrad gave Molly a thumb's-up sign and reached to unscrew the bulb.

Molly eased back on the couch.

Watching Conrad, Zeb said, "I ain't gonna be here much longer. That's why I'm gonna talk to you now."

Conrad plugged in the recorder and set it on the floor beside the old man. Then he pulled up another cane-bottomed chair.

Zeb leaned forward and peered down at the recorder. "Is it turned on?"

Conrad reached down and punched a button. "It is now."

"It can hear what I say?"

Conrad nodded. "Mr. Smoke, can you remember—"

Zeb held up his hand. "I wanta tell what happened back in the old Cherokee country, in Tennessee, before the people were driven from their homes. This is what my granddad told me. When he was a boy, he heard the old folks talk about some people who lived on the Hiwassee River where Shooting Creek comes in. They heard voices of spirits in the air calling them, telling them of the wars and destruction that were coming on the Cherokees. It was the *Nunne'hi* they heard." He squinted at Conrad, then at Molly. "Do you know of the *Nunne'hi?*"

"The Immortals," Molly said and Conrad nodded.

Zeb went on. "The *Nunne'hi* live in their homes under the mountains and under the waters. They told the people, if they wanted to be saved, they could go down and live with the *Nunne'hi*. The people gathered in the townhouse and prayed and fasted, and at the end of seven days they disappeared. Nobody ever saw any of them again. The *Nunne'hi* came and took them away down under the water. They were there when my granddad's father was a boy, and they are there now. On summer days, when my granddad's father was a boy, he would go fishing. Sometimes, when the wind made little waves in the water, he could hear the people talking down there. Whenever he would drag a net in the river for fish, the net always stopped and caught in the place where the people of that town went down. It was being held by the lost people because they didn't want their kinfolk to forget them."

As he talked, Zeb gazed straight ahead, but he wasn't seeing Molly or Conrad or the dim room where they sat. He was looking into the glorious past of his imagination, the past which he believed existed before any Cherokee set foot in Indian Territory.

His wrinkled face seemed to crumple as he said, "When the people were forced to come west, they cried many tears because they had to leave behind forever their relatives who had gone to the *Nunne'hi*."

He stirred and looked at Molly. "I tell you what I told my nephew, Will. When the destruction comes to this place, fast and go to water and you can be saved, like those people back then." Suddenly he pointed at Molly. "I tell you this too. Something's not right about them black stones being with Ed's body. Somebody's messing with powerful medicine."

By dusk, when Molly drove home from her office, most of the snow had turned into dirty slush. It seemed a metaphor for her state of mind. She had been affected by Zeb Smoke in ways that she didn't understand. He was an enigma. A harmless, sometimes confused old man full of stories with hidden meanings? A prophet? A nut case?

A murderer? No, she couldn't believe it.

The investigation was beginning to depress her. More and more, she felt she was wasting her time on the Ed Whitekiller case. Several people were probably glad he was dead. His wife and the mistress he'd dumped, to name only two. Various husbands whom Ed cuckolded. But that didn't mean one of them had murdered him. There was a great leap between the wish and the act, and not many people took it.

Maybe she shouldn't have pressed Dave Highsmith to look more deeply into Whitekiller's death. Maybe, in spite of the opinions of Ed's daughter and friends, it was a simple case of suicide.

Too many maybes.

Homer wasn't in the yard when she got home. Conrad must have taken him into the house. As she unlocked her door, she was forced to admit that she didn't look forward to spending the evening alone. Her apartment, usually a haven, seemed silent, cold, dreary. Homer's company would have been welcome. But what she really wished was that she had D.J. there to talk to.

She tossed her coat and purse on the sofa and went to the kitchen and ground some Kona beans. While the coffee brewed, she chopped onions, ham, cheese, and jalapeño peppers, then dumped them in a skillet with three eggs.

When the omelet was set on the bottom, she folded it in half. Turning down the flame, she let it simmer while she toasted two thick slices of raisin bread, which she'd baked herself. She slathered butter on the hot toast, stacked it on a plate with the omelet, poured coffee, and took it all to the table.

The phone rang in the middle of dinner. Molly tucked the phone under her chin and went on eating. "Hello."

"Is this Molly Bearpaw?" The voice was barely above a whisper.

"Yes. Who's this?"

"Maggie Whitekiller."

"Oh, hi, Maggie. How are you doing?"

"Okay, I guess." She sounded anything but. "I called to see if you've found out something about my father's death."

"I'm still looking into it, Maggie. I'd rather not talk about it until I've reached some conclusions."

"Then you *do* think it wasn't suicide?"

"I haven't formed an opinion yet."

"Oh." She was clearly disappointed. "Well, I have to go now. My mother doesn't know I called you."

Molly hung up with a sigh. So much for throwing in the towel. She'd keep digging in hopes of turning up something comforting for Maggie.

Later, when D.J. called, Molly told him about her visit to Zeb Smoke and the pity she'd felt for the old man who lived in the past, and not even a past that he could remember, but a past that he imagined had existed long before he was born. She told how his voice had been full of longing for the glory days of his ancestors. Her ancestors.

Zeb Smoke had spoken of people who heard spirit voices on the wind, warning them to escape before the coming trouble fell on them. Had Zeb been hearing spirit voices as well, sending out warnings on the wind?

She relayed all of this to D.J., then said, "Now, tell me everything you and Courtney have been doing."

He did, at some length, adding, "I keep thinking how much nicer it would be if you were here too."

A lump formed in Molly's throat. "I miss you," she said with a rare burst of transparency.

"God, I miss you too. Yesterday, I had a long talk with Courtney about you."

Molly would have liked to be a fly on the wall during that conversation. She wanted to ask exactly what he'd told his daughter but instead asked, "What did she say?"

"Not much, except that she'd like to meet you sometime."

Sure. To a ten-year-old, *sometime* was too far away to be threatening. At the moment, Courtney was dealing with a new stepfather. She shouldn't have to worry about a new woman in her father's life, as well.

They talked about the Ed Whitekiller case for a while. "Be careful, Molly," D.J. cautioned. "I don't want you getting hurt again. I love you, woman."

Maybe it was the loneliness that had hit her when she got home. Maybe it was because she'd been afflicted with melancholy by Zeb Smoke's stories. Whatever it was, for the first time Molly was able to say, "I love you too." Somehow it was easier to say it long distance than face to face, but still she surprised herself with her uncommon willingness to be vulnerable. Immediately she wanted to back-track, and she added, "But love isn't always enough, D.J."

He inhaled a deep breath and pushed it out. "Love's all that matters, Molly. Everything else is negotiable."

"D.J.—"

"Honey, I know where you're coming from, okay? There are things we need to work out and it may take a while. Just stop being afraid."

She swallowed. "I used to think love was simple, but it's not."

"Are you crying?"

A single tear slid from her eye, and she brushed it away. "Not enough to count."

"I'm sorry, baby." He sounded torn. "I love you, and I want you, but we can't work out anything on the tele-phone."

They said good-bye, and she hung up, wondering how three simple words could change everything. She didn't un-derstand it, but she knew that the relationship, hers and D.J.'s, was different than it had been before his call. More connected.

Scarier.

She felt as though she were standing on a cliff, looking down a very long distance at a pool of water and working up her courage to jump, knowing there was no turning back now.

19

Thursday

It had dipped below freezing again Wednesday night, but the sun was trying to break through the clouds and rising temperatures were forecast.

Three concrete-block walls were in place at the construction site, the weather having delayed the work only half a day. The workers started on the fourth wall Thursday morning. It still looked as though they'd have the bingo hall enclosed before they knocked off on Friday. After that, the weather wouldn't be a factor in finishing the interior.

Cecil had a little kerosene heater going where he was working, to take the edge off the chill, which didn't do Horace and Franklin much good since they were in and out all the time.

When Moss Greenleigh arrived, Horace noticed right away that he was in a good mood, pleased with the progress they were making. They could start installing insulation on Monday, and they'd be putting up the wallboard by the middle of next week. The council wanted the hall open for business by March.

Horace and Franklin were taking a load of blocks from the wheelbarrow and unloading them near where Cecil was working. "You know that Whitekiller guy who killed himself the other day?" Horace asked as Moss walked into the building.

"I seen him around," Cecil said, looking up and adding, "Lo, boss," as Moss joined them.

Franklin raised a gloved hand in Moss's direction and asked, "He tried to get on this job, didn't he, Moss?"

"Who?"

"Ed Whitekiller."

"Yeah, he applied." Moss zipped up his down jacket and looked unhappy. "The paper said he'd been out of work for five months. We didn't have a place for him here, but I wish now I'd tried to make one. Maybe he wouldn't have killed himself."

"Aw, a guy doesn't kill himself because he gets turned down for a job," Cecil said. "I'll bet you money there was trouble at home."

Franklin lifted out two more blocks. "I think he had experience in construction," he went on. This was Franklin's and Horace's first such job, and with the labor situation what it was, they knew they were lucky to have it. Franklin, of course, claimed to have experience because he'd helped his brother build a garage out of concrete blocks. Which wasn't much of a recommendation, Horace thought; he'd seen the garage.

"I knew him," Horace said.

"Ed Whitekiller?" Franklin asked, as if they'd been talking about somebody else.

Horace nodded. "Not real well, but I was shocked to hear he'd done that. Didn't seem the type." He handed a block to Franklin, who stacked it with the others.

"Never know what's going on in another person's head,"

Cecil mused as he slapped a trowelful of wet cement on the end of a block and set another block beside it. With the side of the trowel, he raked away the excess.

"Ain't it the truth," Moss agreed with a shake of his head. Horace wondered if Moss was thinking of his wife. Recently, he'd heard Moss talking to Cecil about her, saying she was having a bad time, going through the change of life. She flew off the handle or cried for no reason, Moss had said, and when Moss tried to get her to see a doctor, she'd taken it as an insult and threatened to divorce him. That had hurt Moss, even though he didn't take the divorce talk seriously. For one thing, he ran the construction company, which was owned by his wife's family. If there was a divorce, Moss might leave and start a competing company.

Watching Cecil set another block, Franklin said, "I heard the sheriff found seven black rocks in Whitekiller's pickup."

A stunned silence met this information, and then all four men turned to look toward Zeb Smoke's shack. They'd left the wall on that side of the building until last because Cecil said he wanted to see what was going on over there as long as possible. He'd said it like a joke, but Horace thought he was about half serious. Watching that old man make medicine was getting to all of them. Horace had even dreamed about it and woke up in a cold sweat.

"Did you talk to the sheriff about him, Moss?" Franklin asked.

"Yeah, and I got some of the ladies from church to come out. He threatened to get his shotgun if they didn't get off his property. Scared 'em half to death."

"He ought to be in a nursing home," Cecil said, "but I don't reckon anyone can make him go."

"The county sent a social worker out too," Moss said, "but her opinion is that he isn't a threat to himself or others, and he's still able to take care of himself, so there's nothing the county can do."

"That social worker ain't seen some of the stuff we've seen," Cecil said. "She'd change her mind if she had."

Moss looked troubled. "Are you sure about those rocks being in Whitekiller's pickup, Franklin?" he asked.

"That's what I heard."

Moss looked toward Zeb Smoke's house again. "I wish I knew what is going on with him. Maybe I should tell the sheriff about the rocks Smoke left out there behind the bingo hall."

Horace shot Moss a look of disquiet. "My advice is leave it alone." Franklin surprised Horace by mumbling an agreement. Even Cecil, who claimed not to believe in Zeb Smoke's medicine, seemed uneasy when it came to dealing with the old man.

"You see him this morning?" Moss asked. His good mood had evaporated.

"He was walking around out behind his shack earlier," Cecil said. "Next time I looked, he was gone. He's like a puff of smoke. Now you see him, now you don't."

"It's like he can make himself invisible," Franklin added. "Maybe we oughta let it lay, like Horace says. We wouldn't want to upset him."

"He's already upset," Cecil observed.

"Well, let's don't make it worse," Franklin said.

"You don't reckon he could've had something to do with Whitekiller's death, do you?" Cecil asked of nobody in particular.

"Maybe we don't want to know," Franklin told him.

*   *   *

The slush had glazed over during the night, making the streets hazardous. Molly had stayed up late the night before to bake whole-wheat bread, and she took a loaf to Conrad before leaving for work. He insisted she stay for a cup of coffee.

Conrad's warm kitchen enveloped her as she stepped in and shut the door. The toaster oven was out on the blue formica counter—Conrad liked to prepare his prebuttered toast in it rather than the toaster. Actually, he used corn-oil margarine, a concession to his doctor. A few crumbs were sprinkled around the toaster oven and the remains of a pot of hot cereal sat on the stove.

"I made oatmeal," Conrad said. "You had breakfast?"

"Yes," Molly said, turning down the oatmeal.

Conrad rinsed the remains down the sink and ran water in the pot to soak.

Homer, who had been stretched out on the blue-tile floor, got up to greet Molly. She rubbed his head with her knuckles. "You build him a doghouse, and then you let him stay in all night," she chided.

Conrad shrugged. "I know he must be warm in his doghouse, but I keep thinking how I'd feel out there when the temperature's below freezing."

Molly smiled. "It's not the same thing, and you know it. But I'd probably have let him in last night if you hadn't."

They stood there, looking down at Homer like two proud parents. Homer gave them a pink-tongued grin and squirmed all over because he knew they were talking about him. "Are we spoiling him?" Molly asked.

"Afraid so," Conrad agreed and poured her a cup of coffee. "You can do that with dogs, unlike children. Spoiled dogs don't turn into ingrates and monsters later on."

Molly chuckled, wondering how Conrad knew so much about children, since he didn't have any.

When they were seated at his kitchen table, he said, "I found a description of the Cherokee death curse in my library."

Molly held her cup in both hands and looked at him through a tiny rising cloud of steam.

"Wanda Weems was right about the seven black stones, but the curse also required spittle from the victim. That was rolled up in a ball of dirt and buried with the stones. The victim was supposed to die within seven days."

Molly thought about it. "Whoever left the stones must not have known how the curse was supposed to be done."

"Uh-huh."

Homer laid his head in Molly's lap, insinuating his nose under her hand. She stroked him idly and sipped her coffee. "Which might exonerate Zeb Smoke. I had a feeling he knew exactly how the curse is supposed to be performed. Remember, he said something's not right about the stones found with Whitekiller's body."

"He also said he never had anything to do with a death curse."

"Can we be sure he was telling the truth?"

Conrad's bushy white brows inched up. "You can't really consider him a suspect in Ed Whitekiller's death."

"I don't know." She had stopped stroking and Homer nosed her hand again. She lifted his head off her lap and he looked up at her disconsolately before flopping down beside her chair.

"If you're right about his knowing how the curse should be done," Conrad said, "then he's in the clear. Whoever left those stones evidently didn't know."

Molly studied the reflection of the ceiling light in her coffee for a moment. "Maybe." She lifted her cup, shattering the light into dozens of fragments. "But I keep thinking—"

"What?"

"If the stones were buried, nobody but the person who buried them would ever see them."

"I would imagine that's an important part of the ritual," Conrad said. "It's like the way tobacco for the Grandfather Medicine is grown. Nobody is supposed to see it while it's growing but the one who plants it. Otherwise, it loses its power."

"But the stones couldn't serve as a warning—an omen of disaster—if they were buried." Molly drank some coffee and set her cup down. "I keep thinking those stones were meant to be found. If so, somebody is twisting an ancient ritual to his own ends, which could upset the traditionalists, once word gets out. And if they were meant to be found, then Zeb Smoke didn't do it. He'd never make light of Cherokee medicine." She paused. "Oh, I don't know. I'm just rambling, thinking aloud. I'm not even sure Whitekiller's death wasn't suicide."

"Suicide is the simplest explanation." Which is basically what Dave Highsmith had said.

Molly gave him a wry look. "Not for Maggie Whitekiller. She phoned me last night to ask what I'd learned about her father's death. I didn't have the heart to tell her I'd turned up nothing you could call evidence against suicide."

"Poor child," Conrad murmured.

The phone was ringing when Molly reached her office. It was Dave Highsmith. "I asked the Tahlequah City Police to check up on George Butler. He's staying in a Tahlequah motel." He gave Molly the name of the motel.

"Maybe I can catch him there," she said.

"The police were real interested in why I was asking about Butler. Seems his wife put a restraining order on him Sunday night. They served him Monday, so he was in town then." Highsmith almost sounded pumped up. Would wonders never cease?

"Did she really?" Susan Butler must have taken out the restraining order immediately after the beating. But when Molly talked to her Tuesday, she'd acted as if she'd welcome him back home.

"Yep."

"Did you tell the police why you were looking for Butler?"

"I said I just wanted to talk to him, said his name came up as a possible witness in another case."

"Good. I have some information you should know about too. Don't know if it'll lead anywhere. Could we meet for lunch today?"

He thought it over. "Who's paying?"

Cheapskate. "We'll go dutch."

"Here or there?"

"If you come here, you can go out to George Butler's motel with me."

Highsmith chuckled. "Having second thoughts about stirring up the natives?" he drawled.

"No, but I saw what Butler did to his wife."

"Did you now?"

"I'll tell you all about it at lunch."

* * *

By the time Molly met Highsmith at The Shack on Muskogee Avenue, the temperature had risen into the high thirties and the glaze on the streets had melted and was rushing into storm drains in dirty streams. But the wind had begun to rise, which made it feel colder than the thermometer said it was.

Highsmith was dressed for the weather, having pulled a cap with fur-lined ear flaps down low on his head and the collar of his sheepskin coat up. He paused in the doorway and pulled off a new pair of gloves, which he stuffed in his coat pockets. His eyes swept over the lunchtime crowd seated at booths and tables. He nodded in Molly's direction when he saw her and went to the table at the far end of the café near the cash register.

He pulled off his cap and stuck it in a pocket with a glove, then removed his coat and dumped it with Molly's on an extra chair before he sat. Over a sudden burst of laughter from a nearby table, he said, "Full house. The food must be good here." He picked up a menu.

"Have the chicken-fried steak or a burger," Molly advised.

He read through the menu with great deliberation, looking up to inquire of Molly about the meatloaf and pork chops. But when the waitress came, he ordered the chicken-fried steak dinner with corn, mashed potatoes, and gravy. Molly asked for a cheeseburger and fries. They both wanted coffee, which was delivered immediately by a young waitress with large, bouncing breasts.

Highsmith tried to pretend he didn't notice and almost missed his cup when he stirred real cream into his coffee. "Talk," he muttered to Molly.

"Ed Whitekiller had life insurance. A hundred thousand. He'd had it long enough for it to pay, even on suicide."

He leaned back in his chair. "I assume his wife is the beneficiary." Molly nodded and Highsmith said, "She was at work when he died."

"Maybe not." Molly fished a small spiral notebook from her purse and flipped it open. "She's got a student teacher this semester. I talked to him. He says Dot leaves him in charge of the class for long periods of time. She works in the teacher's lounge or"—she flipped to another page—"runs errands. The student told me Dot was absent from the classroom most of Monday afternoon. He didn't—or couldn't—say if she left the building. The secretary wouldn't commit herself on that, either."

Highsmith frowned. "You're saying she could have gone home and knocked her husband unconscious, set it up to look like suicide, and returned to school without anyone being the wiser?"

"It's possible. I got the idea from both the student teacher and the secretary that things are pretty loose around there. Nobody checks too closely on a teacher's comings and goings when there's a student in charge of the class—as long as there are no problems, and this particular student seemed very capable."

"None of the neighbors saw Mrs. Whitekiller's car at the house that day. Of course, most of them were at work themselves, but there's an elderly couple a half mile down the road who were at home. They didn't notice any vehicle but Whitekiller's pickup coming or going."

"Which doesn't mean there was no other vehicle."

"True, but that's speculation."

They fell silent as the waitress set their meals in front of them. "Anything else right now, hon?" she chirped, looking at Highsmith.

Highsmith grinned and his face turned pink. Molly laid her notebook beside her plate. "We'll need more coffee in a few minutes, hon," she said.

The waitress glanced at Molly uncertainly and Highsmith watched her bounce away before picking up his fork. Molly dipped her head to hide a smile and dumped ketchup on her french fries.

"The insurance money aside," Molly said, "Dot White-killer wanted out of that marriage and she wanted custody of her daughter. Maggie's fourteen, old enough to choose which parent she wanted to live with and, from everything I've seen, it was no contest. Maggie would have gone with her father. Dot had to know that."

Highsmith cut a healthy bite of steak and ate it before replying. "Okay, so the wife might have had a motive, but as of now there's no evidence that she went home that day. Did you come up with anything else?"

Molly lowered her fork. She sipped some coffee and wiped ketchup off her chin with her napkin. "The other woman, Susan Butler."

"The battered wife."

"Yes. You should see her. George worked her over pretty good."

"Because of the affair?"

"I think so. Susan and Ed were in a Stilwell motel together last Sunday afternoon. Dot was aware of the affair before that. She admitted it to me."

"But you say she wanted out of the marriage. She wouldn't kill him because he was messing around."

"You're forgetting Maggie." She took a bite of cheeseburger and speared a french fry.

He shook his head. "The guy was out of work. He'd have had a hard time supporting himself, much less his daughter." He buttered a roll thoughtfully. "As for George Butler, we know he beat his wife sometime Sunday. It must have been when she returned from Stilwell."

"My guess is he'd just found out about the affair. Maybe he followed Susan to Stilwell. Ironically, according to Susan, she and Ed had decided Sunday afternoon not to see each other again. She said it was by mutual agreement, but I think he dumped her."

"Which gives her a motive for murder too."

"Right." She took a bite, chewed, and pointed her fork at him. "And Susan knows karate."

He grinned. "You mean the bruise on the back of Whitekiller's head? I don't think Doc Pohl was serious when he mentioned a karate chop, Molly."

"I agree it seems farfetched. I just thought it was interesting that the mistress took a karate class."

"Do you really think a woman could knock a man unconscious with the edge of her hand?"

"If she knew what she was doing, yes. Of course, Susan claims she never left the house Monday."

"Maybe you should check with her neighbors."

"I intend to. We have to consider George Butler a suspect too. He lost it Sunday and beat his wife. That makes him capable of murder, in my book."

"Okay, I'll buy that—if Butler doesn't have an alibi for Monday."

"I phoned the motel before coming here," Molly said. "The clerk has seen Butler coming and going from his room since Sunday night. He told the clerk he's leaving on a sales trip tomorrow. He wasn't in his room when I called, probably out for lunch. But he should be back later today."

"*If* it was murder," Highsmith said, "and so far we don't have evidence that it was—"

"Except that bruise on the back of Whitekiller's head."

"Which he could have gotten from a fall."

Molly shook her head. "I don't think it happened that way, Dave."

"Tell me this. If there was no Maggie, would you be so stubborn about accepting the suicide verdict?"

Molly hesitated. "Yes, I think I would."

He looked as though he didn't believe her. "I'm willing to go along with you for a while. As I was saying, if it was murder, George Butler sounds like our best bet as a suspect. We'll get a better fix on him when we question him. But if we can't prove that one of our three suspects was at the Whitekiller place Monday, we've got no case. It'll have to go down as suicide."

"I don't like it. We can't let somebody get away with murder."

He mopped up some gravy with a piece of roll. "If you can't prove it's murder—" He let the sentence hang while he ate the gravy-drenched bread. "When all you've got is gut instinct, you compromise, Molly. Happens all the time. The criminal-justice system isn't perfect."

"There *is* evidence that somebody besides Whitekiller was in the garage that day."

Highsmith wiped his fingers on the napkin and gave a grunt of impatience. "The bruise again."

"Not just that. What about the stones?"

Momentarily, he looked blank. Obviously he'd dismissed the stones as irrelevant. "What about 'em?"

"Somebody put them in Whitekiller's truck. It wasn't Ed. His wife told you he wasn't a collector. Could it have been Dot herself?" She took a bite of her cheeseburger while he mulled over the question.

"No," he said finally. "When I told her we'd found them in the pickup, I'd swear she had no idea how they got there."

"Then it was probably somebody else." She leaned forward and planted her elbows on the table. She waited while three men got up and walked by them. Then she said, "Think about it, Dave. If Ed didn't put the rocks there, then he'd have thrown them out when he noticed them. Since they were there when the body was discovered, they were put there after he was unconscious."

He was already shaking his head before she finished speaking. "Why would somebody leave rocks with the body? It makes no sense."

"I'm beginning to think the stones were a warning to other Cherokees that the Nation is on the road to destruction. At any rate, that's the meaning the killer meant people to get from the stones." She went on to tell him what she'd learned about the Cherokee death curse and the article mentioning the curse which had run in the local newspaper.

"Good Lord, Molly," he said when she was finished. "That's really reaching."

"Maybe," she admitted, "but can you think of any other reason for the stones being in the pickup?"

He sighed. "Why does there have to be a reason? Maybe Whitekiller picked them up while he was cleaning the garage and tossed them in the pickup temporarily."

"Seven *black* stones? Dave, you can't find black stones just anywhere. And seven of them, that's too much of a coincidence for me to swallow."

He looked at her helplessly. "You're irrational on the subject. That kid has really gotten to you." He finished his steak and wadded his napkin beside his plate. "Look, Molly, if you want to chase after this will-o'-the-wisp indefinitely, be my guest. But if we don't get anything from Butler or the Butlers' neighbors when we check on Susan Butler's alibi for Monday, I'm hanging it up. I've got other things to do."

Oh, right, Molly thought sourly. Can't miss those coffee breaks with the good old boys or the afternoon naps, can we? But she managed to appear compliant. "Fair enough."

20

George Butler was packing a small suitcase, preparing for departure the next day. He was not welcoming but was evidently influenced by Highsmith, whose presence made the call seem official. His gaze lingered on the uniform for a long moment as he deliberated whether to admit them. It must not have occurred to him that Highsmith had no jurisdiction in Cherokee County, and Molly hoped it wouldn't until they'd questioned him. It had probably occurred to Highsmith, however, that no matter how mad they made Butler, it wasn't going to cost Highsmith a vote.

"Come in," Butler said finally, gesturing toward two unmatched chairs. He transferred the partially packed suitcase to the floor. He slumped on the side of the bed, which sank alarmingly with his weight, then he winced and leaned forward. Back problem, Molly thought, and sleeping in a soft bed would make it worse. Butler was probably blaming his wife for that too.

"If this is about the restraining order—"

"It isn't," Highsmith said.

Butler didn't seem to believe him. "I haven't been near my wife since Sunday. If she says I have, she's lying."

"Your wife has nothing to do with this, Mr. Butler," Molly told him. "Not directly, I should say. We're investigating the death of Ed Whitekiller."

A quick tremor passed across his face. Before Molly could decide what it meant, he looked away toward the room's only window. "Who?"

Out in the street, two young boys, wrapped in coats, caps, and scarves, with only their eyes and noses showing, whizzed by on bicycles, sending out sprays of dirty slush. School was out. A car braked with a squeal and a horn honked—sudden, startled sounds in the afternoon quiet. Butler's gaze followed the car down the street and out of sight.

"Ed Whitekiller, your wife's lover," Highsmith said bluntly. The words sounded prim and disapproving, coming from the sheriff.

"You knew about the affair," Molly said quickly before he could deny it. "I've already talked to your wife."

He returned his gaze to Molly. It had turned hard. "What if I did? The marriage was over anyway."

Molly knew instinctively that this was a lie. He wouldn't have been angry enough to beat his wife if he'd already given up on the marriage. "If it was over, why did you fly into a rage when you learned your wife and Whitekiller were together Sunday afternoon?"

Butler had gotten control of himself now. He merely shrugged and looked out the window again. "She was asking for it, believe me." The same litany espoused by all wife beaters. "It was the sneaking around I couldn't take, the way she pretended to be such a loving wife while all the time . . ."

"Mr. Butler," Highsmith interrupted rudely, "we're looking at possible motives for murder. If you know something, we'd appreciate your telling us about it."

"Murder?" Molly saw his instinctive shrinking away from them. "I thought the guy killed himself. Frankly, I figured it was because Susan and I were getting a divorce and she expected him to leave his wife for her. She was probably pressuring him to do it. I figured he'd rather die than live with Susan, who's a real slob." He tried to laugh, but it didn't quite sound authentic, and neither Highsmith nor Molly smiled.

"The paper said it was suicide," Butler went on seriously.

"Some conflicting evidence has come up," Molly said. "We have to look into other possibilities."

The bed squeaked as he rose, grabbed his back, and went to the window, where he hitched up his sagging trousers and faced them, hands in pockets. No wonder he had back problems. He was overweight by probably forty pounds, most of which seemed to be protruding and sagging over his belt in front, pulling against his spine.

"I don't want to get involved in this. I know nothing about Whitekiller's death. I never even met the man."

"What about his wife, Dot?" Highsmith asked.

"Never met her, either."

"Are you saying you didn't contact Dot Whitekiller and tell her about the affair?" Molly asked. Given Butler's fury when he learned his wife was unfaithful, Molly thought it was the first thing that would have occurred to him—after working Susan over with his fists. Just another form of revenge.

"I thought about it," Butler admitted, "but then I thought, she's better off if she never finds out. She's an innocent party, like me. I felt sorry for the woman."

Highsmith glanced at Molly and scratched his chin. "So you never met either of the Whitekillers?" he inquired.

"Never. I knew Whitekiller by sight, but I never spoke to him."

Molly asked, "Mr. Butler, can you account for your time on Monday?"

His jaw clenched. His gaze went to Highsmith, who was leaning back in his chair, fingers laced together on his chest, with an air of waiting on events.

Butler hesitated to see if Highsmith would take charge of the conversation, perhaps put this upstart female in her place. After all, Highsmith was the one in uniform. Moments ticked by. A sudden gust of wind tossed a few wet leaves against the windowpane.

"I was here Monday morning," Butler said at last. "Followed up on some calls by phone, set up some appointments. Went out for lunch—"

"Where?" Molly interjected.

"Western Sizzlin', I think." He paused. "Yeah, that's where I ate lunch Monday. Came back here, watched TV for a while, made some more calls, took a nap. Went out again for supper. Carry-out steak sandwich and malt from Braum's. I brought it to the motel to eat it."

"Can anyone back you up on any of this?" Highsmith asked.

Butler met the sheriff's eyes directly. "There were people around at the Sizzlin', and the kid who took my order at Braum's may remember me. Somebody may have seen my car on the street—it's that green Chrysler out front." He tugged his pants over his stomach. "I can't give you any names. I didn't anticipate having to prove where I was Monday."

Because he didn't kill Whitekiller, Molly wondered, or because he'd counted on the death being accepted as suicide and no questions asked?

"If I'd killed Whitekiller," Butler added, "I'd sure as hell have a better alibi. Think about it. Now, if there's nothing else . . ."

Molly sighed. "Not at the moment." Immediately, High-smith stood, as though he'd been waiting for Molly to admit defeat. At the door, Molly said, "We may need to talk to you again. When will you be back in town?"

"Wednesday or Thursday of next week. Depends on how the sales add up."

Outside, Highsmith pulled up his collar and said, "He's right, you know. If he'd murdered Whitekiller, he'd have set up an alibi." It was clear he was prepared to wash his hands of the murder investigation.

"Thanks for coming over anyway," Molly said. "If I learn anything else, I'll let you know."

"Do that," Highsmith said, but his faint smile said it'd be a cold day in July when that happened.

Molly spent an hour calling on people in the block where Susan Butler lived. The few neighbors she found at home could not recall seeing Susan Butler's car leave the house Monday. Nor could they say it hadn't left the house. Seeing a neighbor's car on the street was such a common occurrence, it hardly registered.

Finally, Molly drove out to Park Hill to see Eva, who, as always, immediately began trying to feed her. Molly accepted a sugar cookie. Eva seemed none the worse for having crawled around the graveyard on Sunday, but she had heard about the black stones and was outraged. "The very idea of somebody exploiting people's beliefs," she fumed.

Having reassured herself of Eva's good health, Molly, for the second night running, went home feeling dispirited about the Whitekiller inquiry. She hadn't come up with anything that would influence Highsmith to continue the investigation. He would argue that she was placing significant interpretations on minor details, like the seven stones, because of Maggie Whitekiller.

But Highsmith couldn't keep her from going ahead with her own investigation. If only she knew where to go next.

By seven that evening, when it was time to leave for the first session of the finger-weaving class at the library, Molly still had not settled on a direction. She was tempted to skip the class, stay home, and wallow in the quandary some more. Maybe talk it over with Conrad.

But she remembered that Moira would be there, and it had been too long since she'd seen her friend. So, dressed in jeans and a red plaid flannel shirt, she grabbed her coat, purse, and the sack of supplies she'd been instructed to bring, and left the apartment.

At the library, she was greeted by the head librarian and directed to a meeting room. Four women and two men were seated around a long table with the instructor, Rachel Locust, at one end. They all looked up as Molly hesitated in the doorway.

"Come on in, Molly," Rachel said. "We're about to start." A plump, pretty Cherokee woman in her forties, Rachel was a noted practitioner in the ancient art of finger weaving. She grinned at Molly, nose wrinkling under coal-dark eyes.

Moira had saved Molly a seat and gave her a hug as soon

as she sat down. "Gosh, it's good to see you. It's been so *long.*"

"Whose fault is that? You've been too busy," Molly reminded Moira as she shrugged out of her coat. She was a little put out that Moira had time for a finger-weaving class—which Moira had never before now expressed the slightest interest in—but she hadn't had time to meet Molly for lunch or dinner in over a month.

Moira threw her hands out, palms up. "I know. I'm sure things will settle down after the first of the year."

"Once you're an old married woman?"

"Yeah," Moira said. Her smile was so genuine that Molly decided she was wrong in suspecting her friend of entertaining second thoughts about the impending nuptials.

Molly took her supplies from the sack and placed them in front of her. A six-inch-long dowel, a large safety pin, and three colors of wool yarn. Little was required for finger weaving, which made it very portable. Molly wondered if she'd turn into one of those old ladies who never went anywhere without their hand work.

Rachel leaned her sweatered forearms on the table, folding capable, blunt-nailed hands under her chin. "This class will meet the first and third Thursday evenings of each month through March. I encourage you to work on your projects between classes. The more work you do at home, the more projects you'll complete. Feel free to call me if you hit a snag. I'm in the phone book. Now, let's start by getting acquainted.

They introduced themselves. The two men were Cherokee—the one named Ralph was in his sixties, retired, and looking for something to do; the other, Wendell, a square-faced man of about fifty with big, beefy hands, said his wife and daughters sold their finger weaving at craft shows, and since he had to go to the shows with them, he might as well have something to sell too. His wife had tried to teach him but lost patience with his clumsiness.

Moira and the other two women, who had done fancy needlework for years, were white. The chunky, mid-fortyish woman with round cheeks was an instructor at the university; the other, a thin redhead, was the wife of a professor. They'd become fascinated with Cherokee finger weaving since moving to Tahlequah.

Rachel glanced around the table. "All weaving uses vertical threads, called warp threads, and horizontal threads, called weft threads. In loom weaving, the warp and weft are separate threads. But in the type of finger weaving you'll learn in this class, we'll have only one set of yarns, using them as both warp and weft threads." She laughed as frowns appeared on a couple of faces. "Don't worry. It'll make more sense as we go along."

She took several examples of her own finger weaving from the large tote bag beside her chair and passed them around the table, commenting on each as she did so.

"These will give you an idea of the variety of things that can be made with finger weaving. Here's a fringed belt in a double-chevron pattern." The belt was eye-catching in mauve, navy, and gray. "And here's another belt. It's been finished with a buckle, rather than fringe. As you can see, that's a diamond design." The red and blue diamonds had been meticulously outlined with tiny white beads. "And here's a necktie, also a chevron pattern, but you can see how different it is from the fringed belt. In this yellow and

green sash and the black, white, and gray scarf, I used varia-
tions of the arrowhead design."

"This looks complicated," the university instructor
mused as she picked up the scarf.

"It may seem so at first," Rachel agreed, "but you should
be able to tackle it by the time the class is over. We'll start
with something easier, a fringed belt with a diagonal-stripe
pattern." She pulled a tangle of yellow tape measures and
four pairs of scissors from her tote bag. "First, we'll cut ten
two-and-a-half-yard lengths of each of your three yarn colors, thirty lengths in all. Then we'll loop the middle of each
length of yarn around your dowel . . ."

Time passed quickly as the novice finger weavers learned
how to secure the yarn on one side of the dowel with a
safety pin while they worked with the remaining threads.
Rachel moved around the table, giving individual instruction as she saw the need. At first, the weavers' entire con-
centration was required to follow the step-by-step pattern
sheets that Rachel had passed out. But when they began to
get the hang of it, they talked, getting better acquainted as
they manipulated their yarn.

After some false starts, unraveling, and starting over,
Molly began to achieve an even tension as she drew the weft
through the opening, called the shed, created by the warp
threads.

"Do men wear these fringed belts?" Moira asked Molly,
the tip of her tongue caught between her teeth as she con-
centrated on following her instruction sheet.

"I don't think so, except on ceremonial occasions," Molly
said. "Why? You thinking of giving it to Chuck?"

Moira hesitated before saying no. The pause seemed
pregnant to Molly, which made her look up from her weav-

ing, but Moira was bent intently over her instructions. After rereading the appropriate step on the sheet in front of her, Moira picked up a thread of green yarn and said, "I'll wear this myself. I can think of a couple of dresses it'll go with."

Luann, the professor's wife, who was seated across from Molly, said, "Molly, that's looking great," diverting Molly's attention from Moira. "Darn." Luann sighed and unraveled about an inch of her weaving. "I keep getting the tension too tight."

"There's a rhythm to it," Molly said. "I used to watch my grandmother do this." A memory had popped into her mind of Eva, seated in her rocker in the living room, weaving and talking to a friend who'd come to call. But she didn't think Eva had done any finger weaving in years. "Maybe I absorbed the rhythm from her."

"Molly's right," Rachel said. "Once you get the rhythm down, your tension will improve quickly. Skilled finger weavers can manipulate as many as two hundred strands at one time."

Luann groaned. "Then any idiot can learn to work with thirty strands," she muttered and began reweaving her unraveled yarn. Beside her, her friend the NSU instructor was making better progress and looking pretty smug about it. The woman had the manner of one who was proficient at whatever she took on.

"How long have the Cherokees been doing this?" Moira asked Rachel.

"They were finger weavers for centuries," Rachel said, "and progressed to using simple wood frames very early to make large items such as rugs and shawls. Spinning wheels and looms were introduced by the English before the American Revolution. Then finger weaving practically died out for a while. It's only been revived in recent years. There are several women who give demonstrations at Tsa-La-Gi." The reproduction ancient Cherokee village, Tsa-La-Gi, at the Heritage Center in Park Hill, was open for tours during the summer months.

Moira asked another question, and another, until Rachel was telling them about the first time she ever saw a Cherokee woman weaving with her fingers, and how that woman became her teacher. Soon the conversation wandered to stomp dances and other things Cherokee.

None of it was new to Molly, but Moira seemed to be soaking up Rachel's every word like a dry sponge. Clearly, this interest in the culture wasn't feigned, though it might be sudden and short-lived. Funny, Molly thought, how you could think you knew a person well when, all the time, there were hidden thoughts and interests that you may never have suspected.

Molly couldn't believe it when Rachel called a halt, saying the library would close in ten minutes. They had been working for an hour and a half; it seemed no more than thirty minutes.

Molly put everything back in the sack and walked out of the library with Moira. She pushed open the library door and they stepped out into the cold night.

"That was fun," Moira said, pausing on the lighted steps to zip her jacket.

"Uh-huh." Molly pulled up her hood. "How about telling me what's going on with you?"

Moira looked at her abstractedly. "I don't know what you mean."

"Tonight, I kept thinking there's something you want to tell me but you're holding back for some reason."

"Nope," Moira said, pulling on her gloves. "You know all my secrets already."

"Like I knew you were interested in the Cherokee culture?"

Moira smiled. "I guess we never talked much about that, did we?"

"You never even mentioned it before this week."

"Actually, I only got interested recently. Felix has a lot of Cherokee clients. It just seems like I ought to learn more about them."

Felix had always had Cherokee clients, and Moira had worked for him for five years. Why hadn't she felt the need to know before this?

The other members of the weaving class passed by them, descended the steps, calling good nights and hurrying to their cars.

"I have to go home and do a load of laundry," Moira said. "I've been so busy lately, things at home have gone to pot."

Moira had rarely had to work overtime in the past. "Has Felix taken on a lot of new clients?"

"A few, and then he's helping Bruce get acclimated. And I may be going out of town this weekend, so I need to get caught up at home before then."

"Bruce . . . oh, Felix's new partner. I haven't met him yet. I hope he's not as intense as Marquita was."

"No, he's pretty laid back. Come by the office sometime and I'll introduce you." Before Molly could ask when, Moira said, "I really have to go."

"Where are you going this weekend?"

"Uh—I'm not sure yet. Well, see you in two weeks."

Molly said good night and got in her Civic. Moira definitely had something on her mind that she couldn't, or wouldn't, tell Molly. Was she afraid to spend time with Molly alone, for fear of making a slip and revealing whatever it was she was being so mysterious about? Maybe that's why she kept refusing Molly's suggestions that they get together. Well, she'd probably tell Molly eventually. Meantime, Molly had other things on her mind.

Had D.J. left a message while she was out? Maybe she'd call him, whether he'd left a message or not.

She heard the telephone ringing as she reached the landing outside her apartment. Fumbling with her key in the darkness, she finally got the door open and ran to grab up the phone.

"Hey! I've been calling all evening," D.J. said. "Where have you been?"

21

Friday

At seven-thirty the next morning, Molly was drinking her first cup of coffee of the day—praline pecan—at her kitchen table. She'd let Homer in to feed him, and he was stretched out beside her chair, sated on kibble but still alert for any other tidbits Molly might offer.

She bent and ran her fingers across his head, and his tail thumped appreciatively. She gazed out her kitchen window at the bare branches of an oak tree, like giant skeletal hands raised in entreaty to the dark sky. She puzzled over Moira's mysterious behavior the previous evening, even though she'd promised herself to forget it until Moira decided to talk to her. But her puzzling led nowhere.

She turned her mind to the Whitekiller investigation. It, too, seemed to be going nowhere, and Dave Highsmith wouldn't spend more time on it unless Molly came up with a good reason that he should.

Leaving her coffee on the table, she got out a nonstick griddle. Homer, his head resting on his paws, watched her expectantly.

She set the griddle on a low flame and cut two thick slices of homemade raisin bread. When the griddle was hot, she dipped the bread in a milk-and-egg mixture and laid it on the griddle. Smelling food, Homer came to lean against her legs and look pitiful.

She melted a chunk of butter on the griddle, lifted the bread slices to spread the butter around, then flipped the bread to brown the other side.

Homer whined and leaned harder.

"I see you," Molly told him. "I may give you a bite if you'll get out from under my feet."

Homer cocked his head quizzically, barked, and slunk away to flop under the table.

Molly transferred the toast to a plate, added a couple pats of butter and let it melt before she poured on the maple syrup. She ate the centers, then set the plate on the floor. Homer slurped the crusts and licked up every drop of syrup. So much sugar probably wasn't good for him, but she was as bad as Conrad about giving in to Homer's longing looks.

As she was pouring another cup of coffee, the telephone rang.

"Did I wake you?" Dave Highsmith asked.

"I've already had breakfast. What's up?"

"I wish I knew." He made an eerie, crooning sound to the tune of the *Twilight Zone* theme song. "Strange things are happening."

"Such as?"

"There's been another death in my county." Highsmith emphasized the pronoun, as though anybody who had the audacity to die in Adair County had insulted him personally.

"Sorry about that, Dave," Molly said, wondering why he was bothering her with it.

"This time there's no doubt about it. It was murder."

This time? Did that mean he might revise his opinion of Ed Whitekiller's death?

"Who's the victim?"

"A man who was working on that bingo hall near Highway 51. Some of the other workmen found him when they came to work at seven."

Molly felt a prickling at the base of her skull. A murder next door to Zeb Smoke? She could still see the old man's piercing black eyes, like holes burned in parchment. With the image came disquiet. Two people had died—one of them known to Zeb Smoke, the other employed on the hated bingo hall looming over his shack.

Highsmith was saying, "I'm using the telephone at a neighbor's place a couple of miles down the road—the same one the workmen used to call me after they found the body. I didn't think about calling you till I'd been out to the site. I'll explain that later. I'm going back there now and wait for the ambulance and the medical examiner. I figured you might want to come out."

"I'm on the way," Molly said.

She wondered if she should call Will Fishinghawk. They would have to question Zeb Smoke. At the very least, he was a possible witness, and perhaps a relative should be with him. She hesitated. Highsmith would undoubtedly prefer to question the old man alone. Molly tried to imagine her grandmother in Zeb Smoke's circumstances and knew she'd definitely want to be with her during any questioning by the police. She looked up Fishinghawk's number and made the call.

Fishinghawk's reaction was interesting. After she'd explained why she was calling, he asked tensely, "How was he killed?"

She realized that Highsmith hadn't said. "I'm not sure. All I know is that he was murdered, and since Mr. Smoke is next door, he could well have seen or heard something. I thought you'd want to be there when we talk to him."

"I'd better be, I guess. I'll try to find somebody to cover for my classes this morning. I'll get out there as fast as I can. Should I contact an attorney?"

Conrad had wondered if Zeb Smoke might take action to make his prophesy of doom against the Nation come true. Now perhaps he had. "I don't think that's necessary at this point," Molly said, "but you do whatever you feel you should."

She hung up, wondering what it must be like to be caught between suspecting an elderly relative of murder and wanting to shield him from the unpleasant consequences.

She glanced at her watch. It was almost eight. If she left now, she might arrive before the body was removed from the crime scene.

They huddled close together in the field, their shoulders hunched against the wind and cold. "His name's Franklin Soap," Highsmith said. He pulled at his nose, which was red with cold, and narrowed his eyes against the northeast wind. It had driven the clouds away, exposing the wan blue sky, but had brought with it more cold from the north. The barren elm trees next to where Molly and Highsmith stood with the two ambulance attendants offered scant protection from the wind.

They were waiting near the blood-encrusted body of

Franklin Soap for Ken Pohl, the medical examiner, to finish his preliminary examination. Pohl, wearing a quilted brown hooded coat that made him look like a bear, squatted next to the corpse. The dead man was tall and slender and was wearing a heavy ski-type jacket open over a gray sweat shirt and jeans. His chest was a mass of shattered bone and tissue covered with darkened, dried blood.

"He's Cherokee," Highsmith said to Molly. "Did you know him?"

Molly shook her head. "I don't think I ever saw him before." She looked up at the sheriff. He'd forgotten his cap, and the tops of his ears were crimson. "Who found the body?"

"One of the workmen. Moss Greenleigh called me," Highsmith said. "He was pretty upset, as you'd imagine. He said Soap's pickup was here before he and the other two employees arrived this morning. They looked for Soap on the site, didn't find him, and extended the search to this field. The one named Kelly actually found the body and yelled for the other two."

"If the pickup was here when the others arrived, it could have been here for a good while," Molly said and he nodded.

He glanced briefly at the legs of the corpse, the only part that Pohl's body didn't shield from view "From the condition of the body," he said, "I'd guess he's been here for hours, maybe all night. They knew right away that he was beyond help, so I don't think they touched him. Greenleigh got in his pickup and went to find a phone. The other two went back to the hall to wait."

Pohl grunted as he came out of his squat, straightening

his thick haunches to stand. "Had to be a shotgun," he said. "You find the weapon, Sheriff?"

"No, just a spent shell. Twelve-gauge. The murderer probably took the gun with him, but a couple of deputies are on the way out now to conduct a search of the area. I called them right after I called you."

Pohl wiped his runny red nose with a wadded handkerchief and squinted at Molly. "I don't expect to find any poison, Molly. That would be overkill, to coin a phrase. So what are you doing here?"

This was Pohl's weird idea of a joke. In the two previous murders Molly had investigated, the victims had died of poisoning. "The sheriff called me, Doc," Molly said.

"Ah. Is this Indian land?"

"Not right here," Highsmith said, gesturing around them at the field. The body had been found near the elm trees in almost the exact center of the open field. "But the victim's an enrolled Cherokee and he worked for the Cherokee Nation on Indian land."

Pohl motioned for the ambulance attendants to remove the body. "We'll take him to the morgue." He looked at Molly. "Come by this afternoon and I'll let you witness the autopsy."

Another example of Pohl's cockeyed sense of humor. Molly had watched him perform an autopsy the previous summer and had to leave to keep from fainting. Pohl would never let her hear the last of it.

Molly snapped her fingers. "Darn, I think I'm busy this afternoon."

Pohl smiled and they stepped back as the attendants began maneuvering the corpse into a body bag. Rigor mortis had set in. "I'll leave you two to do whatever it is that you do," Pohl said. "I'll call you, Sheriff, soon as I can make a guess about time of death. With this weather, it's going to be a very rough guess." He followed the ambulance attendants from the field.

"Have you had a chance to question the workmen?" Molly asked, glancing toward the partially constructed bingo hall. Three men stood in a wide opening where double doors would eventually be installed. Moss Greenleigh was one of them; another was Horace Wilson, who had once lived near Molly's grandmother in Park Hill. Molly thought Horace lived in Tahlequah now. The other man was a stranger to her, but he had to be Kelly, who had found the body.

"Not in any detail. Before we do that, I want to show you something." He led the way to an old Ford pickup. "This belonged to the victim." He pointed at the window on the driver's side. "Look in the seat."

Molly rested her forehead on the window and peered inside. Small black stones were pooled in the driver's seat. She counted seven of them. This was why Highsmith had called her.

"Like with Ed Whitekiller," Molly said.

"Uh-huh. What do you know about the stones, Molly?"

"Nothing but what I've told you."

He grunted. "Then what good are you to me, woman?"

"I'm your conscience, Dave."

He grunted again and led the way to the building, where he introduced her to the man she didn't know, Cecil Kelly, who was in his mid-thirties with laugh wrinkles at the corners of his eyes. He wasn't laughing now.

Molly was glad to be inside, sheltered from the wind. A

kerosene heater in one corner knocked the hard edge off the cold.

"Do you men have any idea who might have done this? Did he have a falling out with somebody lately or marriage problems?"

"He wasn't married," Horace muttered.

"Hell, we know who did it," Kelly said shrilly. He seemed quite agitated. "Look over there." He pointed toward the west wall, which was only partially constructed. "That's where you'll find your murderer. It's Zeb Smoke. He's a medicine man. He's in there right now, planning out how he's gonna kill the rest of us."

"You're the one who found the body?" Highsmith asked him.

Kelly fumbled in his coat pocket for a handkerchief and blew his nose. "Damn right. I got here a few minutes before Moss and Horace. I saw Franklin's pickup and was looking around for him when they got here. Moss saw them black rocks in the truck and I knew right then that old man had done something to Franklin."

"Did you touch the stones?" Highsmith asked.

Kelly's eyes widened, but it was Moss Greenleigh who answered the question. "We didn't even open the door." He appeared almost as agitated as Kelly. "I thought that old medicine man might have put them there. I wouldn't touch 'em with a ten-foot pole."

"Did anybody else touch them?" Highsmith asked, glancing at Horace Wilson. Wilson shook his head and rubbed his bare hands together. If possible, he looked more shaken than the other two; he looked ill.

"Good," Highsmith said, "we might get lucky and find fingerprints."

"I told you who done it," Kelly sputtered.

"Mr. Smoke is quite elderly," Molly put in.

"You think he's harmless because he's old?" Kelly demanded. "That's what Moss has been saying—ignore him, he's harmless. Well, it's bull. Mean people just get meaner as they get older." His voice shook now. "We're living on borrowed time and, Sheriff, you act like we're talking about a traffic ticket here." His mouth twisted and he flung an arm toward Zeb Smoke's house. "He might be old, but he's a menace."

"Aw, now," Moss put in, "he may have put the stones in Franklin's pickup, but that doesn't mean he killed Franklin. He probably doesn't even remember putting the stones there."

"He knows exactly what he's doing," Kelly burst out.

"Why don't you try to calm down, Mr. Kelly," Highsmith suggested. "Let's get back to when you found the body. You said you yelled for Greenleigh and Wilson. How long did it take them to reach you?"

Kelly took a deep breath, rubbed the back of his neck, and looked to Greenleigh for help. "A minute maybe," Greenleigh said. "We weren't far away, and we ran when we heard Cecil yell."

Highsmith looked at Kelly again. "You're sure you didn't touch the body, maybe step on it before you saw it?"

Kelly's face drained, turned gray. "Lord, no."

Highsmith turned to Greenleigh. "You're the one who looked in the pickup and saw the stones. As I understand it, that was before Kelly found the body."

"Yes. We'd already looked through the building and outside, in the john, anywhere he could be. Then I saw the stones. We heard there were some black stones with Ed

Whitekiller's body, so that's when we decided to search the surrounding area."

"What did you do after you found the body?" Highsmith asked.

"Me and Horace came back here, and Moss drove down the road to find a telephone," Kelly said.

"What time did you three get here this morning?" Highsmith asked.

"It was about two minutes before seven," Kelly said. "I remember looking at my watch when I drove up because Franklin's pickup was already here. I wondered if I was late, but I wasn't. Moss and Horace drove up in Moss's pickup five or ten minutes later.

"I was supposed to ride to work with Franklin," Horace said. "My car's out of commission. When he didn't get there at six-thirty, like he was supposed to, I called his house and got no answer. He lived by himself. I live about five minutes away from him, but I waited another ten minutes. I was afraid he'd had car trouble, and I knew if I waited any longer, Moss and Cecil would have already left for work. So I called Moss and he came and picked me up."

Highsmith thought for several moments, then turned to Kelly. "Mr. Kelly, why are you so sure Zeb Smoke killed Franklin?"

"Because he wants to shut down the construction of the bingo hall."

"He's been trying to scare us off with medicine ceremonies," Moss Greenleigh interjected. "Last Monday he did a medicine ceremony out in that field and left behind some black stones like the ones in the pickup."

"Can you show me where he left the stones Monday?" Highsmith asked.

"Sure. Come on, Cecil. Help me find the spot." Green-leigh and Kelly followed the sheriff from the building.

Horace Wilson's sick pallor had faded. "Did you know about the stones in the field?" Molly asked him.

He shifted uncomfortably. "Like Moss said, Smoke's been making medicine around the bingo hall ever since we started work on it. When he did that ceremony Monday, Franklin kept—oh, shoot, poor old Franklin." His voice broke.

Molly waited a minute, then prompted, "What were you going to say about Franklin?"

He swallowed and managed a wan smile. "He kept bug-ging me about old man Smoke, asking me what he was doing in the field. He was nearsighted and wouldn't wear his glasses at work." He shook his big head sadly. "I don't know why he thought I should know what the old man was doing. Just to shut him up, I said I figured he was trying to protect himself from the evil influence of gambling, some-thing like that. Anyway, after Smoke left, Franklin said he was going out there and look around. He even talked Moss and Cecil into going with him." He gazed past Molly to-ward the shack and his face clouded. Molly saw a late-model white car stop on the shoulder of the road in front of Smoke's house, and a man got out and walked up the lane. It was Will Fishinghawk.

"I tried to talk them out of it," Horace said abruptly, al-most angrily. "Moss and Cecil wouldn't have gone if Franklin hadn't been so determined. He wouldn't listen to me." He made a helpless gesture. "He wouldn't listen to anybody when he got his head set. You'd have to know Franklin to understand."

Molly wanted to understand, wanted to get a feel for the kind of man Franklin Soap had been. "How do you mean?"

His face was grave. "Don't get me wrong. Franklin wasn't cruel or anything like that. He didn't really mean any harm. He never did nothing to deserve what happened to him. But he was as nosy as an old woman, and when he got on a subject, he wouldn't shut up. Drove you crazy sometimes. Monday, after the medicine ceremony business, he got off on the blocks being moved."

"Blocks?" Molly asked blankly.

Horace made a sweeping gesture with his arms, indicating the walls that surrounded them. "The concrete blocks. Cecil's the block layer. Me and Franklin are—was—just laborers. We hauled the blocks up here in a wheelbarrow for Cecil, went to Tahlequah or Tulsa when Moss needed supplies, picked up around the site, stuff like that."

"And Franklin thought some of the blocks had been moved?" She couldn't see the remotest connection between Franklin Soap's obsession with concrete blocks and the medicine ceremony, which he'd also been obsessed with, according to Horace.

He drew his eyebrows together, as if trying to order his thoughts. "That's what he said. Kept harping on it. Said they weren't stacked where they were when we left last Friday. See, the guy from the lumber yard delivered 'em early last week, but we couldn't start laying till the inspector gave the go-ahead. He didn't get here till Friday, and we started laying the blocks Monday morning. Franklin kept saying they'd been moved over the weekend. Nobody took it seriously. Franklin couldn't see ten feet in front of him without his glasses. The rest of us knew the blocks were right where the guys from the lumber yard unloaded them early last week. But Franklin was on one of his tangents. He drove us all nuts Monday, talking about it. Finally, he said maybe the problem was some of the blocks were missing. Franklin said maybe somebody stole some of 'em over the weekend."

Molly nodded. She was getting a picture of Franklin Soap as a compulsive talker and complainer, ready to argue with anyone about anything.

Horace said, "When we got here Tuesday, there he was out there counting the damned blocks. Which it turned out was all there." Horace looked pained. "At least it shut him up on that subject. But then he started gritching that Moss didn't appreciate how conscientious he was being about the blocks."

He gave a sigh of exasperation. "You wouldn't understand if you didn't know Franklin. He had to find *something* wrong with something, see. Just to show up the rest of us. Franklin thought he was some kind of construction expert because he helped his brother build a garage out of blocks once, plus he just couldn't ever admit he was wrong."

Molly had known people like that. It would have worn on the nerves, working side by side with Franklin Soap. She wondered, too, if in addition to being naturally argumentative, Soap had stirred things up to relieve the boredom of the job.

Horace ran a hand over his face. "I'm getting off the subject, aren't I? Starting to sound like Franklin. Poor guy. I wanted you to know what he was like, so you'll understand why I couldn't talk him out of messing with those medicine stones. I told all of 'em to leave 'em be. Cecil and Moss went with him anyway, but me, I stayed right here. I don't want nothing to do with that old man's medicine."

"Did Franklin take those stones, the ones Zeb Smoke left in the field?"

Horace's expression turned dark. "He picked 'em up. Seven of 'em. He put 'em back where he found 'em, but the damage was done. Then he nagged me the rest of the day, wanting to know what it meant. He just couldn't seem to understand what a dangerous thing he'd done."

Horace looked toward Zeb Smoke's shack and said, "Is it true they found seven black stones with Ed Whitekiller's body?"

"Yes," Molly admitted.

"Means he didn't kill himself, don't it?"

"Possibly."

His attention was still on Zeb Smoke's house. "I need this job, but now . . . I don't know. I'd rather be unemployed and alive."

"Is it possible that somebody besides Zeb Smoke left the stones in Franklin's pickup?"

He turned back to her. "Who?"

"You said Franklin's constant talking got on people's nerves. Maybe somebody wanted to get back at him, scare him, teach him a lesson."

"You mean Moss or Cecil? Moss wouldn't do something like that, but Cecil . . . no, I don't think so. He acts like he don't put any stock in Cherokee medicine, but he quit making jokes about it the last day or two, after we heard about them stones found with Whitekiller."

"Did anyone see Zeb Smoke around the site yesterday or this morning?"

"No, but we wouldn't necessarily. He slinks around out here like a cat. We'll see him over at his place or out in the field or hiding behind the john. Next thing you know, he's gone. It's spooky."

Horace was obviously spooked, and Molly wasn't feeling all that serene herself.

"Are you and the sheriff going to talk to the old man?" he asked.

"As soon as we leave here. Has the foreman ever had a talk with Mr. Smoke, asked him to keep off this property?"

Horace stared at her as though she were babbling. "What good would that do? You can't turn back medicine with talk."

They saw Highsmith and the other two men walking back toward the building and went out to meet them. "We didn't find any stones," Kelly told Horace. "They disappeared."

"I don't think so," Greenleigh said. "I'll bet they're the same ones that are now in Franklin's pickup."

22

Two deputies arrived as Molly and Highsmith were leaving the construction site to call on Zeb Smoke. They stopped, and Highsmith told the two uniformed young men to search the field behind the construction site, starting in the center, where several elm trees grew close together, and working outward from there.

"We're looking for a twelve-gauge shotgun, boys," Highsmith told them. "And anything else that might have been left by the shooter or the victim."

The two, one named Schwartz, who looked to be in his mid-twenties, the other, Chapman, who appeared to Molly to be too young to shave, trotted off. Molly and Highsmith continued to the road and turned left, with the wind at their backs, toward Zeb Smoke's lane about four hundred yards away.

"Are you sure that Chapman isn't a minor?" Molly asked.

Highsmith grinned. "He gets that all the time. Makes him crazy. It's the baby face. Actually, he's twenty-one."

"You've seen his birth certificate, I trust."

"Yep. He brought it with him when he interviewed. Said

he figured he'd need it. He hates being taken for a teen-ager."

"There are worse things than looking younger than your years."

Highsmith nodded and gazed glumly at Zeb Smoke's listing shack. "Nice place Smoke's got here," he said dryly.

"Maybe he can be talked into moving now."

"Never met a medicine man before."

"They're pretty much like everyone else."

Highsmith was thoughtful. "If Cherokee medicine or politics is involved in this murder, I'm going to need your input."

Molly cut her eyes around at him. "Shucks, I thought you wanted me out here because of my charisma."

He grunted. "And I don't care if the old man *is* senile. If he killed Soap, he's got to pay." As they turned into the lane, he eyed the white Taurus parked on the shoulder of the road. "He's got company."

"Looks like it," Molly said. She'd just as soon Highsmith didn't find out she was responsible for Fishinghawk's presence. The sheriff would complain that she'd destroyed any chance of Smoke's blurting out something incriminating in the first moments of surprise. The old man was expecting them, and there had been time for Fishinghawk to coach him on what to say. But Molly doubted that Zeb Smoke ever blurted out anything before thinking, particularly to a white man, or that he would necessarily listen to advice from his great-nephew.

"Moss Greenleigh thinks the old man's flipped out. Did Wilson mention that?"

Molly shook her head. "He's scared, though, and I don't

think he feels the sheriff's department can do much to protect him and the other men."

"What do you think, Molly?"

"I'm still trying to figure that out."

"You're a big help."

"Give me time, Dave."

They walked the rest of the way in silence. Will Fishinghawk admitted them, and Molly introduced him to Highsmith.

The two men shook hands. "Do you live around here?"
Highsmith asked.

"No, in Tahlequah." He glanced past Highsmith at
Molly, who, standing behind the sheriff, was shaking her
head. Fishinghawk had been about to say something more
but changed his mind. Instead, he turned to the old man in
overalls and a wool shirt who was seated in a chair near the
stove. "This is my great-uncle, Zeb Smoke."

Zeb's nod was barely perceptible. He looked warily at
Highsmith for a long moment before dropping his eyes.
Will invited them to sit on the couch. He pulled a cane-
bottomed chair out from the wall and set it facing them.
"My uncle saw the ambulance over at the bingo hall earlier," Will said, glancing at Molly curiously. "What's the
trouble?"

Molly expelled a silent breath. Will had read her correctly and was feigning ignorance of the murder.

Highsmith unzipped his coat but left it on. "A man was
murdered next door in that field behind the bingo hall."

"My God!" Will exclaimed. "Who?"

Molly thought Will sounded genuinely surprised, but
Highsmith studied him suspiciously. "His name's Franklin
Soap," Highsmith said. "Know him?"

Will denied it with a shake of his head.

"Did you know Franklin Soap, Mr. Smoke?" Highsmith asked.

Zeb ran his tongue around the gap in his teeth and wiped his mouth with his shirt-sleeve. "I know all of 'em working over there by sight. Can't put a name to any of 'em, though."

"When did it happen?" Fishinghawk asked.

"Sometime between five-thirty or six yesterday and seven this morning."

Smoke leaned his chair back against the wall. He hadn't taken his glittering black eyes off Highsmith since the sheriff sat down. Highsmith turned to him. "Franklin Soap stayed at the site after the other men left yesterday. Did you notice the red pickup parked over there when the other vehicles were gone, Mr. Smoke?"

He shook his head. "Wasn't paying any mind."

"And you didn't see a second vehicle drive up to the site after working hours? Whoever killed Soap had to get out here some way."

Again, he shook his head.

Highsmith sighed. "Did you hear anything during the night, Mr. Smoke?"

It was a while before he spoke. Molly could see he resented being questioned by the sheriff and didn't want to answer. Maybe Will had told him he could be taken to Stilwell for questioning if he refused to cooperate. At any rate, he evidently decided to go along for the time being.

"I heard what I always hear," Smoke said, staring a challenge at the sheriff. "A few cars going by." One of which must have been the murderer's, Molly thought. "Coyotes. Sometime early this morning I heard a screech owl."

Some Cherokees believed a screech owl was a harbinger of death. Molly glanced at Highsmith, but he seemed unaware of any hidden meanings.

Feeling too warm, she took off her jacket but left it draped over her shoulders.

"You didn't hear anything that sounded like gunfire?" Highsmith asked.

Smoke pursed his lips. "Could've been that, I reckon."

Highsmith sat forward on the couch. "When was this?"

The old man lifted his shoulders. "Good while before I went to bed last night. It was dark. I don't have a clock, so I can't tell you what time it was."

"Did you go out to see what made the noise?" Highsmith asked.

"Nope."

"You weren't worried?"

He shook his head. "We get coon hunters around here at night pretty regular. Used to hunt coons myself when I was younger. Figured it was a hunter or a car backfiring."

Highsmith studied the old man. It was clear he thought Smoke was feeding him a line of bull. "The workmen say you've been trying to run them off, Mr. Smoke."

Smoke stirred himself, stood, and went to the shelf along the back wall for his pipe and tobacco. His spine was stiff with indignation. They watched him as he filled and lighted the pipe. Will was looking agitated, Highsmith seemed merely irritated. Molly tried to make her face blank.

Smoke puffed on his pipe and, turning, grumbled, "They don't know what they're talking about."

"You haven't been trying to stop the construction next door?"

"Ain't my place to stop it."

"They've seen you performing medicine ceremonies."

"I been making medicine most of my life."

"Are you saying you don't mind the bingo hall going up next door?"

He muttered contemptuously, *"Yo-ne'ga."* He puffed angrily on his pipe. "Ain't what I said, neither. It's evil, and the Apportioner will stop it when the time is right."

Puzzled, Highsmith looked to Molly for help.

"The Sun," Molly said.

Highsmith raised an eyebrow. "Mr. Smoke." His tone was deceptively unthreatening. "You said you used to hunt. Would you mind showing me your shotgun?"

Will's indrawn breath was audible. He jumped to his feet. "I don't like the way this is going, Sheriff. I don't think my uncle should answer any more questions until we consult a lawyer."

Highsmith regarded him with seeming calm, but Molly saw his neck muscles tauten. "That'll just delay it a few hours. Mr. Smoke doesn't need a lawyer to answer yes or no to a simple question—if he has nothing to hide. And while you're talking to a lawyer, I'll be getting a search warrant. But it would be simpler all around if Mr. Smoke would just answer the question."

"You know a lawyer that'd come out here?" Smoke asked his nephew.

"We'd probably have to go to his office," Will admitted.

"Ain't no need, no way," Smoke grunted. He looked at the sheriff. "My shotgun's in the shed. Ain't been fired in a year, maybe longer."

"I need to see the weapon, Mr. Smoke."

Will's voice rose over the sheriff's. "Uncle, this has gone far enough."

Smoke shot him a look of disgust. "I want him off my land, Nephew." He laid his pipe on the shelf and went to the back door. "I'll get it."

"I'll go with you, if you don't mind," Highsmith said. His tone said he was going, whether Smoke minded or not.

Molly and Will exchanged a glance. Zeb Smoke, who wore a heavy wool shirt with his overalls, had gone out without a coat, but Will grabbed his from a chair and Molly poked her arms back in her jacket sleeves. They followed the two men out of the house and across a hundred yards or so of bare ground to a weather-grayed shed with a tin roof and a wood door hung on homemade leather hinges. The door was secured with a piece of rope strung through the rusted handle—the type used on cabinet drawers—and a leather loop nailed to the shed, and tied in a square knot. It took a full minute for the old man's gnarled fingers to work the knot loose, but he stubbornly refused offers of help from Highsmith and his nephew.

Finally, he got the rope untied, threw the door back, and stepped into the dim interior. Old pieces of machinery, buckets of rusted nails, nuts and bolts, tools, and accumulated castoffs filled most of the space in the shed. Molly and the other two men stayed outside around the open door.

Smoke moved pieces of disassembled, unidentifiable tools to get to a pile of gunny sacks in one corner. "I wrapped it in a sack and put it under here to protect it," Smoke said. He threw the sacks aside until the bare wood floor was exposed. The old man looked confused and began grabbing up the gunny sacks and shaking them, but the gun was gone—if it had ever been there in the first place.

Smoke cursed and glared at Highsmith. "I know I put it here! They stole it!"

There was little doubt whom he was accusing. He was gesturing wildly in the direction of the bingo hall.

Will dipped his head in defeat, unwilling to meet Molly's eyes now.

The sheriff grunted as if he'd made a point. "When was the last time you saw your gun, Mr. Smoke?"

He frowned. "A month . . . a week." He looked down. "I don't recollect."

Highsmith nodded grimly. "It was a twelve-gauge, wasn't it?"

Will's head came up and he stared at Smoke, who was glaring at the sheriff. Smoke, who seemed unaffected by the cold, didn't answer, but he didn't have to. It was as if he finally understood that he could be in serious trouble. Something flicked across his lined face. It wasn't fear exactly. Molly didn't think there was much that frightened Zeb Smoke, at his advanced age. Maybe it was self-doubt. The flicker disappeared and his expression became stoic.

Molly had seen the same resigned acceptance in other elderly people. As for Zeb Smoke, he truly believed a destruction was coming on the Cherokees. He probably didn't expect to survive it; maybe he didn't want to. But he wouldn't want to spend his last days in a cell.

What a horrible way to end a life that had been fiercely independent. Molly didn't want to believe Zeb Smoke had gone over the edge, killed two men, but right now it looked very bad for him.

"Mr. Smoke," Highsmith said, "I must ask that you not leave the county for a while."

Smoke snorted. "Ain't going no place," he said as if daring anybody to doubt him.

Walking back to the construction site, their heads bowed against the wind, Highsmith said, "That old man's dangerous. He killed Soap and maybe Whitekiller too."

Molly shoved her hands into her jacket pockets. "You'll never prove he did Whitekiller, Dave. He's not strong enough to have knocked him unconscious and put him in the pickup. And how did he get there?"

"He walked. Or got somebody to drop him off nearby."

"Who?"

"Will Fishinghawk?"

"That's ridiculous."

Highsmith gave a sigh of frustration. "We'll never nail him on Whitekiller without a confession, and we both know what the odds are on that. So let's concentrate on Franklin Soap."

"Anybody could have taken the shotgun from that shed," Molly said. "It wasn't locked."

"Which may be why he left it there, instead of in the house in the first place. So he could say it was stolen. If it *was* there. I'm not sure Smoke even knows." Nor was Molly.

"How much you want to bet," Highsmith went on, "it was Smoke's gun that did Soap?"

Molly wasn't about to take that wager. "Even if you could prove that, it still wouldn't prove Zeb Smoke was the one who pulled the trigger."

"If the weapon's found around here, it'd be damn good circumstantial evidence."

"You'll never get a murder conviction on circumstantial evidence, not in this case."

"It's not my business to convict people. I just gather evidence and take it to the D.A. Hey, I know you're feeling sorry for the old buzzard, but we can't let him get away with murder just because he's old and a couple bricks short of a load."

"There's no history of violence," Molly said, though she knew she was wasting her breath. As usual, Highsmith had his mind made up almost before the investigation started. "Why would he suddenly kill somebody—two men, rather—when he's in his eighties?"

"Not my business to psychoanalyze him, either."

Molly did not respond, and as they reached the construction site, they heard a shout and saw the younger of the two deputies, Chapman, running toward them from the field, waving a shotgun above his head.

23

Saturday and Sunday

Molly slept poorly Friday night, as she often did when she was stuck on an investigation. During the long periods of wakefulness, she vacillated between being certain Zeb Smoke was no murderer and thinking anxiously that he might well be.

Dr. Pohl had been reluctant to commit himself on time of death, but Friday afternoon, when Molly pressed him, he said his best guess was that Franklin Soap died sometime before midnight Thursday.

When confronted with the twelve-gauge shotgun found by Deputy Chapman in a thicket of scrub brush near the boundary between the field and Smoke's property, the old man identified it as the one he'd stored in his shed. He continued to insist that it had been stolen.

Friday afternoon an ebullient Highsmith had called Molly to say he'd conferred with the D.A. and was going to bring Zeb Smoke in for further questioning. Molly had resented the sheriff's eagerness, thinking that his main concern was to wrap up the case so that his life could get back to its usual lazy pace. She had a hunch that Highsmith was working up to a quick arrest, if he could get the D.A.'s approval. She had urged him to wait until Monday, but he'd refused.

"The whole thing's too easy," Molly had insisted. "If Zeb Smoke killed Franklin Soap with his own shotgun, he wouldn't have left the gun in the field where it was bound to be discovered. He's not that crazy. He'd have put it back in his shed or disposed of it where it wouldn't be found."

"So he panicked. Aw, Molly, you're making it too complicated," Highsmith said. "Most murder investigations are simple. The most obvious suspect is usually the guilty party."

As if he'd investigated hundreds of murders, Molly thought, fuming. She had turned down Highsmith's request that she be present during the questioning of Smoke, although she had talked to Will Fishinghawk after the fact.

"They kept saying his gun killed Franklin Soap and advised him to make it easy on himself and confess," Fishinghawk told her angrily. "He wouldn't say a word. Finally, the lawyer told them to arrest him or let him go. I tell you, Molly, I thought they were going to throw him in a cell right then."

"Highsmith won't make an arrest until the D.A. gives him the go-ahead," Molly said. "Do you think he did it, Will?"

"I honestly don't know," Will admitted.

"Did you ask him?"

"Sure. He got his back up, as usual, and refused to answer. I wish now I'd had him declared incompetent and moved to a nursing home."

"I'm not sure you could've made that stick. He seems forgetful sometimes, but most of the time he's as lucid as you or I."

"Would you say that if you knew for sure he killed that man?" Will asked. "That's not a rational response to the bingo hall."

"You're right, I suppose."

"I'm afraid for him, Molly. He won't last a month in jail."

"Where is he now?"

"I brought him home with me. He didn't like it, but he shouldn't be out there where he can stir up more trouble."

"Good. I agree."

Saturday began cold and windless. It was still dark at 6:00 A.M. when Molly finally gave up trying to sleep. She got up and, after making coffee, sat at the kitchen table in her robe with a full coffee mug, and tried to organize the circling thoughts that had kept her awake for much of the night.

From what Conrad and Will had said, Zeb Smoke had insisted all along that the Cherokee Nation's long progressive drift away from the old ways would be dealt with by the ancient gods. So, why would he suddenly take matters into his own hands?

The thing that bothered her even more was the stones found in the pickups owned by Whitekiller and Soap. They definitely connected the two murders. She couldn't escape the conclusion that both men were killed by the same person. Whitekiller's wife and both the Butlers seemed to have motives for murder in Whitekiller's case, but none in Soap's. Had Dot Whitekiller or the Butlers even known Franklin Soap? She'd ask them, but George Butler seemed to be in the clear, since he had been out of town when Soap was killed. She was floundering because she didn't know enough about the victims, particularly Soap.

The deaths were connected, so there had to be some tie, however tenuous, between the two men. Had they known each other? What had they done and what had occupied their thoughts in the days before their deaths?

"The only thing bearing on Ed's mind was finding a job," said Dot Whitekiller, "—and tomcatting around with another woman."

They were seated in the Whitekiller living room. Dot wore an old pair of sweat pants and a man's cotton shirt. She had been running the vacuum sweeper when Molly arrived and she hadn't been pleased to have her work interrupted. But she'd let Molly in and had sent a protesting Maggie to the other end of the house to gather up the laundry and start the first washer load.

"I talked to Susan Butler," Molly told Dot. "She said the affair ended before Ed's death."

Dot glanced toward the hallway in case Maggie had decided to return to the living room. There was no sign of the girl. Dot leaned forward and lowered her voice. "That's probably because I told Ed we were through if I suspected one more time that he was fooling around." She shifted restlessly, obviously wanting Molly to finish what she had to say and leave.

Molly got to the point. "A man was murdered Thursday night about a mile from here."

She grew quite still. "Where? Who?"

"Behind the site of the Cherokee Nation's new bingo hall. The victim worked as a laborer there. His name was Franklin Soap."

There was no recognition in her face. "You didn't know him?" Dot shook her head. "Did you ever hear your husband mention him?"

"I don't think so." She paused, frowned. "No, I'm sure I never heard him mention the name." Her right hand reached for the neck of her shirt and drew the open collar together in an instinctively defensive gesture. "Why are you asking me about this Franklin Soap?"

"Soap's pickup was parked at the construction site." Molly observed her carefully. "Seven black stones were found in the driver's seat."

Molly could hear her swallow as she began to understand. "And you say he was murdered. But his body wasn't found in his pickup?"

"No, it was in a field behind the construction site. He was shot."

Dot wiped her hands on her sweat pants, running them along her thighs, as if they'd begun to perspire. "And the stones, like the ones found with Ed? What do you think that means?"

"Possibly that there's some link between the two deaths. That's why I asked if your husband knew Soap. I thought they might've been involved in something together." Molly lifted a hand helplessly. "I don't know, really. I'm looking for anything that might connect the two men."

She sat forward with a snap. "Do you think it means that Ed was murdered too?"

"I think it's quite possible."

"But the way Ed died . . ." She looked away, shook her head, looked back at Molly. "The sheriff said it was suicide."

"That's what it looked like. But if that's true, if your husband was alone when he died, where did the stones come from?"

She met Molly's gaze. "I don't know. Frankly, I never thought the stones were important. I'd forgotten about them." She looked bewildered now.

"The stones found with your husband have bothered me all along," Molly said. "They were an incongruous detail at the death scene. Your husband wasn't a rock collector. The interior of his pickup was meticulously neat and clean. To leave loose stones to roll around on the seat of his pickup seemed out of character."

"Yes, it would have been. I guess I never really thought about it in that light." She spoke slowly, as if to herself, and when she looked at Molly she said musingly, "I've read about serial killers, how they leave something behind as a—a sort of signature."

"Serial murderers usually kill strangers and they kill in the same way, over and over. About the only similarity between the scene of your husband's death and that of Franklin Soap is the stones left in their pickups. I think your husband was murdered, Mrs. Whitekiller, and I believe both murders were premeditated. I think the stones were left either as a warning to other Cherokees or as an attempt at misdirection."

"How could they be a warning?" she asked blankly.

"There was an ancient death curse involving seven black stones."

She seemed unable to take it all in. "I didn't know that. I doubt that Ed did, either. He never mentioned it." She plucked at her sweat pants, making a crease between her thumb and forefinger, playing her thumb back and forth against the fabric.

"Do you know Zeb Smoke?" Molly asked.

She looked up. "Not well. Ed talked about him sometimes. Zeb Smoke used to tell him Cherokee stories when he was a child." She hesitated. "He lives near where they're building the bingo hall, doesn't he?"

"Right next door," Molly told her. "Did you know that Ed paid him a visit not long before he died?"

Her eyes were momentarily distant. "I think Ed mentioned it last Friday. He'd been to the construction site that day to ask about a job."

"Did he tell you anything about his visit with Mr. Smoke? Did they have a disagreement, argue—anything . . ."

She frowned thoughtfully. "No, he just said he'd stopped by there. Nothing more."

Molly chewed the inside of her cheek. "I wonder if I might have a word with Maggie?"

Dot shook her head emphatically. "I'd rather you didn't. She's still terribly upset about her father. Talking about it seems to make it worse."

Molly thought that talking about it was the only way Maggie would ever be able to come to terms with it. She couldn't think of any more questions to ask Maggie's mother at the moment, so she thanked Dot Whitekiller and left.

Outside, the ashen morning sky had gone back to the pale, ice blue of the day before. Molly stood on the Whitekillers' porch while she buttoned her jacket and pulled on her gloves. As a sudden gust of wind whistled through the porch, a voice hissed, "Miss Bearpaw?"

When Molly stepped off the porch, Maggie stepped out from the side of the house and gestured urgently for Molly

to come closer. The sound of the vacuum sweeper had re-
sumed inside. Molly hurried down the steps and met Maggie at the corner of the house. The girl had come out
without a coat. She pressed her arms against her body and
used the sleeves of her red sweater as a muff, tucking her
hands inside.

Molly glanced toward the front door. "You'll freeze out
here."

"I had to talk to you and I knew mother wouldn't let
me." She looked so miserable that Molly wanted to hug her.
It didn't seem possible that she could have lost weight since
their talk in Molly's office, but her eyes and cheeks looked
hollower than before. "Mother thinks she's protecting me."

"I'm sure she does."

"She doesn't understand how it makes me feel. I'm not a
baby! It's worse not knowing what's happening with the—
the investigation and all." She looked closely at Molly. "You
are still investigating, aren't you?"

"I am," Molly assured her. "But you need to talk to your
mother, Maggie, tell her how you feel."

She dismissed the advice. "What have you found out
about my father?"

"Nothing really definite." Molly spoke carefully. "I
would like to ask you a couple of questions, though."

"Anything."

"The Friday before your father died, he paid a visit to an
old Cherokee man named Zeb Smoke."

For an instant, her eyes lit up. "Daddy liked Mr. Smoke.
He went to see him every month or two."

"Can you remember what your father said about that last
visit? Did he mention, for example, that he and Mr. Smoke
got into an argument?"

"Oh, no," she answered quickly. "Daddy would never have argued with Mr. Smoke. He really—well, respected him, you know?"

"I didn't think they'd argued, but I wanted to make sure. Did you ever hear your father mention a man named Franklin Soap?"

"No." Maggie sounded resigned. "It doesn't seem like you've learned much about my father's death."

"On the contrary, I've learned quite a lot." That may have been an exaggeration, but when Molly looked in this child's miserable eyes she had to give her some small hope. "And I can tell you this, Maggie. I don't think your father killed himself."

Maggie blinked rapidly, and Molly realized she was trying not to cry. "It was an accident, wasn't it?" Suddenly she threw her arms around Molly's neck and squeezed. "Thank you," she whispered.

"I have no proof yet," Molly cautioned. She wanted to say that it hadn't been an accident, either, but before she could think how to phrase it or even if she should, Maggie dropped her arms and gave Molly a misty smile. Then she ran back down the driveway the way she'd come.

A few phone calls on Saturday afternoon turned up a cousin of Franklin Soap and a neighbor who was willing to talk to Molly. Neither of them had any idea who might have killed Soap and, as far as they knew, he hadn't known Ed Whitekiller.

Her repeated phone calls to Susan Butler's house went unanswered. When she stopped by the Butler residence late Saturday afternoon, the house was locked and still, the curtains closed. After checking the garage, which was empty, Molly admitted defeat and went home.

There was a sense of urgency about her investigation since the murder of Franklin Soap. She felt she should be doing something, even when it wasn't apt to lead anywhere.

She called the Butler house again Sunday morning and, again, there was no answer. Perhaps Susan had gone away for a few days.

She had Sunday lunch with her grandmother in Park Hill. Eva had been talking to her Cherokee neighbors and reported that they too were angry because a killer was leaving black stones with his victims, exploiting the beliefs of traditional Cherokees.

Molly wondered aloud if perhaps the killer himself was a traditional Cherokee. Eva had pooh-poohed the very idea, saying no Cherokee she knew would indulge in black magic, and besides, if Molly was up on her Cherokee medicine she'd know the stones were supposed to be buried, which was the first time Eva had indicated *she* knew anything about the death curse.

After returning to Tahlequah, Molly detoured down the Butlers' street and saw a car in the driveway. She parked and went to the door.

She rang the bell and a woman called, "Just a minute!" Then Susan Butler opened the door. "Oh, hello."

"I'm sorry to bother you again—"

"It's all right, only—I'm in a hurry to leave. I was in the bedroom packing when you rang and . . . oh, well, come on in." Her face was almost back to normal. One had to look closely to notice the last traces of the discoloration around her eyes. Her blond hair, shining with cleanliness, tumbled around her face in soft waves, and her makeup had been applied expertly. Now Molly could see that her pale complexion was smooth and flawless.

Susan Butler was dressed in soft blue slacks and a matching sweater. It was hard to believe this was the same woman Molly had talked to before. This woman had purpose, plans. Quite a transformation.

"I've been trying to get hold of you all weekend," Molly said.

"I went to this *really* wonderful women's retreat." Susan was suddenly animated. "It changed my life! A friend of mine called me last Friday from Tulsa. She could tell from my voice that I was really down and she said, 'I'll be there as soon as I can,' just like that. I didn't even have to ask. When she got here, she . . . well, I guess you could say she bullied me into cleaning up—me and the house too. Then she made me go to this retreat with her. I didn't want to. But she wouldn't take no for an answer." Her blue eyes sparkled, and she clasped her hands beneath her chin. For a moment, Molly thought she would applaud. "I'm *so* glad she didn't."

"It's obvious it was a good experience for you," Molly said. "When you answered the door, I almost didn't recognize you from before."

She grinned. "I'm a new woman! I was a real mess last week, wasn't I? Can you believe I had never even heard of *The Feminine Mystique* before this weekend?"

"Er—really?"

"It's the God's truth. And I thought feminists were all lesbians. That's what George always said. Of course, labeling people we fear makes us feel more secure."

"Right," Molly said, wanting to smile. Susan didn't even

talk like the same woman. She had to be quoting these clichés from what she'd heard at the retreat.

"Poor George," she was saying. "He's such an ostrich. And I used to be as bad. Always expecting some man to solve my problems." She threw her hands out expansively. "Not anymore. As soon as I finish packing, I'm going to Tulsa and stay with my friend until I find a job. I'll never be dependent on a man again."

"Then I'm glad I caught you before you left," Molly managed to insert. "I need to ask you a few more questions."

Susan hesitated. "I'm trying to put the past behind me. Ed. George. They're the past. Now I have to concentrate on getting in touch with my inner child, like they said at the retreat." She looked around. The carpet had been vacuumed and no dust was visible on the living-room tables. "My lawyer says I can get the house in the divorce settlement. Then I'll put it on the market. The equity will help me get started in a new place." She had it all figured out. She would walk away and start over with her newly raised consciousness. Molly wished it could be that easy for Maggie Whitekiller.

"There have been new developments in the investigation," Molly said.

"Of Ed's death? Frankly, I still don't think there's much to investigate. He just couldn't stand his drab little life any longer. I couldn't see that before, but now—"

Molly interrupted. "It's looking more and more like murder."

That stopped her, but only for a moment. "I'm sorry to hear that, really I am. I've forgiven Ed for using me, because that's what he did, you know. I'm even trying to forgive George for beating me up—although my lawyer says we may have to show in court the pictures the police took of me afterward, if George won't agree to give me the house and alimony." She looked uncertain for an instant. "I hope that won't be necessary. At the retreat they said we had to quit playing the blame game and get rid of all our old emotional baggage to move on. Have you read *The Games People Play?*"

"It's been a while," Molly said.

"It's a truly great book." She clasped her hands again. "I saw myself on every page of that book."

"About Ed," Molly said.

She looked displeased with Molly for continuing to harp on Ed. "What happened to Ed has nothing to do with me."

"Sometimes people know things they don't know they know," Molly said. "It's possible Ed said something to you that would lead us to the murderer."

She shook her head. "I'd have mentioned something like that when you were here before."

"I'm sure you would have, if you'd recognized the significance. At the time it may have seemed like an innocent remark." They were still standing near the front door. "If you could just spare me a few more minutes, Mrs. Butler . . ."

"Susan," she corrected firmly. After a pause, she added, "All right. Sit down."

Molly took the nearest chair, while Susan Butler perched on the edge of the sofa, her palms planted on her knees.

"I'm particularly interested in the last time you were with Ed, that Sunday in Stilwell. What seemed to be on his mind?"

She lifted a brow and smiled wryly. "We were in a motel

room and he wanted to get back home before his wife and daughter did. What do you think was on his mind?"

Molly answered the question with a smile of her own. "But there must have been other things. What did he talk about?"

She caught her bottom lip between her teeth and suppressed another smile. "Actually, he was too eager to hop in the sack to be very talkative. That's about all men like Ed and George are interested in. If they'd ever had an intelligent thought, it would have given them a migraine. I can't believe I used to be attracted to men with such a low level of expectation." She giggled, then sobered just as quickly. "Anyway, it irked me and I let Ed know it. I told him we were going to have a conversation first, like civilized people."

"So you had a conversation."

She rolled her eyes. "If you can call it that. He asked what I wanted to talk about, and I said something like, Whatever's going on with you. I mean, the motel wasn't what you'd call a romantic setting, and all Ed wanted was slam-bam-thank-you-ma'am. It made me feel as cheap as the motel. Basically, he was humoring me to keep me from walking out."

Molly could easily imagine the scene. "Try to remember specifically what he said."

She shrugged. "He didn't say anything about somebody wanting to kill him, if that's what you think. He talked about making a bookcase for his daughter and a couple of job interviews he'd had, ordinary stuff like that."

"Did he mention Franklin Soap or Zeb Smoke?"

She bent to brush a piece of lint off the toe of her shoe.

"No—" Then her head snapped up. "Franklin Soap, isn't that the man who was shot over in Adair County?"

Molly nodded. "He was working on the bingo hall the Cherokee Nation is building. Ed was out there on the Friday before his death, asking about a job."

"I don't understand. Did he and this Franklin Soap get into a fight or something?"

"No, nothing like that. It doesn't appear that they even knew each other, but there is evidence that the same person might have killed them both. I'm looking for a link. Did Ed mention his interview at the bingo hall?"

"No, he didn't. I'm sorry. I wish I could help you. But he just said he'd had a couple of job interviews and there was no opening at either place."

Molly tried one last question. "Can you think of anything else, anything at all?"

She drew a deep breath and let it out. She was impatient to be on her way. Into her new life. "Let me think. He was making conversation to humor me, like I said. He said something about one of the interviews . . . the man he talked to made him mad."

"How?" Molly asked.

"He was rude to Ed. He said they were out of application forms, but Ed said that was a flat-out lie." She lifted her shoulders. "It was after regular working hours, and the guy was probably tired. Ed said there were only two men there. Everybody else had left."

"Two men? Did he mention their names? Or say anything more about them?"

"No, just that the one guy was rude. He was unloading concrete blocks, I think."

"Did Ed talk to the other man?"

"Not much. I think he was leaving when the other guy got there. Ed got huffy and said something about not wanting to work there, anyway, after he'd sized things up."

"What did he mean by that?"

"Oh, it was just sour grapes. He couldn't afford to be picky. He'd have taken a job in a second if it had been offered."

And Molly had to be satisfied with that.

24

Monday

D.J. called Monday morning, before Molly left the apartment. He was coming home early. Courtney had caught a bug and was suffering from a sore-throat and stopped-up nose. Since Gloria had returned from her honeymoon on Sunday, he had decided, over Courtney's heated arguments, that she would be better off with her mother. He missed Molly and planned to drive all day Tuesday to get there by evening. She would, she assured him, be waiting.

She left the apartment on a little cloud of happiness which lasted until she was blindsided by a call from Cherokee Nation headquarters. She had been so focused on the investigation that she'd managed to bury the problems of her looming unemployment. But the request to be present at an 11:00 A.M. meeting with the chief and representatives of the tribal council, to "discuss the future of your office," brought it back with a resounding thud.

The meeting took place in the office of the principal chief, but the chief herself wasn't there. Instead, Molly was welcomed by two council members, Phil Dry and Marcia Rainwater.

"Chief Mankiller was called away unexpectedly," Marcia explained. "She sent her regrets."

Molly wondered fleetingly if the chief, a warm and compassionate woman, hadn't wanted to be the one to tell Molly that she was out of a job.

Molly shook hands with Phil and Marcia and sat down. They exchanged a few pleasantries as Phil settled himself importantly behind Chief Mankiller's desk and rearranged some papers. Molly surmised that he'd like to sit behind that desk in that office on a regular basis. And maybe he would. Chief Mankiller had announced that she would not run for another term.

Marcia Rainwater kept smiling at Molly, as though she sympathized with her and was trying to think of some way to make what they had to say easier for her.

"We want you to know, Molly," Phil said, "that we are all pleased with the job you've done with the League. I speak for the full council and for the chief." The *but* remained unspoken, but it was there. He's definitely trying to soften the blow, Molly thought and wished Phil would deliver the bad news and get it over with.

"Thank you."

"I believe Chief Mankiller alerted you some time ago," Phil went on, "that the grant which funds your office might not be renewed. Last Friday the BIA notified us that there definitely would be no more money for the Northeast Oklahoma office. It was disappointing but not unexpected. Chief Mankiller pled our case, but the BIA is being hit hard by the new budget cuts."

Molly nodded glumly, unable to work up much sympathy for the BIA bureaucracy when her own situation was dire. "I'm sure the chief did what she could."

"They did say," Phil went on, "that the grant could be renewed at a later date."

Molly doubted it. Given the huge national deficit and a sluggish economy, the federal government would be cutting back for some time to come. Meanwhile, Molly had to eat.

"The council has met twice now to discuss your situation," Phil said, "and we've come up with something that we hope will meet with your approval."

They're going to offer a severance package, Molly thought. A month or two's salary, three, if she was lucky. She would be grateful for anything and gathered her thoughts together to say so.

Marcia Rainwater sat forward in her chair. "We're all very excited about this, Molly. It's something we've needed for a long time."

Molly looked at her blankly. What was she saying, that they'd never given anyone severance pay before?

"Officially, you would be assigned to the tribal police force," Phil said.

Molly turned back to him. "What—I mean, are you offering me another job?"

"Why, yes." Phil laughed. "Forgive me, Molly. I should have spelled that out in the beginning."

The rock that had sat in Molly's chest since the phone call requesting her presence at this meeting slowly began to crumble. "It's just that I thought . . . well, never mind that. You're asking me if I want to be a tribal policewoman?"

"Not exactly," Phil corrected. "You wouldn't be a uniformed officer. We'd create a new position. Call it something like Major Crimes Investigator—we could even give you a small raise. As Marcia said, we've known for a while that we need a liaison with whatever law-enforcement agency has jurisdiction when a tribal member is involved in a major crime."

"You've been doing some of that all along," Marcia added eagerly. "We were impressed by your work with the BIA investigator on that murder at the museum earlier this year. You wouldn't even have to move your office." It almost sounded as though Marcia thought Molly needed coaxing.

"We understand," Phil said, "that you will probably want to think it over before reaching a decision."

"No," said Molly hastily. "I don't have to think it over. I want the job."

Marcia relaxed. Phil smiled. "I told them you'd accept," he said. "You've got a knack for investigative work, Molly."

"I'm nosy, you mean," Molly said.

He chuckled. "I would have said curious and tenacious."

"Otherwise known as stubborn," Molly said. Lord, she was so relieved she could jump up and down.

"It's settled then," Marcia said and beamed at her.

"You'll start the new job in January," Phil said.

Standing, Molly found she was shaking. Having your hopes dashed and put back together again in the space of a few minutes will do that. She managed a reasonably dignified thank you and went to the door.

Where Phil's voice stopped her. "By the way, Sam Davey will be by to see you after the first of the year." Davey was chief of the Cherokee Nation Police Department. "He'll issue you a weapon at that time."

After the council members' complimentary remarks, Molly could perhaps be excused for basking in the warmth of being appreciated, not to mention securely employed once more, even if it meant being issued a weapon. (She'd deal with that later.) But the feeling didn't last. The compliments only increased the pressure to tie up the White-killer and Soap investigations to prove their confidence wasn't mislaid.

As far as Highsmith was concerned, the cases were solved, and he was busy trying to pull together enough evidence to arrest Zeb Smoke.

Molly spent the afternoon going through her notes, looking for connections, significant details she'd missed before. She lost track of time, surfacing only when her hunger pangs were too insistent to ignore any longer. It now was after six and already getting dark beyond the office windows. She had sat in the same position at her desk for hours and felt stiff all over.

She groaned and stretched and put on her coat. She'd take the case files with her. After dinner—a big bowl of beef stew at The Shack—she drove home.

Conrad's house was dark, and she remembered he'd mentioned a Friends of the Library meeting tonight. She was disappointed. She'd wanted to talk to Conrad, tell him about the new job and discuss the investigation.

Homer met her at the stairs. He couldn't talk through the investigation with her, but he was company and she let him in the apartment. After a week of D.J.'s absence, she was feeling awfully lonesome.

She'd cook dinner tomorrow, she decided, and hope D.J. got there in time to share it with her. She'd make a list and shop for groceries in the morning. Her thoughts gave her pause. What was going on here? She rarely cooked. She didn't *like* to cook. Yet she was actually pondering menus and making mental lists.

But it would be fun to surprise D.J., show him how

much she'd missed him. It wasn't as though she were setting a precedent.

She called Will Fishinghawk to check on Zeb Smoke. "I
took him home," Will said.

"What? I thought you were going to keep him with you
for a while."

"Hah! You don't keep Zeb Smoke anywhere he doesn't
want to stay, unless you tie him down. When I got home
from work today, he was waiting for me. Said he was going
home. We argued for a while, and finally I told him he
could badger me all he wanted but I wasn't taking him
home. That's when he got his coat on and started walking."

"But it's miles!"

"I thought he'd come back once he realized I wasn't coming after him, or he'd get a ride. I waited almost an hour
and then I couldn't stand it any longer—it was cold out and
I got to worrying that he *wouldn't* get a ride. So I went
looking for him. Found him walking along the road a couple of miles out of town. Believe, me, he'd have kept walking until he dropped. I was mad as hell, but I took him
home."

Molly tried to work on the case files, but she couldn't
hold her eyes open. She closed the folders, turned Homer
out, made a cup of coffee, and settled down with a new
mystery novel.

But even a story by one of her favorite authors didn't
keep her from dozing off and, finally, she put the book
aside. It was too early to go to bed, so she paced the room
and thought about the Whitekiller and Soap investigations
some more. The little alarm that had niggled at her when
she was talking to Dot Whitekiller Saturday was back in

her head. There was something she was overlooking. What *was* the link between the two murders?

The answer didn't come. She sat down and rested her head on the back of the sofa. She dozed and jerked awake some time later.

As if her mind had never stopped sifting through her notes as she napped, she was immediately conscious of details, phrases she had read over and over.

She tried to relax and let her thoughts run free.

Franklin Soap had worked at the bingo hall. Ed Whitekiller had gone there a few days before his death to apply for a job. It was a link as fragile as a spider's web, but the only link she had found.

Had they both heard or seen something they shouldn't have? The easy conclusion was that it had involved Zeb Smoke. But Smoke had been Whitekiller's friend; Soap had had nothing to do with him, had probably been afraid of him.

Leave Zeb Smoke out of it, then. What about the construction site?

The man Whitekiller had talked to had been rude to him, which had angered him, caused him to respond with what Susan called sour grapes.

Ed got huffy and said something about not wanting to work there, anyway, after he'd sized things up.

. . . there were only two men there. Everybody else had left.

One guy was rude. He was unloading concrete blocks . . .

That was on Friday, but Horace Wilson had said the concrete blocks were delivered earlier in the week. Perhaps that meant something, but Molly couldn't figure out what.

Another puzzle. Monday morning, the day of his death, Whitekiller had told his wife that he had one more contac* to make, that he had a good feeling about it. Yet, Sunday afternoon, according to Susan, he had no job prospects. What had happened between Sunday afternoon and Monday morning? He hadn't left the house, so, whatever it was, it must have happened in Ed's mind.

And what did it have to do with Franklin Soap?

She had never even met Soap, but after going through her notes so many times she almost felt she'd known him. He'd been stubborn, inquisitive, opinionated, argumentative, a man who wore other people out with his compulsive talking. He'd talked about Zeb Smoke and his medicine. And harped on the blocks being moved.

That had been on Monday, following Whitekiller's visit to the construction site on Friday.

Soap had said the blocks weren't stacked where they were when the workmen had left the previous Friday, or some of them were missing. But he'd counted them and they were all there.

It was starting to make a vague kind of sense to Molly. Franklin Soap had known something. Was he the man unloading concrete blocks when Whitekiller showed up? Perhaps they'd talked. Had Soap told Whitekiller something that got him killed? That hardly seemed likely, since the two men didn't know each other and Whitekiller hadn't mentioned it to Susan Butler.

Okay, so Soap knew something—or somebody thought he did—and Whitekiller somehow figured it out for himself. Something Whitekiller thought he could use to get a job.

Molly got up for a drink of water. The luminous clock on her range read nine-thirty. She wasn't sleepy anymore. She stared out the kitchen window at the few stars visible between the branches of the oak tree.

The man Ed Whitekiller had talked to at the construction site had been eager to get rid of him. Why? Because Whitekiller had seen something he shouldn't have, even though he hadn't figured out what it meant until later?

Was it possible that Zeb Smoke had seen whatever it was that Whitekiller saw? The old man had been hanging around the site since construction began.

Molly knew she wouldn't be able to sleep now. Was Zeb Smoke awake too, alone in his little shack, worrying that he would be arrested for the murder of Franklin Soap?

The old man could well hold the key to the murders, if only she knew what to say to make him talk to her. Even if he knew nothing, the murderer couldn't count on it. Mental alarms went off all over the place.

Molly went to her closet and grabbed a coat. If the shack was dark, she wouldn't stop. But if he was awake, she had to talk to him.

Wispy clouds raced across the moon. Molly's gloved hands gripped the steering wheel as she sped along the deserted highway. Now that she'd decided to check on Zeb Smoke, she felt a desperate sense of urgency, as though time were speeding faster than she was toward a violent climax. She took three deep breaths, but her foot pressed a little harder on the accelerator.

Zeb Smoke had said he had nothing to do with death curses, and now she believed him.

If the old medicine man hadn't dropped those black stones in the field, then somebody else had put them there.

Why? So that, when they were found, it would be assumed that Smoke had left them as part of a death ceremony? If that were true, it had to be the killer who planted the stones, which meant that he was already planning to murder Ed Whitekiller and leave black stones with the body. Then, if Whitekiller's death wasn't accepted as suicide, investigators would eventually hear about the stones found in the field, which would lead them straight to Zeb Smoke.

The stones were the key to solving the case. Ironically, without them, Whitekiller's death would probably have gone down as a suicide. The killer might just have outsmarted himself.

Molly saw the flames as soon as she rounded a bend in the road a half-mile away. Either the bingo hall or Zeb Smoke's shack was on fire.

She bounced over the rutted road until the Civic was shaking and banging and threatening to come apart. She could see now that the flames were shooting from the roof of the shack. She braked at the end of the lane and the Civic slid halfway around. She jumped out and ran down the lane, shouting the old man's name and praying he'd already gotten out.

But she didn't see him. She shouted again and noticed a movement near the sagging fence between the house and the bingo hall. "Mr. Smoke?" As she started toward the fence, she heard a faint cry from inside the house.

Dear God, he was still in there.

She ran back to the door. She covered her mouth with one arm and tried to open the door with the other. It was locked—or jammed. The fire crackled ominously and she heard another cry from inside. Frantic, she sobbed and drew back her foot and kicked with all her strength.

The door creaked open and she fell into billowing smoke. She gasped for breath and cried, "Mr. Smoke!"

She heard a feeble cough somewhere to her right. She began to cough too, so hard that she was near to choking. She held her breath as she crawled into the smoke.

A few feet inside, she crawled into the old man. He was curled in a fetal position against the wall, his arms around his head. He didn't move when she touched him. She grabbed his feet and crawled backwards toward the open door. He seemed to be unconscious, but he weighed less than she did.

She dragged and hacked her throat raw and, somehow, she maneuvered him down the steps and away from the house.

She fell on the ground, coughing violently. She thought she'd never stop. She coughed until the beef stew she'd had for dinner was a puddle on the ground.

The fire crackled and roared and there was a loud crash. She struggled to sit up and wiped her face with her coat. Beside her, the old man stirred.

She gripped his shoulder and shook him. "I have to get you out of here." She got to her feet, swayed, and caught herself before she fell. "Come on, you have to help me. You need a doctor." She shook him harder, and this time he groaned.

She grabbed him under both armpits and heaved. "Get up, you stubborn old fool! I won't let you die here!"

She got him on his feet, with one of his arms around her shoulders, holding him upright with an arm around his waist. "Walk!" she ordered. "That's it. That's good. Now another step."

Stumbling over the rocky ground, they reached the

Civic. She got the passenger door open and dumped him inside. His head fell back against the seat. He was only semiconscious, but he was alive.

She'd left the Civic half in the bar ditch, nose first, where it had come to rest. When she tried to back out, the tires spun. She remembered that movement near the fence and panic tore at her throat. Get a grip, Molly, she told herself. She tried again and, suddenly, the tires took hold and she shot backwards into the road and slammed on the brakes just in time to keep from ending up in the ditch on the other side.

Her heart pounded like a kettle drum.

She shifted into low. That's when she saw two bright headlights hurtling toward her in the rearview mirror. She thought of the man she'd seen beside the fence near the burning house, the man who must have set the fire.

The car was nearly on her rear bumper now. She hit the gas, roared forward, shifted, and shifted again as she accelerated. She only had time to realize that it was a pickup or a four-wheel-drive vehicle because the lights were too high to be a car, when it rammed the rear of the Civic.

Her reaction was instinctive. Even as her head whipped back, she stamped on the accelerator and shot down the middle of the graveled road, taking a gentle curve on two wheels. There wasn't time to fear for her life or wonder about what was happening or even if the old man in the passenger seat was still breathing. All of her attention was focused on keeping the Civic in the middle of the road and trying to anticipate each curve before she got there and slowing down just enough to keep from flipping the Honda.

The truck rammed her again and she headed for the

ditch. Whipping the steering wheel frantically, she managed to get the car back on the road. The other driver meant to force her off the road, and she knew she and the old man would die if he succeeded.

They were approaching a sharp S-curve. If she didn't slow down, she'd never make it. The other vehicle had found enough room to pull even with the Civic on the right, and she could see it was a pickup truck. Inches separated the two vehicles. She would have to turn right toward the pickup to make the first part of the S-curve. The road shoulders were narrow at that spot, and the ground sloped steeply down to woods on the right. On the left, the bar ditch was shallower and there were a hundred yards of open land between the ditch and the woods.

She had only one chance. Instead of slowing as she approached the first leg of the curve, she speeded up and jerked the wheel left, in the opposite direction. The Civic bounced across the bar ditch and into the field, where it came to a jarring halt. The engine had stalled.

In the sudden quiet, she heard the squealing of tires that seemed to go on and on, then the night-splitting sound of metal crashing against a solid barrier. A horn started blaring and didn't stop.

Molly sat in the Civic, shaking and fighting hysteria. She turned the key and got a grinding sound. She tried again and again, but the Civic wasn't going anywhere. Even if she managed to start it, she didn't think she could get it back on the road. She'd gotten where she was only because the Civic's tires had left the ground as it flew across the ditch.

The pickup's horn still blared.

She touched the old man's face. His breathing was deep and regular.

She fished a flashlight from the glove compartment. She covered Zeb Smoke with her coat, took the keys and got out, locking the door. Cold penetrated her sweat shirt immediately. She ran back toward the road. The pickup had gone off the highway on the other side and hit the trees. The front end was now in the driver's seat.

She crept up on the driver's side and aimed the flashlight beam. Nausea pushed at her throat. The driver's chest was covered with blood, and he slumped sideways against the mangled steering wheel. She closed her eyes and swallowed hard.

Then she looked again, quickly, to be sure. Her hand shook and the light jerked erratically. It was Moss Greenleigh, and he'd never known what hit him.

She ran back to the road and headed for the house she remembered seeing at the other end of the S-curve. Behind her the pickup's horn wailed, an anguished death dirge in the cold night.

25

Tuesday

Molly bumped into the sheriff as she was leaving the hospital. Zeb Smoke was resting comfortably. He'd regained consciousness during the night and tried to get out of bed. Now they had him in restraints and Will was with him. When Zeb left the hospital, he'd stay with Will for a while. Then, if he couldn't live alone, he'd have to go to a nursing home.

"I thought I might find you here," Highsmith said. "I want to check on old man Smoke and then I want to talk." She had phoned Highsmith last night to tell him what had happened, but she hadn't wanted to go into the details then. Her throat had been raw—it was still sore—and she'd been exhausted.

"He's resting. Let's talk first," Molly said. "The hospital cafeteria?"

It was too early for the lunch crowd. They got coffee from the self-serve counter and sat at a table next to a long, unadorned window.

Highsmith sampled his coffee, grimaced, and dumped in some nondairy creamer. "Okay, how'd you know who did it? And why the hell didn't you tell me?"

Molly sipped carefully. The coffee tasted like the bottom of the pot, but the heat soothed her tender throat. "I didn't know who did it, Dave, but I didn't believe it was Zeb Smoke. If you hadn't been so intent on convicting him, you'd have realized it too." She was doing her best to be charitable. She'd never know when she might need Highsmith's cooperation again.

"What were you doing out there at night?" he asked crankily, as though he thought she'd been up to something behind his back.

"I was worried. I thought about the case and it finally dawned on me what the connection between Whitekiller and Soap was. The bingo hall."

"Whitekiller didn't work there."

"No, but he was out there on the Friday before he was killed. It had to be the link. I figured both men saw or heard something the killer didn't want known. It occurred to me that, whatever it was, Zeb Smoke might have seen or heard it too. I drove out to his house to see if he'd talk to me and found the place on fire. Greenleigh set it. He'd read about the death curse in the newspaper and started leaving black stones where they'd be found."

"Yeah, the big church man. Advocate for the homeless. What a hypocrite. Wait a minute. Are you saying Smoke didn't do a death curse and put those stones in the field behind the bingo hall?"

"I'm convinced he didn't. Greenleigh dropped the stones in the field where one of the other men would find them and assume Zeb Smoke left them there as part of his medicine ceremony. Greenleigh had already decided to kill Whitekiller, after Whitekiller tried to blackmail him that morning. The stones would tie the death to Zeb Smoke if we started asking too many questions."

"So he left stones in Whitekiller's pickup to frame the old man for the murder," Highsmith mused, "then came to see me, pretending to be so concerned about Smoke, insinuated Smoke didn't have all his marbles so I'd think he was crazy enough to commit murder."

"Exactly, and after Soap was killed, it looked like you were buying it. Then Smoke came back home. Greenleigh realized you'd let him go because you didn't have the evidence to hold him. Or, even worse, Smoke was no longer a suspect, in which case you were still looking for the killer."

Highsmith had the grace to look embarrassed.

"Greenleigh figured if Smoke was dead, the investigation would be stymied and eventually closed. I dragged Smoke out of the house and got him in my car and that's when Greenleigh showed up." She waved a hand. "I told you all of this part last night."

"It's a weird time to be out questioning people." He peered at her and added grudgingly, "But it's lucky for the old man you went."

Molly took another swallow of the bitter coffee. "According to Susan Butler, Whitekiller first went to the site after working hours. He probably drove out to see Zeb Smoke, saw a pickup still at the site, and went over to talk to somebody about a job. Another man showed up. We know now that one of the two men was Moss Greenleigh. Whitekiller got mad, said he didn't want to work there anyway, after he'd sized things up. Greenleigh may have reacted strongly to the remark, though I don't think Whitekiller meant it as a threat—not then. Greenleigh probably saw him go to Smoke's house after leaving the site. Later, Whitekiller thought it over, realized why Greenleigh had reacted so strongly, and Monday morning he went back out there and tried to blackmail Greenleigh into giving him a job."

"Cecil Kelly told me Whitekiller was there Monday. He came to my office this morning when he heard about Greenleigh. Nobody heard what Whitekiller and Green-leigh said."

"Did Kelly tell you what was really going on at the con-struction site?"

Highsmith nodded.

"Why didn't he tell somebody before this? It might have saved Franklin Soap's life."

"He was afraid to." Highsmith drained his cup. "Hang on a minute." He went to the self-serve bar, refilled his cup, dumped in nondairy creamer, and returned. "I'll tell you everything Kelly told me, but first you go ahead with what you were saying."

Molly propped an elbow on the table and rested her chin in her hand. She hadn't had much sleep. She needed a nap before D.J. got home. "Whitekiller told Susan Butler that when he was at the bingo hall on Friday, somebody was un-loading concrete blocks. When I talked to Horace Wilson, he said the concrete blocks had been delivered earlier in the week. Even when I saw the discrepancy, I couldn't figure out what it meant. Until I remembered something else Hor-ace told me. The day of Whitekiller's death, Soap kept say-ing the concrete blocks had been moved."

Highsmith lifted an eyebrow but gestured for her to continue. "According to Horace," Molly said, "Soap was always griping about something, so he didn't pay any attention. But Soap was right. The blocks had been moved—or rather the first ones delivered, the ones that met the architects' specifications, had been taken away and cheaper blocks unloaded. The new blocks had to be unloaded before the old ones could be put in the truck, so obviously the new ones couldn't be stacked where the old ones were; they had to be stacked beside them. Greenleigh got the inspector out to okay the blocks, then traded them in for cheaper ones that didn't meet specification. He was skimming, substituting cheaper items for the ones specified and pocketing the cash difference."

Highsmith sighed. "That's what Greenleigh was doing, all right. Cecil Kelly confirmed it. Greenleigh had skimmed money on previous jobs. He must have accumulated quite a nice little bundle. His wife's family owns the construction company, but Greenleigh ran it, and his wife was talking about divorce. So he was getting it from all sides. Just when he thought he'd talked his wife into staying, Whitekiller tried to blackmail him. He knew his wife would go through with the divorce if she found out about his dishonesty. He'd lose her and the company, too."

And the whole town would have known that a pillar of the church was nothing but a common thief, Molly thought.

"By the way," Highsmith said, "Cecil Kelly was the one switching the blocks the first time Whitekiller was there."

"I suppose," Molly said, "he was getting his cut to keep quiet."

"No, just assurance of work on all Greenleigh's projects. It was never said in so many words, they never even talked about the scam, but Kelly knew the blocks he laid were below spec. Evidently it's not hard to tell if you know what to look for."

"Which is why Whitekiller, who'd worked construction before, figured it out," Molly said. "And Greenleigh had seen him go into Smoke's house. He had to be worried that Whitekiller had told the old man what was going on at the construction site."

"Yeah. Kelly said the other people hired by Greenleigh were novices. Neither Soap nor Wilson ever worked construction before, so Greenleigh figured they wouldn't know what was going on. Till Soap started shooting off his mouth."

"If only Kelly had come to you earlier . . ."

Highsmith acknowledged this with a grimace. "He was afraid he'd implicate himself. And his story is that he never believed Greenleigh would commit murder to cover up his scam. Until after Soap was killed, that is. Kelly feels guilty as hell, if that's any comfort to you."

"I'm not the one who needs comfort, Dave. Maggie Whitekiller does."

"Murder's a mighty big thing for a victim's kid to deal with."

"But easier than suicide. Trust me."

He gave her an odd look.

She finished her coffee, grimacing as though it were medicine. "I'm going to find Maggie and then I'm going home. I'm giving myself the rest of the day off."

"Nice work if you can get it."

"Parts of it," Molly said. Not the part where she had to tell Maggie the truth.

*   *   *

Molly found the girl standing in the deserted foyer of the high school. In jeans and a jean jacket, she was hugging a notebook and an algebra textbook to her chest and gazing through a glass door toward the circular drive.

When she saw Molly coming up the walk, her impatient frown cleared, her expression shifting to recognition. Molly saw a touch of anxiety too.

Molly entered the foyer with a gust of wind. "You need a ride home?" she asked. Her words echoed in the hollow silence that all schools have when the students are gone.

"No. My mother's picking me up." Maggie hugged her books closer. "You've learned something about daddy, haven't you."

"You were right all along," Molly told her. "He didn't kill himself and now we have the proof."

Her eyes widened and she almost smiled. "I knew it!" she burst out passionately. "I knew he would never leave me on purpose. It was an accident."

Molly wondered if she'd been right in thinking Maggie could handle the truth. The girl looked so fragile. She touched Maggie's arm. "Not that, either. He was murdered."

For a moment, Maggie seemed paralyzed. "But who?" she asked in a cracked voice and closed her eyes. When she opened them, tears had gathered.

Molly gave her a very condensed version of the facts. It took about two minutes. Maggie listened intently, twice wiping a tear from her cheek.

When Molly finished, Maggie swallowed and said in a thick voice, "I'm glad Moss Greenleigh is dead."

Molly squeezed her arm. She was glad too. Had Greenleigh lived to be tried, Maggie would have haunted the courtroom. Every day would have reopened the wounds. Now she could start to heal.

"Are you going to be all right?" Molly asked.

"I think so." She wiped her eyes with the back of her hand. "The counselor talked to me. She's trying to help, but I'd rather—" She paused, glanced down.

"What?"

She looked up. "Can I come and talk to you sometime?"

"Whenever you want."

She really smiled then, through a mist of tears.

This time Molly did not resist the urge to hug her, books and all.

"It's nothing to joke about, Molly," D.J. said. They'd eaten dinner—chicken cacciatore, baked squash, asparagus, and grilled parmesan tomatoes. They'd made love. Now they were nestled, spoon-fashion, on Molly's sofa bed.

"I'm perfectly serious. I want you to teach me how to shoot."

He raised up on one elbow and peered down at her in the dim light. "Sounds like dragging an old man from a burning house and getting run off the road by a murderer in a pickup truck finally brought you to your senses."

"Not exactly. A gun wouldn't have helped much last night. By the time I realized we were in danger, the pickup was ramming the Civic's rear end and I had to drive for our lives." She'd had the car towed to town. The garage mechanic had assured her it would be in driving shape by tomorrow.

"I hope you never have a closer call. If he hadn't crashed into those trees . . ."

"It must have been my sudden veering in the opposite

direction from the one he thought I had to take. It caught him off guard, diverted his attention just long enough for him to miss the curve."

"And it scared you into deciding to get a gun."

"It scared me, all right. I hope never to be that scared again. But the gun—well, there's something I failed to mention about my new job. They're going to issue me a weapon."

His mouth tilted in a lopsided grin. "That means you have to get a license, and to do that you have to pass a gun-safety course. I get it."

"You'll teach me?"

He ran his thumb over the arch of her eyebrow. "We'll start tomorrow."

Molly wished he wouldn't sound so eager. She knew she had to do it. That didn't mean she had to like it. "Wait till I begin the new job. That'll be soon enough."

He wrapped her in his arms and stroked her hair. "Poor Molly. I know you hate guns, but you'll feel differently when you've gotten used to one, learned how to handle it properly."

She pressed her face against his shoulder. She didn't believe him. "Promise?"

"Promise." He kissed her hair, then moved down, lingered for a long moment over her mouth, then moved lower.

The phone rang. D.J. swore. It was after midnight. Nobody phoned this late unless it was important. Molly groaned and reached for the receiver.

"Molly, I know I probably woke you, but don't be cross. I have to tell you something."

"You didn't wake me, Moira."

"Honest?"

"I wouldn't lie to you."

"Oh, good. Guess where I am."

"In your apartment. At the Tulsa Doubletree with Chuck. In Paris." Moira was giggling. Giggling? Moira?

"Wrong, wrong, and wrong."

"How many guesses do I get?"

"You'll never guess, so I'll tell you. I'm in a bed and breakfast in Eureka Springs and—" She paused. Molly could almost hear the "ta-da." "—I'm married."

"There must be something wrong with this line, Moira. I thought you just said you're married."

"That's right. We eloped. So you can forget about the bridesmaid dress."

"Boy," Molly said with an exaggerated sigh, "is that a load off my mind."

Giggle. Giggle. "Now you won't have to worry about it."

"I wasn't worried about the stupid dress. What I meant is, I'm glad you finally did it. I'm tired of talking you through broken engagements."

"Oh, Molly, I'm so happy."

"Great. Congratulations. And congratulate Chuck for me."

"Oops, I forgot to tell you. I didn't marry Chuck. I eloped with Bruce."

Molly's jaw dropped. "Who?"

"Bruce Hilldebrand."

Felix's new partner. Felix's new part-*Cherokee* partner. Moira's recent interest in Cherokee culture was finally clear. Good Lord, she'd known the man all of two months. Molly swallowed a tart reminder. "Well, as long as you're happy."

"I'm delirious." Molly heard a deep, male murmur in the background. "I have to go now, Molly. My husband wants me." In every sense of the word, Molly was sure. "Talk to you when we get back."

Molly hung up.

"Moira, huh?" D.J. said. "I take it she finally married that Chuck guy she's had on the string for months."

She went back into his arms and lay her head on his chest, listened to the deep, steady beat of his heart. "No, she didn't. She eloped with Felix Benson's new partner, Bruce Hilldebrand."

D.J.'s laugh rumbled in Molly's ear. "You're kidding me."

"I wish I were. This is the same woman who's had an aversion to marriage for as long as I've known her, though she kept trying to convince herself otherwise. I can't believe it. She's known this Bruce only a few weeks, D.J."

"I guess she just had to meet the right man."

"I guess," Molly murmured and closed her eyes. D.J.'s arms tightened around her.

She knew all about the right man. The right man could make you do things you swore you'd never do. She murmured drowsily.

"Sleepy?"

"Uh-huh."

"Sounds like I'd better go."

Molly snuggled closer. "Would you like to stay?"

He was still for an instant. He had given her plenty of previous opportunities to suggest it, but she never had. She'd felt the need to hold back that much of herself. But suddenly it seemed silly for him to get up in the middle of the night and go home.

"Stay all night? You sure?"

She smiled and lifted her head, took his face in her hands. "The invitation was not issued without considerable thought, Deputy Kennedy. Of course, if you'd rather go . . ."

"Now you're toying with my affections, woman," he growled.